BEST OF THE WRONG REASONS

Visit us at www.boldstrokesbooks.com

BEST OF THE WRONG REASONS

by
Sander Santiago

2021

BEST OF THE WRONG REASONS

ISBN 13: 978-1-63555-867-8

This Trade Paperback Original Is Published By
Bold Strokes Books, Inc.
P.O. Box 249
Valley Falls, NY 12185

First Edition: April 2021

Credits
Editors: Jerry L. Wheeler and Stacia Seaman
Production Design: Stacia Seaman
Cover Design by Tammy Seidick

Acknowledgments

Thank you, Bold Strokes Books, for making a dream a reality.

To:
Ethan
Amy
Mom

Chapter 1: Fin

"You okay?"

I wasn't okay. I was on the phone with my mother, sitting in the car in the middle of the road, incapable of moving forward. I was twenty-seven years old, and the only person who could still make everything okay was my mom. "I'm fine."

I checked the rearview mirror, but no one was behind me. Small town, middle of the day on a Wednesday...naw, I could have idled at that stop sign for hours and seen no one. I considered staying. In ten minutes, I would have been late; in forty I could have missed the whole funeral.

"How are things going with you?" I said to her. I let the phone rest in my palm while I stared at the screen. The clock on the phone showed the call was nine minutes long and counting.

"The way it always goes," Mom sighed, fed up. I could picture her sitting in the treatment chair, her bare feet up, a book on the armrest.

"Rose, is that Frank again?" I heard Lucas, my mother's in-home nurse, ask.

I groaned, slumping forward in the driver's seat, letting my forehead thump against the steering wheel. It was bad enough I had to call my mother for help. I didn't want Lucas to know. "Don't tell him it's me."

"Oh, Fin, you're on speaker."

"Mom!" I cried. "Take me off speaker."

"Fin, just go to the funeral," she told me for the thousandth time in a week. "It's not that big a deal."

But it *was* a big deal. The funeral was for Margery Starr, so her son, Orion, would be there. Orion Starr was a big deal. Orion Starr was the "crush of my life" big deal. He was the "guy who sparked my sexual awakening" big deal. He was the "guy who I haven't seen in six years" big deal. And I needed reassurance I wasn't some creep trying to stalk him at his own mother's funeral.

I had heard about the funeral through the gossip hotline that was the local drugstore while I was filling Mom's prescriptions.

"You knew that foreign family, didn't you, boy?" the craggy pharmacist asked me.

"Who?" I wondered, not sure why the guy was talking to me about anything besides two-a-day vitamins.

"You's the only carrot-top in this town...musta been you...all them years back...and that Mexican kid riding round on that blue motorcycle."

"Oh...Orion, yeah, I knew him." I thought about telling the pharmacist Orion wasn't Mexican, but it didn't seem worth it.

"Yeah, well that kid's mom passed. You going to the funeral?"

That left me speechless. I looked up the obituary and the details for the service as soon as I got home, not believing it until I saw her photo on the town news site. My heart left me then, taking a red-eye flight straight to Orion. I made up my mind to go to the funeral right then. Executing that plan was harder than it sounded.

"Fin?" Mom cooed into the phone.

I jumped, the memories popping like bubbles. "Yeah, Rosey?"

"I—"

"Where are you?" Lucas said.

"Lucas," I groaned.

"Don't *Lucas* me."

"What...what if he's at the funeral?" I sighed, relenting.

"He *should* be at the funeral, it's his mom. And you should be there because you knew her."

I rolled my eyes. Sure, I knew Margery. What I didn't know was if I was going for her or if I was going just to see Orion again. My guts bunched up, and I adjusted the AC to blow on my sweaty face.

"Mom?"

"It's okay, Fin. You know I would be there if I could."

"Treatment is more important," Lucas and I said together. Cancer didn't wait for you to help your grown-ass son get his shit together.

"At least I get ice cream today," Rose said.

"Who said?" Lucas laughed. We both knew Rose was just trying to wheedle a treat out of him, not that she had to try hard.

Despite my irritation, I had really come to respect Lucas. And maybe worship him a little. Having him around for the last three years had been refreshing, if not a blessing. Lucas Laverty was a giant, hulking man with warm, brown skin, green mohawk, full sleeve tattoos, and gauged ears. Mom and I knew we loved him his first day.

"Fin, any intention for going is the right intention," Mom offered knowingly.

"And it's not like you are gonna jump the guy in a church."

"Lucas," I groaned. I could hear him laugh, the sound growing smaller as Lucas moved away from the phone. "Fuck."

"Don't cuss at us, Frank," she scolded.

"What if I just—"

"*Frank*, get the fuck off the phone and go to the damned church."

"Damn. Fine."

"Bye, darlin'," Lucas said.

"Love you," Rose said. And the line went dead. Something deep in my heart ached. I took my foot off the brake and the car rolled forward into the intersection. I had to go. I knew I had to go. I gassed it and headed for the church.

❖

On the church steps, I sent Mom a happy face and a sad face text. She sent back a reassuring text, reminding me I had known Margery Starr for many years and showing up to her funeral wouldn't be "too weird." It sure as hell felt weird. Maybe it was some divine intervention that put me in Georgia the same summer Orion's mother passed away, bringing us both back here from the vast reaches separating us. *Okay, right, sure, Fin. And maybe pigs fly.*

If I was really just there to support Orion, why was my heart doing backflips? I mean, Orion and I had a long history. For the first half, all I wanted to do was make out with the guy. The last half I spent trying to forget him. Being supportive was the right reason to go. The heart palpitations, on the other hand…well.

Just do it, I ordered myself, and that gave me enough willpower to put my hand on the door. I paused anyway, my excitement, my dread, my guilt making my whole body sweat. The momentum was lost, and I stepped back, staring at my shadow cast against the glossy wooden doors.

Mom sent a thumbs-up emoji just as I was about to turn and run. That was a dirty trick. A thumbs-up meant Mom was proud of me, and now I had to earn it by being a decent human being and going inside the church. I pulled at the sturdy material of my light blazer, airing myself a bit against the heat and my own chaotic nerves as I went in.

Churches were nothing new, especially this one. My father, grandfather, and grandmother had passed through that sanctuary on their way to being cremated. I could have found my way to a pew in my sleep. I silenced my phone as I folded into a bench near the back. If anyone heard me come in, they didn't indicate it. I was relieved. The pastor was just starting. I took in the room. A few people were seated already, patternless and solitary. One man leaned heavily on the pew in front of him, and a woman whimpered into a handkerchief. Then there was Orion.

I tried to ignore the visceral reaction Orion created in me. I had not physically seen him since he walked out that night a long time ago. And I was over him. *Right?* I shook my head to clear it. Either way, I would have known Orion anywhere.

"Today we are here to honor Margery Nicole Starr," the pastor intoned. The sound made me flinch, reminding me why I was there in the first place. I sighed and turned to the front of the room, fishing a handkerchief out of my coat. I noticed the coffin for the first time as the pastor started telling a story.

The proceedings were the shortest I had ever sat through, but they were nice, and they reminded me of the unceremonious way the Starrs lived their lives. I sure as shit cried my eyes out, which was embarrassing. I hated the pomp and circumstance around death, I hated the idea of someone being so unreachable. It wasn't just Margery, either. It was everyone. I urged myself to regroup, wiping my face.

The casket would be left at the altar for a while so people could say their goodbyes, then she would go off to be cremated. Instead of going over to pay my respects, I just sat watching Orion. He stood and looked awkwardly around the room…well, not the whole room, because he didn't see me. I knew I would have to offer condolences at some point, but the distance of time between us kept me rooted. I watched him talk to other people. Then they left. We were alone.

I turned away as Orion approached her casket. I knew it was a private moment. I instead looked down at the pew in front of me until he turned and came up the aisle. As he stomped toward the door, he kept his head down. I didn't expect him to see me. I hoped he would, but I felt like the whole event could have passed without him noticing me. I was relieved to think he would pass me by and it would be over in a few seconds. He would never have known I was there. I shifted to watch him leave.

Orion, probably hearing the pew creak, turned so fast I almost jumped. Our eyes met, and I couldn't stop the stupid smile from forming. Orion just nodded and was gone. It had happened so fast, it might as well have not happened at all. But every part of me was disappointed, like the air had been knocked from my chest. All we had been, all we were, seemed reduced to that simple, sorry nod. And I was a little heartbroken.

Memories and emotions started to fill me, the sound of the church door slamming still echoing in the room. I stayed in the pew as the seconds stretched. I felt like a teenager, Orion passing me indifferently in the halls at school. Orion had been aloof, showing up at school only on the rarest occasions, usually with a guitar in tow. I had been a member of the soccer team and felt mostly like an octopus, reaching six feet before seventh grade. Too many differences for teenagers to reconcile. As I sat alone in the church, I thought back to the time when Orion had never looked at me, only through me.

After a solid minute, the circuits in my brain reconnected and I nearly groaned. *This is what you get.* Frustrated and feeling too young, I went to do what I had come for, or what I *should* have come for. I went to say goodbye to Margery Starr. I stood on the platform with the dark and beautiful coffin and I thought it suited her, even though being cremated suited her more. She had been almost as mysterious as her son, so seeing the coffin was a little like seeing a flower under glass. Pretty, but unsettling.

"See ya around, Marge," I offered aloud. She used to call me by my full first and middle name. *See ya around, Franklin Ian. See ya around, Marge.* I remembered us standing at the bus station. I had said my goodbyes to Orion the night before, and I wasn't supposed to be there. I went anyway. I let her pull me into her sunny presence, she was so proud. And I was so heartbroken. Orion and I hadn't been anything more than friends then.

I refocused on Marge. I had seen her around town a few times over the year I had been living with my mom. No matter when I saw her, she always smiled and asked how I was. I didn't even think about her getting worse when I hadn't seen her for a few weeks. Now she was gone. And so was her son, probably miles away by now.

"He'll be fine," I said, slipping my hands over the cool wood, not knowing if that was true, but desperately wanting it to be. I turned to leave, trying not to knock over the wreath of flowers. The sun was blazing through the stained glass, broken colors tinting patterns onto the seats of the pews and the worn wooden floor. I slipped my hands into my blazer pockets just as my phone buzzed with a new text, probably from Rose.

The thought of Mom stopped me at the door, and I had to choke back a sob. *Rose.* I couldn't physically stomach thinking of how close she had been to a coffin of her own. I stood still a moment, gasping at the thought. My need to keep her with me, to keep her safe, was so strong some days, I could have bent steel with my bare hands. She didn't like that I got angry or scared about it. So, I took a breath. And another. It steadied me. *Rose was alive, Margery was dead, Orion was a stranger.* On the heels of that reality check, I left the church.

CHAPTER 2: ORION

Shit, I made it. I blew past the "Welcome Back to Painted Waters, Home of Painted Waters Orchard and Tilly's Whiskey," sign. That fucking sign, freshly painted by 4H every year. It welcomed you back—*back*. As if anyone wanted to be back. You either stayed gone or you never left.

The motorcycle wobbled, and I focused on the road. I don't think I'd looked around since I left New York almost three days ago, and I didn't really need to look at Painted Waters. It was the same. The old roads were still buckling, the ancient trees trying to take back the land. The new streets were lined with ordinary houses, and the trees were all small and new, leaving everything to bake in the sun. I had to cross town to get to the church, which meant I got a high-speed view of every place in my past. Looking around was like rummaging in a junk drawer, just a bunch of crap you couldn't get rid of and didn't need.

At a stoplight I took a second to take my helmet off and wipe my face. The light changed from red to green and back to red. I was one of the people who never left the town, not really. As long as Mom was here, I was here. She wanted me out. She wanted me to be something, but I just wanted to be home. Now she was dead—*is dead*. And I am in Painted fucking Waters to get her ashes, then—well, I don't know what after that.

A voice inside me stirred and sang. *I left but we both knew I wouldn't stay gone, now you're not here and I have no way home*. It was a lyric to a song something inside me was writing. Most days the lyrics or melodies that would pop up in my head would become real songs. But my life had become so loud, I couldn't hear the music. With Mom dead, the haunting memories of my past had voices again. They were like debt collectors calling for money I didn't have.

You remember, they chanted, *when you got arrested—*
When you crashed your bike—
When you ran away—
When you let your mother die alone—

"Fuck me." Some of those debt collecting memories were out for blood. And if I had a better sense of humor, I could probably find a song in that. I missed her. She had made Painted Waters close to bearable. And she was gone.

I patted the baby blue crystal paint of the motorcycle's tank. Resigning myself to being just on the north end of human, I slammed the helmet back down over my face. If I stayed where I was, baking on the highway, I could easily pretend Mom was alive. I could pretend she was so busy with work I never got to see her and she never got to call. I could pretend. I would rather pretend. I looked once into the side mirror, first seeing the dusty horizon and the country road bubbling in the haze, then my own reflection. I juiced the bike, rolling through the red light.

❖

I made too much noise coming into the church. I tried to keep my head down for as long as I could, the red carpet leading me down the aisle to the front of the room. I didn't know where to sit or if I should cross myself or something, so I just dove into the second row of benches and tried to be fucking small.

I could look but there would be nothing left to see, the singer in my head crooned. I did look up then. Alone at the front of the room sat the shining coffin, my mom's coffin, dark wood draped in colored shapes of light from the glass windows. My heart hummed for a moment at the beautiful, painted fractals of light on glassy wood. It was only a second, but it had been like drawing together stitches, momentarily healing something.

You are such a romantic. The voice was Mom's from a memory a lifetime ago.

A womanly voice whimpered, and a door at the back of the church opened and shut. I became suddenly aware other people were in the room. I ignored them, keeping my eyes on the polygons of color on Mom's coffin.

The ceremony was short and to the point. I heard only Mom's name, Margery Nicole Starr, spoken and repeated like a single, reverent word. It became a mantra. *Margery—Nicole—Starr. Margery—Nicole—Starr. Margery—Nicole—Starr.* The other thing my mind chanted was *I want this to be over.* At some point I shed tears, but I don't know when. I just wiped my face when the preacher said the last few words of some prayer and a bunch of voices whispered "Amen."

I didn't want to stay once it was over, but I owed Mom something, so I guess I had to be nice to her friends. Only Mom's neighbor, Chrissy, and the preacher talked to me. I just nodded along so they would think what they were saying mattered. I figured agreeing with their version of grief was better than trying to explain my emptiness.

Eventually they were gone. I heard the doors to the church open and close a few times, so at some point I assumed I was alone. *More than ever before.* The silence felt large, like the church couldn't hold the nothing, like I wasn't containing my own emptiness. Mom had had a warmth like the sun on your face. From the coffin, there was nothing.

I went over to it, trying again and again to take a breath that would make a difference. I placed my hands on the lid. The contact of my palms on the hardwood was painful, like touching a bruise. There was nothing to say. Or at least nothing I could think of. Besides, it wasn't goodbye yet. I had to wait however long it took to get her ashes, then had to figure out some way, or where, to spread them. I held on to the lid of the coffin. I held on to the last whole, physical form of my mother. I held on to myself. And then I had nothing left to hold on to. I slammed my fists into my back pockets and turned to leave.

I was halfway down the center aisle when a flash of orange caught my eye. I glanced over, expecting light from the stained windows, and froze midstep. Fin. And to make it worse, he smiled at me. My brain flatlined in the wake of it. The most I could manage was a quick nod before rushing out of the church.

Why the hell is Fin here? Last I heard from him, he was in Rhode Island. It's not like the guy would come all the way to Painted Waters just for Mom's funeral. I practically ran down the steps of the church to where I had parked. Fin was the source of a whole lot of debt collecting memories—bad memories I owed a great deal of accountability to. I felt overwhelmed, but I managed to let out a breath I had been holding and suck air back in.

With nothing else to fill me, those old, complicated feelings floated around inside me like smoke. I had just touched the handlebars of the bike when it occurred to me Fin was there for a reason, Fin had a reason for doing everything in his whole life. And I wanted to fucking know why he was there.

Fin. Mom is dead. Fin. Mom is dead. The thoughts were too conflicting, too loud. So I latched on to one and held it there so the others couldn't get in. I wanted to know what Fin was doing there. I hopped on the bike, revving it loudly in the quiet lane. I pulled it alongside the sidewalk that led into the church. Parked in the afternoon shade of the church steeple, I waited.

I had been there for a handful of minutes before I realized I had no idea what I was going to say to him. I could blurt a bunch of questions at him, but who was I to demand answers? Especially from Fin. The list of shit I owed that guy was long. *Remember when you left town without telling him you never planned to come back, remember how you walked out on him, remember how you strung him along, remember how you don't deserve him?* Yup, I had done all that to Fin and more probably. I had moments to decide if I wanted to stay and see what he wanted. I mean, I wanted to stay, but should I? Would it do more harm than good?

I turned to grab my helmet off the lock when I noticed the second helmet locked to the passenger seat at the back. I had bought that on impulse. Somewhere around year four of the six since I had last seen Fin, I needed to replace my helmets. The sales guy talked me into a pair of black helmets. The only passenger I had ever had on the bike had been Fin. Not even Mom. And certainly not any other guy. And I have never planned on ever letting anyone ride with me again. But I had bought them anyway.

I still had no idea what I would say to him when he stepped out into the sun. His face was scrunched with some unknowable thought. I wanted him—wanted to *talk* to him, I mean. He was still as thin as ever. He was dressed in a cream-colored suit, white shirt underneath. I could just barely tell he was wearing biking boots. Between that and my extra helmet, it was a sign of something.

He looked so surprised to see me that I reacted before thinking. I nodded the same nod that had passed between us ten thousand times. *Get on, let's go.* For some impossible reason, he started toward me.

What the fuck am I doing?

CHAPTER 3: FIN

I stumbled into the sun, wondering where I had left the car. I noticed a shape through the glare. When the spots cleared, I realized I was staring at Orion. And Orion was staring at me. My guts dropped into my shoes, and I felt myself tense. I hadn't expected to see him outside. Honestly, I hadn't expected to see him ever again. Orion offered me a slight, familiar nod. He was inviting me on the bike, inviting me to go wherever it was he intended to go.

Orion had communicated what he wanted with only a slight nod, the way a few notes fill your mind with the words of a song. It was an old song, but I remembered all the words. The man was a fucking siren. I had no business getting on that bike. I had no business feeling the way I felt. And yet, the allure of Orion and his bike overpowered any reasonable portion of my brain. Besides, I could tell Orion was on the edge, fraying. I had promised Marge he would be okay, and getting on the bike seemed like a way to keep the promise.

I undid the buttons of my jacket, hoping to look cool, and I started toward him. It seemed to take forever to walk over, especially with his eyes on me the whole time. Orion slipped his helmet from the second seat and pulled another one from the latches at the back. He handed it to me, and I took it. Damn, that bike was as enticing as he was. The sight of the two of them was enough to wake up my inner teenager.

We stared at each other and I didn't miss the suspicion in his eyes. I couldn't blame him. I felt it, too. Neither one of us seemed to know what the fuck we were doing. We pulled the helmets on without a word.

I slid into place behind him, the motion familiar but underpracticed, and I put my hands around his waist. Fire scorched through me at the contact, and I had to work hard to stamp it out, reminding myself we were leaving a funeral. He brought the bike to life. We left the church in the dust.

I knew where we were going as soon as Orion made the left in front of Jerry's Peach Orchard. I closed my eyes to the memories, but I could map that route in my sleep: a right on Pinenut Drive, stopping for the new light the city put in last year, a hard curve left, and then out of town. Instinctually, anticipating the drop of the large hill, I tightened my grip on Orion.

When I opened my eyes again, we were twenty minutes outside the city. The trees had taken back most of the road, forming a dense canopy, the light dim and the air cool. I had to resist the urge to put my hands out wide and pretend to fly, like I had so often as a teen. Instead, Orion turned hard onto an unmarked service road. Then the bike stopped and the ride was over.

I dismounted, removed my helmet, and looked around. I blinked away the sad memory of our private goodbye on the bridge the night before Orion's bus left town. He had simply said, *I am leaving*, and I had said, *I know*, and he said, *I don't know when I will see you again* and my heart fell out of my body. I was so naive then, at eighteen, thinking that was the worst he could hurt me. I hadn't been back to the bridge since.

I tried to ignore the memories. I didn't understand how he still had any impact on me at all. I must have spent the last six years kidding myself. And we hadn't even said anything to each other. I told myself our history didn't matter, that the only thing that mattered was Orion's heartache over his mother.

I looked at him, trying to see him all at once. It was like looking at a solar eclipse without the proper tools. The way Orion drove the bike said a lot about how he was feeling. I used it liked a codex to unlock him. Considering the high speeds, sharp turns, and the fact that he had missed a stop sign, this version of Orion had the potential to do some serious damage, mostly to himself. The teenager in me was scared for my old friend, and I let that be enough. Emphasis on friend.

Orion pulled off his helmet and tossed it to me the way he always had. I pinned the helmets to the back of the bike, watching tensely while Orion shuffled through the saddlebags. The first thing he found was a T-shirt. I felt my skin warm and prickle as Orion pulled off the leather vest and the black polo, suddenly revealing tan flesh. I looked at my feet, my whole body thrumming. I forced myself to think about anything else. *I am an adult who doesn't need to panic when a hot guy takes off his shirt—correction, his funeral shirt.* That thought filled me with enough guilt to dim the arousal. When I dared look back, Orion was again rummaging through the bags as if nothing had happened, the Leather and Lace band logo on the shirt pulled across his chest as he moved.

Needing relief, I pulled off my blazer and folded it. With surprising familiarity, Orion took the jacket from me and added it to the contents of the saddlebags. The gesture embarrassed me for a reason I couldn't place. Stepping away from him, I untucked my dress shirt, rolled up the sleeves, crammed my hands in my pockets, and stared down the slightly muddy, slightly buggy trail to the bridge.

I started down the path, and Orion slowly followed. The first time I had come to the bridge was also on the back of Orion's bike. Only then I had been sixteen and carrying a birthday cake. It was small, round, made for three or four people, and read *Happy Birthday Principal Yeager*. Orion had stolen it and had offered me a piece if I held it while he drove. It was a terrible, mildly dangerous plan, but to a young guy with a crush, it was perfection. I would have held on to a live velociraptor if it meant going anywhere with him. That was the first time we'd talked to each other, and that was all it took.

I said none of that out loud. We just walked on in silence, Orion always slightly behind me. The bridge was an old railroad pass over the shallow water and muddy rocks below. The state diverted the river years before either of us had existed. Years after that, it diverted the railroad. The bridge seemed hidden from all of humanity. The vast, dense forest was in one direction, town in the other.

I picked up a few rocks before the rails opened to the riverbed below, I tossed them one by one out into the distance, listening for the splash or clank. As we moved out over the river, the height reaching nearly thirty feet, Orion passed me and went straight to the middle of the bridge. He sat, straddling one of the rails. Even though he never said so, I knew Orion was afraid of heights, but the abandoned place had always been his favorite. I had freaked him out a few times by sitting at the edge. Orion never sat at the edge.

I dropped the rest of my rocks through the slating, some clinking against the metal, some thudding against the wood. It was amazing how you could spend a whole day feeling like you were seventeen again. It was all too familiar. Birds tittered and the sun slipped through the leaves. It was one of the better days I had seen in a long time. Or maybe it was one of the first days I had decided to let soak in.

Orion pulled the flask from his pocket and drank, looking out toward nothing. He offered me the flask as I took a seat next to him. I took it, breathing through the burn of the whiskey inside. I passed it back, and he took an easy swig as if the flask were full of nothing more than water. I remembered him drunk almost as well as I remembered him sober, and that made me worry. He tried to offer the flask to me again, but I declined. We sat almost at ease for a while. We didn't look at each other, just watched the wind blow the leaves on the trees and the sun start to sink.

Then Orion spoke the first words. "Looks like you finally figured out how to grow a beard."

I laughed. After all the years, I never would have guessed that would be the first thing he said to me. I looked over my shoulder at him. He offered a half-cocked smile and a shrug, which was as close to a laugh as he came most of the time. I shrugged. "Yeah, turns out you have to stop growing taller in order to grow a real beard."

I felt Orion take a hard look at me, doing a full appraisal of the man I had become, but I did nothing to acknowledge it. Who knew what he thought of me? I sure as hell didn't know what I thought of him.

"Quit before you reach seven feet?"

"I didn't want to seem show-offy," I said. Orion shrug-laughed again, taking another draw from his flask. I took a chance. "O?"

"Fin?"

"You hanging in there?"

Orion looked down into the creek. I knew to wait out his thoughts. Orion didn't look up when he answered. "I...I don't know, Fin. Probably not."

"Yup."

I understood then what Orion needed from me and what I had

wanted to give him. Sitting like we were on that bridge was how we had met, how we had managed Orion's moods in the years after. I was there to protect Orion from himself.

"I'm nearly a real doctor now," I started. Orion nodded and looked at me. "Yeah, I…don't know what you remember, but I am almost done with school. Mom needed me back here for a while, so I came down. It is complicated, but I have…"

And I told Orion about how the botched paperwork at my school delayed my graduation. Then I continued to talk about anything that came to mind. I felt a little like I was composing one of my emails. In the last six years, Orion and I sent each other a total of eight emails each. *He emailed you first*, my pride offered as a reminder, the New Year's Eve after he left me alone in that hotel. Anyway, my emails were always these long-winded explanations without much direction. And the conversation on the bridge was going about the same.

Orion continued to get drunk. Drunk was better than some things for Orion. But he also looked like he was listening, nodding along, or making an expression that matched the mood of the story I told. I was surprised because Orion seemed to truly want to hear what I said next. The thought made me blush, but I tried to play it off by ignoring it.

❖

My single shot of whisky had been my only. If I could get Orion home before he got the idea to go to a bar or something, I could keep him from doing something crazy for at least one night. Or I assumed I could. I was using predictions from 1942 to try and predict the winner of the Kentucky Derby in 2020. I only *remembered* Orion. He could be completely different in the present.

I had a motorcycle license and was planning to drive us both back. I knew—or used to know—Orion wouldn't want to leave the bike behind, so he wouldn't want to walk. And no way in hell was he driving with or without me. By the time the sun had fallen below the trees, Orion had burned through the flask and an assortment of shooters he had with him. As he finished one off, he would line up the little plastic bottles on the iron rail, like a little army. Soon I was staring at the setting sun through the silhouette of Orion's grief.

I had recounted nearly every aspect of the last six years to him save a major one. I didn't tell Orion I was back in Georgia because Mom was sick. It's not like he asked. It was always in the back of my throat, just like it had always been on the tips of my fingers for three years. Orion's mother had been sick, and it seemed cruel to unburden my own worries on the guy. Or maybe for a long time I felt like I was failing my mom because I could do nothing to stop her pain, to keep her alive, and that made me a coward, at least in my own mind. I couldn't bring myself to explain that to him, not today.

I looked at my watch. It was just after eight thirty. Rose would be out cold from the medication Lucas had given her at seven, so she'd never hear us come in. I gave it half an hour more just in case. I had to take Orion home, but I saw no reason to subject him and Rose to each other. Rose Ness was a patient and beautiful woman, but a drunk Orion rarely sat well with anyone. Or at least he used to, my brain reminded. Besides, I was sure a mother, even Rose, was the last thing Orion needed.

At nine, when I had run out of things to say, I was ready to put up a fight to get the bike keys. I stood, held out my hand, and said with all the force and confidence I could manage, "It is time to go. Give me the keys."

Orion made an effort at a laugh. "You kidding?"

"No, give me the keys to the bike. You're coming back to my place."

Orion scoffed, a cruel edge creeping into his voice. "Why? Just leave me."

"Sure, so you can pass out and die of exposure."

"What is so bad about that?"

"Animals will eat you, develop a blood lust, and…that would ruin the town aesthetic," I said, crossing my arms. I felt suddenly exposed. I couldn't tell Orion I cared about him, even after all the years, all the space, all the pain. I did care, at least enough to make sure he was okay for the night.

Orion laughed and smiled, his eyes shining with drink and the growing twilight. "You're funny."

"Orion. Let's go before it gets too dark. Give me the keys to the bike."

"That…that is not a *bike*, that's my wife, and we are…exclusive." Orion made a show of crossing his legs to demonstrate his unwillingness to leave the bridge.

"O, get up, let's go. Quit jackassing around." I risked kicking Orion's shoe.

Orion growled, but stood. He only looked at me, a curious stare perched on his face. He didn't say anything, he didn't have to. I knew enough to know. "I can drive it. I mean I am licensed, and I know you aren't gonna want to leave it in the woods. So…"

Orion blinked a few times and slipped his hands into his shallow front pockets, not to retrieve the keys, just to store his hands as if he were at risk of forgetting them. I grunted but pulled my wallet from my pocket. I had a bike of my own, left behind with my apartment and work in Rode Island. I handed the slightly bent ID card to Orion.

Orion grinned. "This is a bike license. You need a *wife* license."

"You are such a baby." I snatched the card back.

I was starting to get anxious. The fading light would make the landscape and Orion all the more harsh. My next move came to me as a lightning bolt of instinct, a chance I had to take while Orion still had sense of humor enough to put up with it. I put my wallet away and casually, but quickly stepped up to Orion, my height working to my advantage. Orion didn't step back or flinch. I reached around him, put a hand in his back pocket, and took the keys for myself, unhooking them from the chain with one hand.

Orion look both impressed and annoyed. "Fine."

I started for the bike without waiting or looking behind me. My heart caught up with the situation. The proximity of Orion, the strong smell of leather and booze, made my mind puddle a bit. I didn't wait for Orion to catch up, I just went about unlocking the helmets and starting the bike. I had to breathe, to focus on getting us home.

Orion stopped a moment at the edge of the road. He stared and swayed. His stare, the way he scanned me made my hot blood boil hotter. I pulled on the helmet to try and block my own blush and held out the other to him. Orion could cruise me all he wanted, I just needed to get him on the bike.

Orion stumbled nearer and begrudgingly took the second helmet. He put it on. "I have wanted to get behind you for a long time."

My heart contracted, and I cleared my throat. The innuendo was funny, but it was also ironic in that Orion had never been "behind me"—under me, sure, but never behind. And despite his intention, his remark was hurtful because of the way things had ended that night. I wasn't prepared to think about any of that. "This is as close as you're gonna get tonight, so you better enjoy it. Fall off, and I get to keep the bike."

I tried not to think too hard about what I had meant by "tonight" as Orion slid in behind me. I pulled us onto the lane. Orion held me a little tighter than I expected. We rode in silence for a while. The moon was bright but couldn't compete with the failing light from the sun. Fireflies drifted in dizzying circles over green lawns and amongst the moss and vines that dressed the trees. I tried to focus on the road, not on the lewd comment Orion had made, or the way he had stared, or his hands around me. I took a deep breath. Then another.

"Fin." Onion's voice cracked in my helmet.

"The hell?" I laughed, surprised.

"It's Bluetooth."

"That's awesome—I am Iron Man."

"No...no...my bike...I am Iron Man, you're Jarvis."

"Fine."

"Fin."

"O."

"Thanks...I...it's been nice...seeing you."

My stupid, nostalgic, sappy heart did a backflip, and it took me a beat or two to find an answer. "It's been nice to see you too."

"And, uh...the funeral...thanks for coming."

"Yeah. Marge was a good lady."

Orion fell silent and I didn't fill the space. The house was in view before he spoke again. "If I knew you could drive like this, I would have let you haul me around a lot more."

His voice was soggy. It was the first sign of tears Orion had shown since leaving the church. His grip on me tightened slightly. I thought about rubbing Orion's hand, but it seemed smarter not to.

"Well, you know what they say," I said instead.

"Do I?"

"Sure...once you go bike, that's all you like."

Both of us laughed, a real and decently long laugh.

"Whatever you say, Fin."

I pulled the bike into the yard and right up to the front door. What was I going to tell Rose in the morning?

"Where are we?" Orion asked, his voice ringing through the helmet and across the quiet lawn.

I pulled off my helmet. "My house. Don't you remember it? Here, wait here, I'll put the bike in the back."

Orion slid off, handing me his helmet. He stared at the house like it was something he should have known. I pushed the bike into the barn. Standing in the doorway, I looked at the bike and felt the same way I had when I saw Orion that afternoon, like seeing it all at once but not at all. If Orion was the sun, then the bike was Apollo's chariot. Then I had to roll my eyes. *You are the sappiest fuck.* I shut and locked the barn and went back to the front of the house, fishing the door keys out of my pocket.

"What happened to the tree? And the house wasn't blue the last time I saw it either," Orion hummed, standing a bit too close to me as I aimed the key into the lock.

I was shocked. I had forgotten a peach tree used to be in the front yard. I turned to look at the slight dip in the grass where it had been. Then I surveyed the baby-blue exterior of the house. Things were different. "The tree was destroyed in a storm four years ago, maybe. Mom made me paint it blue because the peach color made her miss the tree."

"Rose." Orion spoke the name as if it were a holy word. Maybe to him it was. I let us into the house.

"I will sleep here," Orion proposed, making a stumbling dive for the couch.

I scooped him under the arms before he could reach the cushions, grunting under the weight of him. "Ha, fat chance."

Orion growled but complied. I didn't feel bad. There had been a time when he was crashing on my floor two out of every five nights, and a pile of busted concrete would have been more comfortable than the living room couch. Orion just probably didn't remember. He stood back up and pushed into my room. He did a lap around then sighed.

He turned and looked at me. "Come on, Fin. Can't we go to the bar or something?"

"No. As a medical professional, I am going to say you've had enough."

"I could take more."

"Stop that."

"What am I supposed to do? It's like nine thirty."

"Go to sleep," I suggested. He just blinked. I sighed. "You were just ready to fall asleep on the couch and now."

He eyed me like I was crazy and ran a hand over his hair. That hand in his hair wasn't a good thing. It had once meant he was anxious and overwhelmed. I looked around the room trying to find something for him to do. I spotted my tablet on the bedside table.

"Here, play with this, I am going to get ready for bed," I said, handing him the device. He was such a kid about the games on a phone or tablet. *Had been*, the voice inside me chided.

He thumbed it open. "I am too drunk for this."

I laughed. "Exactly, so fucking make a bed and lay down."

He grunted as he tapped. I heard a music app chirp to life. It wasn't a game, it was just mock instruments. But it seemed to engross him. He set the tablet down on the bed, watching the instructions, and started to undress. I left the room to give us both a minute.

When I came back from the bathroom, I could hear gentle music coming from behind the door to my room. It was more than just someone following along in an app, pecking at fake keys or strings. It was real and full and beautiful. It was something dark and bluesy, just the way he liked it. Most importantly, it was new, unheard before this moment. Orion had always been like that. Most people liked him because he could reproduce their favorite song. I liked that, sure, but I liked more that he was creative enough to bring new music to life. As soon as I opened the door, the music stopped.

I turned off the overhead light in favor of a bedside lamp and stripped down to my boxers. Orion had reclaimed his old spot on the floor by the door that led to the backyard. I had stopped in the hall for more pillows and another blanket, so I tossed them down to him. He grunted his thanks, and I heard the tablet chirp off.

"You don't have to stop on my account."

"Naw, you're right about sleep," he said, his voice drowsy. I just grunted and turned out the light. I jammed the button on the boom box, and my night music started to play.

"Ugh, I did not miss Chopin," Orion growled.

"This isn't Chopin and I can't sleep wi—"

"I know, I know, without music. I guess I would have thought you would have grown better taste—" Orion's voice was cut off as I threw a pillow at him.

"Fine," he mumbled from around the plush material. I heard him shuffling on the floor and knew he was going to keep the pillow I had tossed at him. That was fine. We fell into stillness and silence, the classical music syncing into an odd discourse with the cicadas and crickets.

"Fin."

It was so soft, I almost didn't hear my name being called. "O."

"My mother is dead."

"I know...I am sorry, Orion," I murmured. I rolled over and reached down. I ran my hand over his hair once, softly. It brought me some comfort to be able to offer him that small, deliberate touch. Orion seemed soothed, letting out a sigh, nestling into his pillows.

CHAPTER 4: ORION

Somewhere a latch clicked gently. To me it was an explosion. I nearly jumped out of my skin and was instantly transported to a world of pain. My head felt like it was going to burst open, my muscles collapsed under my weight, and every single part of me felt the loss of my mother. Tears burned in my eyes at the sudden sensation.

Oh God, just take me now. I sat up hoping it would settle the room. It didn't. It just sent the floor up over the ceiling, and I knew I was going to vomit. I stood and started for the bathroom. Even though I wasn't completely sure where I was, my body seemed to know the way. I didn't even knock.

"ORION!" I heard Fin screech—*wait, Fin? Like actual Fin?*—from behind the shower curtain as I plowed into the bathroom, the door slamming against the tub with a high, cracking pop. I stumbled against the tub, nearly pulling the shower curtain down. I could sense Fin jumped back, heard him hit his elbow on something metal inside the shower.

"Shit—Fin! I'm sorry, I just—"

Then I was face first in Fin's toilet barfing. It gave me time to remember what a gigantic asshole I was. I was half dressed, barfing in the bathroom of a guy I royally ghosted, after a night of binge drinking over the death of my mother. *Orion, you are just the bee's knees.*

"O, you okay?" Fin called, still hiding in the shower.

I wasn't, but I couldn't tell him that. I was done barfing, though. When I was sure no more would come, I slumped against the toilet and the floor, the cool tile and porcelain going a long way to ease my suffering. I used some of the toilet paper to wipe my mouth and then tossed that into the bowl. The room reeked of whatever dude shampoo Fin was using and my own barf.

"Naw…yeah…maybe," I said, running my hands over my sweating face. The smell that fogged my general area threatened to send me back to the toilet, so I pulled the handle.

Fin screamed.

There was a heartbeat, then a flash of curtain and skin as Fin dove out of the shower. I saw everything, *everything,* before he was able to get a towel around himself. Then he turned on me, his breath heavy and his face angry. I scrambled to my feet, not understanding the sudden panic.

"What happened?" I cried.

"Really? You don't remember?" he grumbled, wiping water from his face.

I thought it out, staring at Fin. A series of flashes went off and I remembered. In the old Ness house, if you turned on a faucet anywhere, flushed a toilet, or even if the sprinklers came on at the neighbor's house, the shower water would go suddenly scalding hot, then painfully cold. Fin was funny, his face crunched in concentrated rage. The rest of him however, was an unintimidating bright pink. Being a sympathetic guy, I slumped over laughing.

"Damn it, Orion," Fin hissed, raking wet, red hair from his face. He stood dripping and glaring, but I could see the slightest hint of amusement behind his pursed lips.

"I…just…I am sorry, Fin." I giggled, leaning against the wall to steady myself.

The Fin from last night on the bridge seemed like a painting of the person I had known. Fin's beard was a dark red, intentionally trimmed and shaped into a professional look. The hair on his head, a lighter red, was cut into the latest trend I had seen on billboards. Even his accent had softened, the drawl barely there at the ends of words. Despite all that, the freckles, the pale, almost translucent skin, and shadowy hazel eyes were unchanged.

I had seen Fin look many ways, but time, age, and distance had changed what I remembered. It's not like I couldn't lurk on the guys social media when I wanted a good dose of *look what you fucked up*, so I had seen pictures of Fin over the years. The man sitting with me on the bridge last night seemed like yet another picture of a person I had known.

I saw the real Fin standing in the bathroom. The effect was jarring, and I stared because I was a thirsty creep. I let the seconds stretch, taking in the water glistening on his hard, subtle abdominal muscles. I felt paralyzed by the lazy splatter of freckles on creamy shoulders and lean arms, stretching as Fin tensed under my gaze. The tattoo was new, less than two years old. My brain even took a mental snapshot of Fin's big hand clenching to keep the towel closed over his hips. *Oh man, this is gonna haunt you.* I was just lucky I was too hungover to spring wood. A song rambled: *it's a high price to pay for the memory/but I will take what I can get/It's another day in our history/don't make me end it yet.*

Fin seemed unamused, his skin going from pink to pinker. He snapped to catch my attention and pointed for the door. I laughed and moved to leave. As I crossed, I caught a peripheral glimpse of myself in the mirror. I was half dressed, hair falling in chaotic patches over my face. Overall, I looked like a guy who would throw up in your bathroom. I would have been embarrassed, but I was too distracted. Fin cleared his throat again.

"Yup...I am going back to sleep." I hummed, that too-comfortable feeling creeping up. I noticed some toothpaste on the sink, and without thinking too much about it I took it up and squirted some in my mouth. The intense mint made my eyes water, but I swished it around anyway.

"You're feral," Fin grumbled, but I could tell he was trying to hold back a laugh. I responded by swallowing.

"Oh my God," Fin sighed. He looked me over. Not in a sexy way, but in a medical way. I was being examined. I liked Fin's eyes on me anyway. I wanted to say something, but I had nothing—many nothings, so I continued to leave.

"Wait." Fin stopped me, a hand on my shoulder. I waited as he opened the cabinet over the sink and retrieved an aspirin bottle. He held it out to me like he was offering me a dirty tissue. I took the whole bottle. Shaking it, I offered Fin a salute and meandered back to his room. I chugged the glass of water on Fin's nightstand, sending pills down with it. Then I flopped on the bed, intending to slide to the floor again.

Chapter 5: Fin

I waited for the water to return to normal before I stepped back under the flow. Up until the moment Orion barged into my bathroom, I'd had a pretty normal morning. I started with a run, ending at the church so I could pick up the car I had abandoned when I jumped to Orion's aid. When I got in to drive back to the house, I remembered I had no idea who Orion was, not anymore. The thought filled me with prickly irritation. What was I doing? As I drove, I became infuriated with my instinct to take care of him. I didn't owe him shit. The easy comfort we had found on the bridge was annoying. I hated that I had spilled my guts and Orion had said four words at most.

I was a ball of crabbiness when I went to wake Rose, but she was already awake sitting up in her bed, book on her lap. I knew as soon as she looked at me she knew Orion was in the house. We watched each other the whole way as I walked her to the yard. This time last year I was practically carrying her from one room to another. Now she moved without even needing to lean on me. She looked at me out of the corner of her eye, and, of course, I just blushed. I could tell my mother anything. The telling wasn't what worried me. I wasn't sure I wanted to know what she would say. The porch swing was right under the bathroom window, so she probably heard everything.

I laughed ruefully as I scratched shampoo into my hair. I was irritated Orion had barged in, seen me naked, ogled me. *Ogled me.* That thought gave me pause. Orion had looked at me like he was attracted to me, and that irritated me only because I still wanted him to be attracted to me. I stuck my head under the flow, hating myself for wanting that.

Briefly I remember that night in the hotel six years ago. He had wanted me then. *Only for the night, as it turned out.*

The unfiltered, sleazy way Orion had stared sent a bolt of lightning through me. I wanted him as much as I wanted him to want me. It didn't help that he'd been wearing only briefs and his tight T-shirt, hair falling in a sexy mess, molten gold eyes. I had dreamt of that look from Orion for a long time, and now that I had seen it again, my mind wasn't about to let me forget it. At some point, that certain ache started to pool in my dick, bringing on a weird combination of irritation and horniness. I didn't have time to manage a hard-on, so I flipped the tap to cold and let the frigid water kill it.

I toweled off and dressed in a hurry, proud of myself for thinking to bring clothes into the bathroom so I wouldn't have to change in front of Orion. *God—fucking—help me.* I went to check on him first, because *of course* I had to check on him first. I tried to tell myself it was my Hippocratic oath, my duty as a future doctor.

I was surprised to find Orion passed out on my bed. I surveyed him both as a medical professional and as a friend. Orion looked pale, ill in the growing light of morning. I remembered other long mornings with Orion in similar states of hangover in high school. His brown skin, black hair, and gold eyes dulled by the demons he tried to drown. His hair was longer than I had ever seen it, inching past his shoulders. The past few days, months maybe, must have weighed on him more than he let on. I could see it in the purely exhausted way he slept. My irritation faltered.

My room was at the back of a one-story house that had a door leading out to the backyard. Orion would come and stay when nights with his mother were too hard, always sleeping on the floor. I had certainly tried. I had certainly wanted him. I had made suggestions both platonic and sexual, but Orion never accepted.

I thought we were going that way, as certain as a sixteen-year-old could get. I had even come close to kissing him once in high school, but his brother interrupted. One day things changed and at the same time hadn't. We had the same friendship, but Orion stopped making advances and started actively avoiding mine. I was sure something had happened, but I never learned what. Eventually I accepted things as they were.

Then college—

I shut down the thoughts about college. There in my room I only saw an older version of the vulnerable, tough guy I had convinced to be my friend a decade ago. *The same guy who keeps running away from you.* I sighed, brushing that feeling away. I wrote Orion a note and slipped it under the motorcycle keys on the nightstand. Piano music continued to play as I shut the bedroom door. *With Rose—be back by 10—eat whatever.*

With Orion tucked away, I tried to let it be Thursday as usual. Mom and I had things to do, after all. I made Rose a half bagel with light cream cheese, about all the breakfast she could handle. I shoved the other half in my mouth and chased it with a swig of milk from the carton. I made myself scrambled eggs and some sausage, piling it all on a biscuit in a makeshift sandwich. Then I trotted out of the house.

"Ready," I mumbled, joining her in the front yard.

Rose nodded as she closed her book. She gave me a weird look, but accepted the bagel. "I am. Are you?"

"Yeah, let's go." Mom and I hopped into the car and started for town.

That was the routine for Thursday. I drove Mom to a follow-up appointment, I picked up coffee while she was with the doctor, we would go home, I would make some lunch, then we just hung around the house. I waited for her in the car as usual. I could always feel her coming, like a soft breeze, and when I looked up she was waving at me as she crossed the sunny lawn in front of the hospital. She was perfection, her bright wig almost as blond as her natural hair had been, and a slight golden tan had returned to her skin. I felt time reversing around me. I was seventeen, and Orion was somewhere in town, and my bright, ethereal, healthy mother was coming toward me. She had even put on weight over the last few months. She got in the car, and I clumsily handed her a coffee as she buckled in.

"You all right, Fin?" she said, looking over my face.

"I...yeah, you look great today, Rosey," I said, my voice sounding younger to my ears.

She laughed, disbelieving. "Sure, Fin."

"What did the doctor say?"

She waved me off as she sipped the coffee. I waited. She waited. "Well?" I pleaded.

I had long ago gotten kicked out of the appointments for asking too many questions, making too many suggestions. Lucas said I made *real* doctors angry. I was desperate to know what happened, but I was used to having the results filtered through Rose. I started the car and pointed us toward home. I looked over the sunny pastures and saggy buildings as we made our way back to Painted Waters.

"Well, they took blood this week and said last week's was better than the week before. They think it's working, Fin."

I grunted. It had been working once before, then it turned. I wasn't ready for that kind of disappointment again. I was hopeful, anyway.

"Now, you tell me," she said politely, shifting to look at me.

"Tell you what?"

"Who is the third coffee for, Frank?" she hummed, eyeing the untouched travel mug in the cup holder.

I gulped. I sipped my coffee. "Rosey, there's something I need to tell you."

"Relax, Fin. Orion can stay as long as he wants."

I felt my face burn. "You knew he was here…with me, I mean."

"Of course, I am your mother. I know. Besides, after all the commotion in the bathroom—"

"Ah! You heard that! Mom it's not…it wasn't anything."

Rose laughed. "Fin, relax. It sounded like Orion got you with the flush. Besides if it had been anything else, the bathroom is a good enough place—"

"Mom!" I screeched, turning to stare at her.

"Fin, you just ran a stop sign."

Rose braced as I slammed on the brakes. In a very mom way, she coolly held her own coffee out over the floorboards and placed a hand over the one intended for Orion. I cussed and pulled the car to the side of the road. I killed the engine and wiped spilled coffee from my hands before speaking.

"Mom…"

"Franklin Ian Ness, I am not naive. And even if I *wanted* to pretend, I couldn't because you have told me about everyone you have ever been with. I am okay with my adult son having some fun." She paused to sip her coffee. "Though, I can't say that I approve of you picking up guys at funerals."

I felt my face grow warmer and slumped in my seat. "It's not like that."

Rose cooed and put a hand on my knee. "I'm teasing. This is Orion. I know what this is like."

"I didn't mean...I don't want..."

"Fin, having feelings for someone is *okay*. They are normal. You don't have to be ashamed or afraid or embarrassed. Feelings are viruses, Dr. Ness. Everyone gets them. Have you guys talked about what happened when he came to visit—what, six or seven years ago now?"

I sheepishly thumbed the lid of my coffee cup. We hadn't talked about it. We would probably never talk about it. Rose and I had talked about it, me on the phone sobbing the morning after he left. She had come up the weekend after, out of the blue, and I cried again then. She knew all about my feelings on that night, but Orion knew none of them.

Rose cleared her throat, pulling me out of my thoughts. "If you've calmed down enough, we should get going."

I started the car back up.

"Your boyfriend's coffee is getting cold."

I growled and pulled the car onto the empty country street.

When we got back to the house, I left the coffees with Rose in the kitchen and wandered back to my room. The door was open, and I could see the empty bed from halfway down the hall. The music had been turned off. Orion had made the bed and even folded the blanket he had used, draping it on the foot. I sighed and sat near my pillows. My note was where I had left it, but the bike keys were gone. What had I expected? I was about to leave and pout back to my mother when I noticed dark scrawling at the bottom of the note. It was a return message from Orion. *COULDN'T STAY. LAWYERS. MEET TOMORROW? 4?* And he left his phone number.

I couldn't move. My pulse raced and my hands got clammy. I hadn't felt this kind of excitement and dread since I lost my virginity. I stared at the phone number and resisted the urge to plug it into my phone and send a million texts. Guys I dated in the past used the word *overeager* more than once. *Wait! "Dated." Ha.* No, this wouldn't be a date. It was just to hang out. I was in town, he was in town. That was all. I took a breath. I gently placed the note back where I had found it, memorizing the number at the bottom just in case. I couldn't erase the stupid, happy smile on my face as I rejoined his mother.

"No Orion?"

I shrugged. "No, he had a thing, but we're going to meet up tomorrow."

Rose whistled and held up a hand for a high five, which I gave her.

"Come on, Mom. Let's make some grub."

Rose stepped between me and the fridge. "Actually, Fin…let's go to work."

I eyed her. Rose worked at a bakery owned by my Aunt Fay one town over. She had to quit when she got too sick, but on good days, better days, Lucas or I would drive her over, and Fay would let her bake whatever she wanted.

"I feel so great," she said. I grabbed the keys.

❖

The bakery crew cheered Rose when we came in. A young guy hugged her as he handed her an apron. I was introduced to those I didn't know and was bombarded by questions from those I hadn't seen in a while. Eventually Fay came out from the back and good-naturedly yelled at everyone to return to work. Fay's Bakes was a standalone building in the middle of Main Street with green brick and a white awning over the windows. Inside, white and green iron furniture established a gentle garden theme. I loved the glass cases full of cakes and pastries and the smell of baking things.

I tried to keep out of Rose's way, watching like a hawk from a small table for any signs of stress or fatigue. I saw none, I only saw the glowing joy she exuded. A lifetime of memories filled my chest. I had spent thousands of days at that table watching, eating, reading. Even Orion had graced the little space a few times. I had cried my eyes out there with Fay when Rose told her about the cancer. The sun changed the light to a soft red. I traced the patterns on the surface of the table, hoping to commit those small details to memory.

We had dinner at Fay's and got home just after nine, with six loaves of fresh bread and a dozen cupcakes. Rose was pretty much asleep as soon as we got in the car. I did my best to help her to bed, mostly carrying her to her room and pulling off her shoes. I wasn't tired, so I went to my room with the intention of working. Before I even turned the laptop on, I was staring at the note. Orion's intense, all-capital print looked harsh under my own loopy scrawl. All of my irritation for him was gone, replaced by curiosity and interest.

I never expected him to offer to meet up. In fact, I expected him to disappear. Orion had lived in a dozen cities in half as many years. There wasn't ever anything to tether him. *Plus, he left you before.*

Then I remembered Marge Starr was being cremated. I considered my own father, ashes spread in a field, except the tiny vial I owned. My heart suddenly broke for Orion. I knew what the waiting meant. I knew what it took to wonder how the whole life of a person could fit into those tiny jars of dust. In that moment I knew there wasn't much difference between Orion at twenty-nine and me at fourteen. *Grief was grief.*

I was a dick for thinking I had any reason to be worried about what he thought of me. And yet Orion wanted to see me again. I couldn't pass up finding out why. And I was sure Orion *wanted* it. Orion didn't make false offers. I leaned over and picked up the note. *Just be cool, Frank.* I had debated all day about how to answer, but the only thing I was able to agree with myself on was that I shouldn't include an emoji. Slowly, I plugged the number into my phone.

Hey, it's Fin. 4 is good. Pick me up.

That was all. I didn't expect Orion to text back. He had never been one to text, even when we were in high school. My phone was set to let me see if messages had been read, so I watched until that little check mark and time signature popped up. I laughed and tried not to think too hard about it while I worked.

CHAPTER 6: ORION

I felt guilty penning the note to Fin. I just chalked it up to the debt collectors, just another one I owed Fin. *Mr. Starr, your account with Mr. Ness is vastly past due.* That thought made me laugh a little, in an ironic way. I shouldn't bail on him with just a note, but I had to leave. The crazy thing, or not crazy thing, was I wanted to see him again. I wanted to see Fin again without the grief and the booze. *You are here for Midge.*

I scratched my phone number at the end of the note. My head whirled, so I choked down another handful of aspirin and pulled on the clothes from the night before. I had to do something to show him I appreciated him not letting me implode. I started to straighten up. Fin's room seemed older. The bed was in the middle of a wall and took up most of the space. On each side of the bed was a nightstand, opposite it a dresser and a desk against the wall. All of that was in the same place but little stuff was different. The posters were gone, the YA books were gone, the soccer gear was gone. None of those things had been replaced, at least not by something new. They were just things that were gone. Not gone, however, was the picture of us at the lake on Fin's eighteenth birthday. I left without looking hard at the picture.

The bike and I made it to Mom's house in record time. I didn't look at the place. I let it be there, and I moved around the space trying to get done what I needed to. I managed to shower and find something nicer to wear to meet Mom's lawyer. I had to drive into Atlanta, which was three hours from town. *Shit.* I felt sober, and that was a very raw feeling. Thanks to Fin and my inability to acknowledge my mother's house, I managed to leave in enough time to grab some breakfast.

It is a long drive, so you better figure out what to think about, the highway remembers everything you have ever felt, I sang in my head merging onto the highway. I had blazed through Mom's house—*my* house so fast I hadn't taken in anything. *My house.* I wasn't ready for a house. The only things I owned outright were clothes, the bike, and at least one of my guitars. Now I owned everything that had belonged to my mother.

The vibrating on my body spiked suddenly. I had drifted over the shoulder, the tires drawing out the screams of the corrugated road. I corrected the bike. I probably wouldn't make it to Atlanta thinking about the shit she left behind. Mom's liver had failed due to years of alcohol abuse, and what did I do? Got shitfaced. *Hello, Mr. Starr, Your bar tab is due, the final total: an entire lifetime of being the most ironically shitty son.* Mom had been dead less than a week, and I'd been drunk pretty much since.

Again the vibration and screech of the rumble strip forced me out of my head. Thinking about Mom was killing me. *Fin.* Well, there was a very different thought. I had felt like a stranger walking out of his room, and I guess in the grand scheme of things I was. I still felt like I knew him. He sure as hell knew me, he had proved that. I decided I was going to think about him since Fin guilt didn't feel as big as Mom guilt.

It had been so easy to be with him again, even without the booze. In the light of a sober day, I knew I deserved none of the kindness Fin had shown me. I wouldn't have blamed the guy for just saying *sorry for your loss* and bailing. I honestly wasn't worth any of the phone calls or emails.

Those emails, *geez.* I was always happy whenever a new one showed up. *Always.* I opened them hoping I could figure out how to be the friend Fin wanted, that I wanted to be. But then I would read the damn things. They were always full of stories about medical school and marathons and boyfriends and birthdays. That was the real reason my emails and friendship would never be worth Fin's time. If I tried to match Fin story for story, my emails would be full of long stints of unemployment, binge drinking, a one-night stand, and an internet thing that never went anywhere. Naw, I was not the sort of friend Fin needed.

So why leave the note? It was a fair question. Maybe I wanted to thank Fin. And the only way to do that was to see him again. Or did I just want to see him again? I changed lanes around a semi-truck and surveyed the area. I had made easy progress thinking about Fin, so I fished around for other memories. Eventually, my mind drifted over the events of the morning, and the pervy floodgates were opened, pouring high definition images of Fin in a towel into my brain. I had seen Fin in towels before, but we both had been too young to appreciate it. Then there was that amazing night in the hotel, but that was tainted by me abandoning him the next morning. So this new memory of fully grown Fin in a towel was something I totally shouldn't have.

Somehow I made it to the lawyer's office.

"Hi...uh...Orion Starr for...Mr. Shipley?" I told the secretary. I hadn't thought about what to say to a secretary, so when I spoke to her I stuttered. *Can I see my dead mom's lawyer now?*

"Mr. Shively," she corrected gently. And even though she was kind, it miffed me. "Have a seat, Mr. Starr. He will be with you in a moment."

She was bright-eyed and looked just a bit too young to be a secretary. I hesitated for a moment thumbing a beat on the desk, expecting her to say more. There wasn't. My only option was to back slowly into a chair. *Smooth, dipshit.* The waiting area was ugly as hell. It looked like the seventies and the sixties had a baby and it fell into a vat of toxic waste, then someone pinned it to the walls. I sat staring into the Stanley Kubrick carpet for ten minutes, sweating the whole time.

"Orion," Mr. Shively said, coming around a corner, his arms wide. His voice made me jump. Mr. Shively looked like Colonel Sanders, if the Colonel had lost fifty pounds and found a real tie. I wasn't about to hug the guy.

"Sir, I am Mrs. Starr's son," I tried, hoping for better than I'd managed with the secretary. I stood and offered a hand. Mr. Shively shook it with too much energy and held on a few seconds too long, pulling me down the hall.

"Yes, Mr. Starr. Yes, indeed. Your mother explained everything, and she was very clear and careful about her estate. Your brother is out of the country?"

"Yes sir."

"Fine, fine. Your mother liked to keep things simple, so I don't plan to take up much of your time." Mr. Shively sat me down in his equally ugly office, one of us on each side of a big Craftsman desk.

"Your mother has left everything to you and your brother," Mr. Shively said, his tone conclusive. I waited, expecting more. Mr. Shively just shrugged.

"What is *everything*?"

Mr. Shively tapped the side of his nose as if I had guessed something correctly. Then the lawyer ran through the list of belongings: house, car, savings, retirement. There was a lot more than I remembered. I could tell I looked shocked because halfway through the list, Mr. Shively gave me one of those "my poor boy" smiles and slowed down his reading.

"Your mother put everything in your and your brother's name. I spoke with Mr. Corvus Starr on the phone and he wanted to offer you a trade—your share of the savings for his share of everything else. Now, what I have done—"

"Fucker." I laughed, rubbing my face. Mr. Shively stared at me. I wiped my hands on my jeans and shrugged. "I knew my brother would try to pull something like that. He has never been attached to a place, and it is easier with cash."

I immediately felt like I had shared too much.

Colonel Shively stared like he didn't understand for a second, then chuckled loudly. "Margery—Mrs. Starr said the both of you would behave this way. She had me draw up this deal. Everything else for the cash. If you agree all you have to do is sign."

I leaned forward for a pen.

"Don't you want to read it?" the Colonel cried.

I wanted to laugh at the guy. I just shrugged. "If Mom put this together, then that's enough for me."

"Read it," the Colonel insisted, shaking his head, shoving the papers to my side of the desk.

I took the papers, clumsily holding the pile on my lap. The Colonel explained a few more things, which I can't say I heard. I just thought of Mom and everything she had tried to tell me about her estate when we first found out she was sick. I believed so hard she would get better that I didn't let any of it sink in. I hadn't realized how well off she had been. I had nearly ten acres of land, a house paid in full, a car paid in full, and whatever value all the stuff in the house had. The retirement and investments were still being worked out by accountants, but there it was. Mom's whole life boiled down to the dollar. Corvus had traded his share of all of that for $50,000 and the right to never come back to this country. The Colonel gave me a list of appointments that would happen over the coming weeks, starting Saturday morning with a land appraiser. I took everything handed to me with little ability to digest it all.

"Orion, I know it is a lot. Take your time. Read through it, we have another appointment scheduled for two weeks."

I nodded. The Colonel showed me out. All in all, the appointment lasted two hours. I carefully crammed the papers into my saddlebag and left the city.

I was *trying* to avoid Mom, so naturally, I couldn't outrun her on the way home. The only Fin memories I had left would make me look like an ass so, he was out. That left me and a lifetime of Mom memories. *Let's do this.* I resigned myself and let the most persistent memory in. I had been living in Tennessee at the time, just out of college with nothing better to do. Marge had come to stay with me for a few days out of the blue. Well, I thought it was out of the blue, so I took her to Graceland.

We sat by each other on a bench eating foil-wrapped burritos. They were warm and the sun was out, staving off some of the February gloom. I remember watching her fiddle with the food, her face creased with a thought. I had been told we didn't look much alike, but that we acted alike. She was as tall as me, which wasn't tall at all. Her black hair had been long then, making her olive skin look warm. I was always jealous of hers and Corvus's softer hair and lighter features. Her eyes were black, mine gold. We shared gestures, a way of talking with our eyes, using our hands, and moving through the world.

"Hunter," she sighed. My nickname.

"Midge," I said around a big bite of burrito.

She took a deep breath. "I am sick—like really this time. The doctors said my liver is failing. I need a new one or I won't survive the next few years."

She didn't sound worried or scared or angry. I could only look at her and chew. Sure, I had heard her, but what the fuck did it all mean? It was like hearing somebody say "you're drowning" while you were actually drowning. She watched me, trying to see if she could tell what I was feeling. My brain caught on something she said, and it looped and looped and looped. *I need a new one—I need a new one.* Sure, that was simple. I swallowed, shrugged, and leaned my elbows on my knees.

I said as calmly as I could manage, "So, get a new one."

She smiled. "I am on the list."

"Why are you smiling?"

I had to swallow again, not food but emotions, I guess, *pain* of some kind trying to rise in my guts. I felt that gulping sensation people get when they wanted to cry or puke. I didn't want to do either.

"Hunter, you're so funny. You're so like me." Her voice was unsurprised and determined.

"I bet Crow shit bricks." I shrugged, feeling suddenly like I wished he were around. She would have told him first for sure. He was easier to tell that sort of thing to.

"If I had a real brick for every time Corvus shit one, I could build a second house. He was angry, and then he said what I know you will say next."

"That you can have my liver or part of it or whatever." She could have had every organ in my body if she needed it.

She sighed and petted me. "And I know what you'll feel no matter how this goes."

I didn't answer, just picked beans out of the burrito and tossed them to a squirrel.

"Come to Georgia. My doctors can test you. If we match, then fine. But if we don't, I want you to promise me something."

I waited.

"If you aren't a match, or if you are and it goes wrong, if something happens, I don't want you to feel guilty."

I sighed.

"Don't sigh at me. We are cut from the same cloth, son. I know you will feel guilty anyway, but if you promise me and *remember* that you promised, then at least you can be reminded that I don't blame you for anything."

I hugged her with one arm. I knew she wouldn't be satisfied if I didn't answer. "I promise to try."

She kissed me, leaving a warm smear of lipstick on my face. "I am just—"

"If you say you're sorry, I am going to flip this bench."

She looked at me, and I had to force myself to look at her.

"Shouldn't I be? Sorry, I mean?"

That nearly killed me. She'd had complications for years because of the drinking she had done. Decades as an alcoholic, three years clean. *Three years*. I didn't blame her even a little. She used to cry that she should have quit sooner, that she should have been different.

"Ma, we forgave you. I forgave you for what was your fault a long time ago. The rest wasn't your fault."

"You are such good boys."

"Eat your burrito. I paid good money for that."

Mom jabbed me under the ribs. "*I* bought this burrito. *And* that one. I hope you like my money, squirrel."

"That's my pet."

She tried not to laugh, matching my serious face. "What's its name?"

"Midge."

She jabbed me again. "Hunter," she smiled, scooting toward me suddenly.

"Midge."

"Knock knock."

"Oh, no. No! Ma—"

"Indulge me! Knock."

"Who's there?"

"Rude Starfish."

I started to take a bite. "Rude star—"

I didn't get to finish. Mom latched her open hand on my face, covering me with bits of burrito as she laughed loud and full. I tried to glare at her, feeling my face break into a smile. She pulled her hand away.

I blinked. "Why?"

"It's a rude starfish, Hunter. It does what it wants." She finally started to eat her burrito. It had made me laugh then, and it made me laugh as I drove through the summer evening back to our home.

I *had* gone to Georgia and I *had* been a match, and I *had* given her part of my liver. It started to fail six months ago. Now she was gone. Thoughts of blame and guilt swarmed me all the time. But I made a promise. She was the only one with any real power to blame me, and up to our last conversation, she hadn't.

The last time I heard her was a voicemail saying she loved me, I was not to blame, and she was going to the hospital because she wasn't feeling great. I put the bike fully in park and killed the engine. The road was silent aside from my breathing. I pulled off the helmet, squished my eyes shut, and crammed the heels of my hands into my sockets, hoping that would keep the tears down. I wasn't going to lose my shit in the street.

When I was sure I wouldn't cry, I looked up. *Why am I always about to break down right here?* I was back at the welcome sign to town, and I wanted to walk over to it and rip it from the ground. I hated that fucking sign. The sight of it let another memory slip in past my already lowered defenses. We had to move to Painted Waters because I had been kicked out of my Atlanta school for fighting. I got arrested and people there couldn't let it go. I had to repeat a grade, so I turned nineteen halfway through my senior year. I was sure as fuck at fault, and I had been less than happy about it.

"Home sweet home, son," Marge said as she slowed the moving van. She even made a show of taking a picture of the sign. Then she took a picture of me, capturing my scrunched, grumbled face for posterity.

"Welcome to Painted Waters, home of Painted Waters Orchard and Tilly's Whiskey," she said.

"Looks more like tainted waters," I said, crossing my arms.

"That sounds about right for whiskey, but for us Tainted Waters is home."

From that point on, we called the town and the alcohol "tainted waters." It started out as a bitter way to jab at each other, but it eventually made us laugh. We tried to let Corvus in on the joke, but he never actually lived there. He left the country when he was eighteen. I had only been fourteen. The memory of first arriving in the moving van was short and was gone quickly. I sighed, gunned the bike, and went home. *To Midge's home. To my home.*

❖

The place was a two-story country house made of planks of dark wood. It didn't look different, which made it scary. It should have been different. Things *were* different because Mom wasn't in it. I took a deep breath and shut down the memory flow. I couldn't take any more. I flipped to autopilot as I climbed the porch and went to my old room without looking around. I did the expected bedtime things—found pajamas, brushed my teeth, and found a phone charger.

Just as I was about to collapse on the bed, my phone buzzed with a message from a number I didn't know. I almost ignored it and went to a game but when I thumbed the phone open, it automatically went to the message. *Fin.* How could I have forgotten about Fin? How could I even think of Fin with everything going on?

"Tomorrow at four," I said out loud. *Tomorrow we will remember, we will begin again, we will chase the past away. Tomorrow will be something, tomorrow will be everything because tomorrow will change our yesterday.* Okay, that sounded too much like a musical.

I tossed the phone on the bed and followed it. My bed was in the dead center of the room, a desk serving as the headboard and a trunk full of random shit as the footboard. I flipped off the lamp on the desk and blinked in the darkness, crickets and cicadas taking over the sounds in the space.

I was so fucking tired, and hoped being so tired would let me sleep. As I stared up, a weird light hazed my vision like a dream, then I remembered the glow-in-the-dark stars glued to the ceiling, burning in hues of unearthly green. I thought back to that summer. I had spent almost a week lying on the couch feeling hot and annoyed. One day Mom came home loaded down with red signs and wooden stakes.

"What's that?" I'd asked, half interested.

"I am having a yard sale," she said, dumping all the crap onto the coffee table. That was disconcerting, because we'd had a yard sale before we left Atlanta. I wasn't sure what was left to get rid of.

"What are you gonna sell?" I said, rolling on the couch to watch her.

"Well, I have this pile of boxes here. I figured if someone cared about them, they would have ended up in a room by now."

I stared at her, my mouth hanging open. She was calling my bluff. I had left all the boxes, crates, and baskets containing my things in the living room where the movers had dumped them. Even my bed was propped up against the wall. I had been camping on the couch as a way of silently protesting the move. She had tried talking to me, bribing me, yelling at me. None of it worked. She was threatening to sell all my stuff unless I picked a room. I wanted to high-five her and flip her off at the same time.

I raised an eyebrow at her. She stared at me, her face cheery. I scanned her to see if she was bluffing, but her old jeans, paint-stained work shirt, and ponytail told me she wasn't. She finally just shrugged, looked over the pile, and picked up a canvas guitar case. That guitar was my most prized possession.

"What do you think these are going for nowadays?" she said, picking up a packet of yellow stickers and a Sharpie.

"God damn it." I caved. I jumped up off the couch, snatched the instrument from her hands, and stomped up the stairs. I heard her cap the Sharpie with a triumphant sigh.

I wandered into the few upstairs rooms. There were more downstairs, but the upstairs was cooler because that's where the central air worked best. Mom had picked the master on the left, so I skipped the room right next to that, leaving two on right to pick from. One was big with a pitched ceiling and two large windows. The one closer to the stairs was dark, with a round semi-hidden window near the corner. The darkness appealed to my dramatic emo ass, but something made me go back into the first room. It was bigger, lacked carpet, and was finished in a bright pine. When I first looked up, I couldn't really place the blotches of plastic. After I found my glasses, I could see the stars.

I spent that day hauling my shit up the stairs. Mom hovered nearby, lording her victory over me and helping with the big stuff. I piled it all into the room I wasn't going to take until we could get to the bed. Sometime after night fell, Mom and I finally pulled the bed parts up the stairs and set it up in the center of the room. Mom dressed the bed as I fished blankets and pillows out of space bags.

"Why this room, Hunter?" she asked, looking around skeptically.

It was easier to show her. I wouldn't have been able to explain why those stupid plastic stars made me so comfortable. The room had been bright with sunlight all day and I turned on the lights as soon as it was dark, wanting to give the little plastic bits as much juice as I could. I shut off the light and Mom gasped when her eyes adjusted, the glowing stars making the room brighter than you would expect. She turned in a circle, then crossed the room to me.

"You are such a romantic," she teased, patting my belly as she left the room. "Go to sleep, you have school tomorrow."

❖

Around one a.m., I woke in a cold sweat. I had dreamt of death, of being dead, but I didn't want to try and figure it out. The light on my phone blinded me as I woke it. I had only meant to check the time, but the screen opened to Fin's text. I took that as a sign. I found an old hoodie and some sandals and went out into the night.

Fin's house was across two fields and a small orchard. It only took twenty minutes walking. I didn't knock or hesitate. I just went in the back door that was never locked. Fin was sleeping, but he must have had suspected I would come because a pillow and a few blankets were waiting on a chair. I put together a bed on the floor and went to sleep.

I woke again to the sound of Fin's running alarm, but I only listened as Fin changed and left. It took a little more effort than I remembered to pull myself up from the floor and out into the early morning. It was bright, but it was still cool. I started across the field for home.

Then, almost like a second alarm sounding, something occurred to me. *What the fuck am I doing? I am sleeping on the floor like some teenager. I am twenty-fucking-nine.* I stopped stone still in the orchard, halfway between my house and Fin's. I suddenly felt like an idiot. I'd snuck out of my house to hide from the ghost of my mother and slept on Fin's floor. Does anyone ever stop being eighteen? Almost thirty, and I still couldn't figure out how to feel like a real adult.

For some reason Fin, or the idea of Fin, triggered those thoughts. There was something irritating and challenging about him. Fin had a life beyond Painted Waters. Fin had his work, his future degree, and a thousand other things that proved he had done something with himself. And most importantly, he slept through the night in his own fucking bed, not on some near stranger's floor. I wanted to measure up. I wanted to be someone who seemed half as capable as Fin.

I sighed and started walking again. I didn't know why I suddenly wanted to be someone worth Fin's time. Okay, that was a flat-out lie. I fucking knew why. But it was hard to believe I still wanted it. And if that wasn't fucking enough, I had a date with him that night. A date with *the man* that Fin was now, not the boy I had known in high school. And I was a grown-ass adult.

I got home and tested my new resolve. Instead of running to hide in my room, I went into the kitchen. I didn't get very far before the ghosts and guilt started to overwhelm me. But I didn't run. I watched each memory play out. When it was over, I looked around and saw the kitchen. It was like waking up. The room had a yellow accent wall with burnt orange ceramic tile on the floor. Pictures lined the walls, and knickknacks rested in assorted places. Table, chairs, center island, pots hanging from a rack over the inlaid burner. The ovens and fridge set into the dark cabinets that lined the walls.

I felt a smile break across my face. I was hurting, but I hadn't run. I was guilty, but I hadn't run. Whether this made me an adult or not was shrug-worthy, but it did *something* for me. I tested the same remedy out in the living room to much the same effect. Then Mom's room. That room was hardest. It smelled like her. I sat on the bed and mused over the items I could see, looking finally into the mirror that sat on her dresser.

I had to squint at the reflection. I stood and got closer. My own reflection surprised me. I looked tired, like I had been drinking, like I had been crying. My hair was in a ratty version of a ponytail. Who knew what my beard was trying to do? I didn't have any of the usual jewelry. The shirt I had on was too big, and my sweatpants looked the way things did just before they went into the trash.

Like something whispered to me, Fin crossed my mind. I sighed and backed away from the mirror. My new adult resolve wasn't going to let me go out on a date looking like a mess. And my new adult resolve also wasn't going to let me panic over the idea of a date. I looked at the clock on my phone: ten a.m.

"Nap time," I said out loud.

I got in a two-hour nap. Then I took a shower in mom's bathroom and trimmed my beard. It took a while to find a decent outfit, and I managed to find a new set of contacts. As I passed her dresser, I noticed the box she kept her earrings in. She had been annoyed when I showed up with the first set of holes, but as I added more she got over it and started buying me earrings as stocking stuffers. I didn't have any of mine with me. Hers were much nicer. From them, without giving much thought to the type, I filled all six holes of my right ear. I looked in the mirror and saw myself, really me, for the first time in months.

CHAPTER 7: FIN

I wasn't completely surprised to find Orion on my floor when I woke up. Sure, there was a little shock at having another person in the room, but it felt familiar. I didn't bother him. I just went about the morning as always. I had been promised four p.m., and that was enough for me. Besides, he was on my floor for his own healing, not to see me. I knew what it took to recover from the death of a parent.

My run had barely started when my dad came to mind. I thought about him a lot, but I didn't feel for him much anymore. At this point, he had been dead for almost as many years as he had been alive. I had expected to feel more while sitting at Marge's funeral, held in the same church Dad's had been. I hadn't felt anything. That morning, however, with each thump of my shoes on the sandy road, feelings for my father crept up on me.

I'd been fourteen when he was killed. The funeral was a mock ceremony designed to have all the bells and whistles of a proper military funeral. Dad had been cremated long before that day, though. And I had been presented with a silver tube of his ashes. I didn't wear it anymore, but I *had* worn it for years. As I rounded a corner, one of the last moments I'd had with him came back to me.

"Where are you going?" I had asked early one morning, restless even then.

"Milk the cows, go for a run. What are you doin' up?"

I just shrugged.

He shrugged too, side-eyeing me. "You wanna come? Get one in before school?"

"I dunno, Pop, wouldn't wanna make you feel bad."

"Feel bad for outrunning *you*?" Dad laughed without missing a beat.

That was enough to get me going. I went for my shoes. I had played soccer for years by then, so I wasn't new to running. I also knew Dad had hurt his knee during his last deployment, so for a young, lanky teenager with no body control, and a seasoned, achy Marine, we were pretty well matched. Silently, we slipped from the house and stretched in the middle of the lane on the chilly October morning.

"Call it," Dad said, holding up a penny he'd found in the street.

"Heads," I shouted, stretching muscles still too new to be stiff.

He flipped the coin into the air and let it fall back to the gravel. Leaning to stretch out his legs, he observed the penny. "Heads it is. Guess we are on your pace."

"Right, well, we are going to the park, just in case you get too far behind."

At that point I was nearly as tall as him, but he was still bigger, huge with curated muscles. His hair had grown out a little while he was home on leave and it was fire truck red, darker than mine. Standing in front of the mirror every morning of my life, I remembered what he'd looked like and hoped I measured up. Back then, with dew still coating the grass, that lanky teenager was a scarecrow compared with his dad. Maybe I was still a scarecrow by comparison.

When he was ready, Dad stood tall and strode to the edge of the road. He waited, half smirking, for me to give him the go. I had known then that sharing that moment with him was important. I even remembered pausing, trying to hold on to it. I wanted to remember him as a giant, a hero, and a secret Whitney Houston fan. It was as if I had paused to absorb a lifetime of my father's presence. But it was still only a moment. With a smile and a nod, Dad and I started to jog.

As I remembered it almost fourteen years later, the familiar awe washed over me. Step for step, Dad had kept pace with me, never mentioning his knee, never complaining about a hill or a dirt trail. I used to think it had been the Marine side of him, to keep quiet and get things done. As I got older, however, I understood that was how he was. I still wanted to be like him. I was approaching the age my father had been when he passed, but I knew I wasn't even close to his patience. The whole run, step for step, all my father had done was smile at me.

And then he was gone.

The beeping of a car horn startled me out of my memory. Apparently, I had stopped like a doofus in the middle of an intersection. I felt my face turn red. I waved to the car and trotted out of the way. I wiped my face on my shirt, wet with sweat and tears. I smiled and started my run again.

When I got back, Orion was gone. I met Mom in the kitchen after my shower. She was making her own breakfast, looking well rested and happy. I wanted to protest and take over the task for her, but I knew better. She would just push me away. I watched her for a few minutes. Then I had a thought.

"Rosey Posey," I sighed, leaning on the counter, picking at the tomato she was chopping for an omelet.

"Fin," she said, swatting me away.

"You ever wonder what Dad would have done about your cancer?" I muttered. I wondered how similar our versions of the man were. She talked about him as much as I could ever want, but I always wondered if I was remembering my father right. We played the *you ever wonder what Dad* game a lot.

"Well, what did I do? I cried, I screamed, I hit things, and eventually I just figured out how to do *this* every day. Your father probably would have shrugged and said, 'at least there is something we can do about it.' Why?"

"I thought about him on my run. Never thought about what he would have done with you being sick."

Rose said quietly, "It would have killed him."

That afternoon Rose went to the hospital for treatment with Lucas, and I went to a coffee shop to try and get some work done for school and my internship. My whole day felt like it had a big gap in it, like I had gone from running and thinking about Dad to pulling on a button down on over my T-shirt. I had come home around three and worked on preparing for my maybe date. I got an "oh shit" feeling as I tried to get my expectations under control. It's not like I knew what Orion's intentions were. At five till, I went into the kitchen. Mom and Lucas both let out catcalls and complimented me. I just blushed and tried to act like I didn't hear them.

"Now, ladies and gentleman, if you look to your left, you will see the rarest form of gay, a Gingerus Doctoricus about to do its mating dance." Lucas faked a whispering, wildlife show voice.

"Fuck off, Lucas. I don't think it's a date."

Lucas and Rose looked at each other.

"Is he coming to pick you up?" Lucas asked.

"Yeah."

"Did you know where you are going?" Rose said.

"No."

"Plannin' on gettin' laid?"

I gulped and felt my face burn. "I am going to go wait out there."

"It's a date," Mom and Lucas said together.

Lucas grabbed me before I could leave the room. "No, he has to come to the door if he wants to take my baby out."

"Lucas, you're younger than me." He just put his massive arm around my shoulders and directed me to a chair at the table. Being a giant, he had the advantage, so I didn't really have much of a choice but to sit where he put me. "And it's not a date."

"When was the last time you were on a date, son?" Rose asked. I growled, I guess, but I didn't answer.

"Ugh, just let me have this! Can't you just pretend you know other people besides your mom," Lucas said as the doorbell rang. I shot up from my chair just to have Lucas slam me back down. He was already across the living room before I could recover. "I'll get it."

I tossed a pleading look at my mother. Rose just laughed and followed him.

CHAPTER 8: ORION

I pulled up to the house and parked the bike along the side. I got that weird sense of vertigo, like my present self had collided with so many past ones. I had pulled the bike alongside that house thousands of times, and doing it again felt like coming home. *Almost home.* I had given back my right to call this place home when I fucked up with Fin years ago. Still felt it, though. I didn't actually know what I was doing, and looking at the house made me less sure. But *adult me* was going to follow through. I pulled off the helmet and tossed the bike keys inside it, then tucked it under my arm for something to hold on to.

I stooped to get Fin's blazer from the saddlebags. I had found it just before leaving. As I flapped it out so it might not look so shabby, I thought about how Fin looked two nights ago. The lanky, overdressed redhead looked amazing on my bike, his face dark with concentration and annoyance. The memory sent a weary trickle of sensation through me, some distant notion of attraction moving lazily through the muck of guilt and sorrow I was now made of.

Without my permission, my brain started playing memories of Fin taking off the blazer and untucking the shirt, his skin flashing. I tightened my grip on the blazer and felt my face break into a grin. It took more effort than I wanted to admit to resist the urge to hold the blazer to my face and see if smelled like him. I am sure it would have.

I tossed the jacket over my shoulder and strode up to the door. I rang the bell. *Rose.* The name made my hands start to sweat. I had been in town three days, and I had yet to see her. I wasn't even sure she was real. My memories of her were rose-colored; she was an ethereal being, a wisp, a fairy, a—

I heard a commotion inside the house. I anticipated the sound of the door opening, bracing for Fin or Rose to show up, and then I nearly fell back into the yard, stunned. A gigantic, scrubs-wearing Incredible Hulk cosplayer stepped into the doorway. He dwarfed me. *Holy Hot Jesus, the guy was huge.* I closed my mouth and blinked, then waited, expecting The Hulk to speak. All he did was cross his huge, tattooed arms over his chest.

"Fin home?" I said after a minute.

To my surprise, he laughed, voice softer than I expected. "Of course he is. He's been waiting for you."

But The Hulk didn't move.

"Lucas!" Fin hissed, trying to get around the beast.

The giant man blocked the door, Fin practically climbing him. All three of us stilled as a soft voice sighed from somewhere in the house. I tried not to laugh as the giant man held Fin to the side, letting Rose out into the sun.

"Lucas! Orion, I am sorry," Fin garbled from around The Hulk's arm.

"Orion!" Rose cooed, holding up her arms as if to welcome me. No, she *was* welcoming me. For some reason, I hadn't expected that.

"Rose," I said. I took in the warm smile and bright eyes. She looked just as I remembered and nothing like I knew her.

"This is my nurse, Lucas Laverty."

I cocked my head at her. "Nurse?"

"Fin didn't tell you? No matter, ask him later. I don't want to keep you."

"Good, we'll go," Fin said, his voice muffled behind Lucas.

Rose grinned. "Lucas, go inside."

"But I have questions! Who are you and what do you want with my boy?" Lucas bellowed, stepping up behind Rose like a giant guard dog, still managing to hold Fin off with one hand.

"Lucas," she hissed at him. He grumbled but backed up only slightly. His large frame was steps inside, where he watched in amused silence.

"Hey, O," Fin said, stumbling forward.

I ignored the creep in the doorway. The sight of Fin was like standing too close to a bonfire. Dark jeans, soft looking T-shirt, red plaid overshirt, and perfectly styled hair. I was glad I had the good sense to clean up. I felt that attraction again, going from a trickle to a brook somewhere far away inside me. Those hazel eyes met mine, and I could feel the warmth.

I looked at the smiling Rose instead. I really looked at her. Having a nurse meant someone was sick, or hurt, or…I couldn't conceive anything after that *or*. My mother had her *or*. Grief was suddenly like ice all over my body. I forced my face into something passive. The harder I looked, the more I could see it. She was ten years younger than my mom and she looked great, but I could see what was behind her eyes. I knew the look of someone who was fighting.

"Hi," I finally said. I remembered Fin's blazer. "You forgot this." I handed him the coat.

"Hi. Thanks." Fin blushed.

Rose looked between us and laughed. "You two. Doesn't really feel like so many years."

"Mom," Fin growled, turning only a shade redder.

She put up her hands and gave me a once-over. "You on the bike?"

"I am."

Her eyes sparkled. She turned to her son but spoke to me. "Orion, give Fin your bike keys and helmet."

"What?"

"It's going to rain tonight. You can take the car. Fin can put your bike in the barn." Fin looked like he would burst into flames.

"Mom—" he tried to protest.

I sighed. I suspected what would come next. I had hurt her son and he probably told her since Fin told her everything. So, she knew what an asshole I had been. I couldn't blame her for wanting to get her two cents in now. There were a million reasons why that beautiful, perfect mother wouldn't want her son out with me. I held the keys and helmet out to Fin and gave him an *it's okay* look. Fin looked like he wanted to jump on the grenade for me, but did as he was told, tossing the coat into the open door of the house and hitting Lucas in the chest.

When Fin was out of earshot, Rose looked me over once, then started. "Orion, it's really good to see you, and there is something I want you to know—"

Here it comes.

"I am so sorry about Marge," she cried and engulfed me in her small arms.

I really hadn't expected that. Occasionally, my mind would slip back to when people didn't have to console me or feel obligated to mention my dead mother. That reality was decimated every time someone told me how sorry they were. It made me *feel* the loss that much more. And it made me sorry, too.

"Oh, Orion, you know our home is always open to you. Since I know you would never actually ask, I just want you to know that if you need anything, it is here, okay?"

I let myself be hugged and even hugged back. "Thank you, Rose."

When she released me, her eyes were soft and watery, but she hadn't cried. "That being said, do you plan to sleep with my son?"

I laughed out of sheer surprise, before I even knew I was laughing. She eyed me. I shrugged, not having an answer, not having really thought about it.

"Well, somewhere in all that skintight leather, you'd better have protection."

Nothing about seeing her again was at all like I thought it would be. She wasn't mad. Fin didn't seem mad, either. *Am I the only one who remembered that I was a dick?* That seemed pretty doubtful, so I decided to just go along with it. I put my hands in my pockets and smiled my most innocent smile. Rose laughed like she wasn't buying it and put a soft hand to one of my cheeks, pressing her lips against the other.

"You have grown to be a very handsome man, and I heard good things. Marge was very proud," Rose said. That made my stomach flip. Fin had pulled the car out of the garage and was waiting in the drive. I only noticed when she looked over my shoulder to him.

"You better get on," she said, giving my face a light pat, her voice dipping only slightly into her accent.

"Thanks, Rose...I...well," I said, unsure of what to say. Rose went back into the house, letting Lucas out.

"If you hurt my boy, I have access to enough chemicals to take down a herd of grizzly bears. I will find you."

I tried not to laugh, backing away from the huge man. Rose just gestured at her nurse in a "there you have it" way.

"Bye." I shrugged and went to the car.

I felt Fin's eyes on me as I buckled in. Rose and the nurse had disappeared inside the house, and the fact that we were alone together was making my hands sweat.

"Do I need to apologize for anything?" Fin said.

I laughed and shook my head. "No, not even close."

Fin put his hands on the wheel. "So where to?"

"Wherever you want." I hadn't planned anything, and it only just occurred to me that maybe I should have.

I watched Fin think it over. His face was tense with concentration, but then he grinned at me. I waited, getting the impression he was waiting for me to figure it out. But then I did get it. I knew exactly where we were going. I sighed and pretended to be unsurprised. Really, I was pretty fucking excited. I was ashamed I hadn't thought of it. Fin revved the engine and peeled out of the driveway.

"*Oh!* Hotlanta, someone build me a time machine and send me back to the future! A blast from the past just blew into my place," Grace screeched as we entered the diner.

"Hey, Willy," Fin chirped as Wilhemina Grace sashayed toward us. She put her arms out to me for a hug, dodging Fin.

"Get out of my way, Frank. You was in here two days ago, an' I promise you just the same. But you!"

Grace stopped and waited for me to complete the hug.

"Ms. Grace," I sighed, letting her engulf me.

The continued press of surprised and sympathetic people made a part of me ache for the solitude of a dark road or my bed. It was fucking exhausting to have people be happy to see me. But I let the suffering part of me absorb the life being shared with each pair of arms that came around me.

"I swear it'a snowed ten inches on Tuesday 'fore I expected to see you in here," she said, swaying with me in her arms. "I guess if Fin found ya, it was only a matter of time."

Wilhemina Grace had been the owner of Grace's Place since she was nineteen years old. It was the sort of backwoods, down-home diner people wanted when they went looking for a good, greasy meal. Inside it was dark wood with bright lights strung on cables like in a mine. The walls were lined with photos and posters from the eighties. Fin and I had spent most of our weekends and most of our money at Grace's. She loved us. She had cheered for us and celebrated us and always seemed to be waiting for us to come through the door. Fin had been coming his whole life, and it quickly became another place I called home. *Grace. Rose. Marge.* I was feeling suddenly full, and it hurt.

"I'm here for Mom." I didn't know how else to say it.

Grace pulled back and looked at me. Her big eyes were soft and warm. "I know, child. I *am* sorry about your mama."

"It's okay."

"Willy," Fin interrupted, some impatience in his voice.

"Frank, I swear you like a flea on a dog when it come to my food," Grace growled, pinching the back of Fin's arm as she went back toward the counter.

"How about some burgers?" I called after her.

"And ice cream," Fin added.

"I ain't in need of you tellin' me what to do, child. I know what you want. I know what everyone wants when they come here," Grace squawked, her voice drifting into to the kitchen.

"I think I missed her," I whispered to Fin as we sat at our usual booth, the last one in the center row. It had the best view of the bar, the stage, the pool tables, and the door. We'd never sat anywhere else.

"She missed you, that's for sure," Fin said. "She always asks me about you."

I squinted in confusion. Fin opened his mouth but didn't say anything as a waiter stepped up to the table.

"Can I get y'all a drink?" He was just a teenager, with the bored, tired stare of a kid ready to get off work.

"I'll have a beer," Fin said.

I almost laughed. "Beer and ice cream, Fin?"

"Just order."

"Make it two beers."

"Can I see y'all's ID?"

Fin and I exchanged a look. I hadn't expected to have to prove my age in this place. It was almost ironic since I had a beer here on my nineteenth birthday.

"I don't care no way, but Ms. Grace makin' us ask everyone. So, I am askin'."

We complied.

"Franklin? Din't he just call you Fin?"

"My initials are F.I.N." The kid didn't seem to hear. He handed Fin his ID back and moved on to mine.

"Y'all live in New York? O—rion...ain't that the guy in space?" the kid asked, still staring hard at the card.

I nodded.

"Your last name Starr?" That made the kid lose it a bit. "Bet I like that. That's some woke shit!"

I wasn't sure if the kid liked my name or was just making fun of it, so I tried to blend into the booth. Fin hung his head, laughing.

"Cas!"

"Yes, Ms. Grace."

"Get over here and get this food where it need to go. Frank and Orion don't need you bother'n 'em anyway."

The kid practically tossed the ID at me before stomping off.

"This will be weird," Fin said.

"What?"

"He didn't ask us what kind of beer we wanted."

I laughed. "Right. I'll get 'em."

As I slid out of the booth, I remembered something from an email. Fin had mentioned trying out new beers while at med school, the hobby of a friend of a friend. But he mentioned liking one. "Fat Tire, if they have it?"

Fin's eyebrows went up. "Uh...yeah."

I tried not to think too hard about what it meant that I remembered that as I approached the bar. I waited for Grace to finish with some customers at the other end, surveying the room before my eyes landed on Fin. I watched him pull the silverware out of his napkin and type a message into his phone. Most of my favorite memories of Painted Waters were weird amalgams of Grace's Place, motorcycles, and red hair.

"You gonna burn a hole in him starin' like that," Grace said. She was wiping the bar with a cloth like she had always been there.

I shrugged and tried to sound innocent. "Can I get two Fat Tires?"

"Oh, no. Don't you go pull that with me, I see this." Grace pointed at Fin.

"Gracey, I have been here for three days. I am here for my mom. There's nothing to see!"

She tisked but turned to draw the requested beers. "It been ten years and three days since you met him. And. You. Still. Starin'. So, ain't nothin' changed. I can see that, too."

She held the beers just out of reach, keeping me at the bar probably trying to see if I would talk. I wondered how she could see how I felt about him. I wonder if she knew about that night six years ago. I wondered what she thought of me. I wondered if she could see how my whole world was different because my mother was dead.

"He a good man, Orion."

I didn't answer. I didn't even twitch. It was an Old West style standoff, and I wasn't going to draw first. She had gotten older since I'd been gone. Everyone had, but her age was coming on faster, maybe because she was old when I met her. The creases by her eyes were deep.

"Fine, quit starin' at me like that. Here, take your beer, I ain't gonna talk to you if you don't wanna say nothin'," she said, finally handing me the beers. I winked at her, and she turned away, muttering to herself. I crossed the creaking wood floor back to the booth.

I almost made it when a high-pitched scream rang through the bar. I looked, already knowing what I would see. Lin ran full speed toward me. She was dressed in what could have passed for a leather bra and a leather skirt draped in silver chains. She launched herself into my arms. I needed her near me, so I pulled her as close as I could with my hands full. Any confusion about Fin, Rose, Grace, or Mom fell aside.

Fin took the beers from my hands, laughing. I hugged her, and she ran her hands over my face and shoulders, making cooing sounds and kissing my cheeks. I considered weeping. Last I'd heard, she was on tour in Washington state. She had mentioned coming to Georgia to be with me, but I told her she didn't have to come. But there she was, her small body transferring energy like a lightning storm.

"How did you find me?"

"O! Don't be dumb. I will always find you. I would have come sooner, but the band couldn't get here until today. I was hoping you would still be here. *I am so sorry about Mom!* Grace said you would come, said she could feel it in her bones. She promised to put up the band if we played a few nights. I had hoped…but I know how you get when the only thing you have to answer to is that bike. And I missed you, O."

"I told you not to come," I sighed.

"Fuck off," she said in my ear.

Lin had been my only other friend in high school and we'd stayed friends, really friends. She was the lead singer of a blues band called Leather and Lace. We would get together when one of us was near the other. We talked as much as we could but had not physically seen each other in over a year. She sent me postcards from whatever city she happened to be in and always signed them: *We're starving, but we're too happy to care. Love with all the leather and lace, Lin.*

"It is good to see you," I murmured into her bare shoulders.

"And *Fin*," Lin said, reaching out to him. She didn't let go of me, just pulled Fin into our awkward hug. He was pressing against my back and with Lin pressing against my front, I was somewhere between heaven and nirvana.

"I love seeing you both, you're so fucking gorgeous in all variations of the term," Lin said, winking at Fin.

She finally released us, and we all scrunched into the booth, Lin and Fin looking back at me. There was a moment of quiet awe where we all just stared at each other. Then the waiter brought food and we settled in to enjoy each other's company. Lin told us about the trouble she had getting to town, picking fries off Fin's plate and sipping my beer.

"That damned bus. If it wasn't paid off, I'd scrap the thing. O, look at it for me before we leave?"

"I will." Fixing things with engines was a hobby I picked up from Mom. She spent most of my life restoring old cars and selling them for the fun of it.

"O," she said, sounding like she was about to start an interview. "Did you quit? Did you apply to that thing—the school? Are you moving back here?"

The look of surprise that crossed Fin's face made me feel a little guilty. Lin, being Lin, was ready to lay my whole life out on the table. I didn't mind. I wanted Fin to know, but I should have been the one to tell him. He had told me so much, and I had said, "hey get on my bike," and that was it. I was grateful to Lin. She was ruthless, peeling information out of me that I had no idea how to just offer up.

"I quit. I'm not sure what I'm going to do," I offered sheepishly.

"What do you mean? Did you apply? Are you gonna leave Georgia? The house?" Lin's grand plan was for me to stay in Georgia and live in my mother's home while I went back to school. I wasn't sure why she wanted that for me.

"What am I gonna do with a house?"

Lin glared at me. "Live in it. *Be* somewhere."

I shrugged. She sighed but pressed onward in her interrogation. "What did you hear from—what was that last place?"

"Doesn't matter. They said no, too," I said. I risked a glance at Fin. Fin was staring down at his half-eaten burger.

"A *no*! Damn it. Where to next?" she said without any real disappointment, only her resolution to move forward.

"I am done—"

"Nope. *No*! You only applied to three programs. You will keep trying. One will say *yes*, and it will be perfect."

"Programs?" Fin said, asking the question like it was risky.

"Master's programs. Can you believe this guy, Finny? He has a good degree in English with a minor in Education and Vocations, and he is half-assing it to find a master's program. He needs to—no, don't let him give you that 'pity me' look, because he needs to do this. He has spent the last year as a dog groomer in Shit, New York, and he can—you piss me off, Orion Starr." Lin snatched the nearly empty beer glass away from me. Fin laughed behind his hand, and I rolled my eyes.

"Get Finny to help you. He can probably improve your applications or something. Doc McHottie over here has nearly finished med school, and in one piece." Lin coughed, chugging the last of the beer.

"I wish you wouldn't do that," a man said, leaning on my side of the booth. He was tall with long hair down his back. He smelled a bit like a really nice men's bathroom, fresh but in a covered-up way. I glanced at him, then shrugged at Fin. Fin just raised an eyebrow to me and looked at the man.

"What? Chug or choke?" Lin said, wiping her mouth on her arm.

"Sounds like your sex life, Lin," the guy spat before stomping off.

"It's gonna be my next band name," Lin said to his back.

"Ouch. Who was that?" Fin whispered.

"That's the bassist, Zane. He's mad 'cause he can't tie me down—in a figurative way. I slept with him once, and now he thinks I am *only* gonna sleep with *him*. I'm not ready for that, though. Look at all the pretty people in the world," she said, leaning into Fin. Fin laughed and turned a bit red.

"Oh, Finny, don't look at me like that. Don't be so virginal."

I tried to keep a straight face. Part of me wanted to be furious with her. She knew about that night, and her joke sounded like a mean jab to me. But I stayed quiet because I could tell Fin didn't take it that way. He just groaned and covered his face, turning even more red.

"Thanks, Lin."

She giggled. "Orion knows about everyone. Why else do you think I went to the same college as you? I've been his spy this whole time."

I felt like I was going to die of embarrassment. I tried to kick her under the table, but I barely managed to bump her shin. I glared at her and she winked at me.

"Oh, you're not off the hook, Starr. I've told him all about you, too."

I ran a hand over my face and groaned. She laughed, nearly cackling. She had kept me informed about Fin for as long as they were at the same college. I had a hard time meeting Fin's eyes for a few seconds.

"Lin," a woman said, approaching Lin's side of the booth.

"Jessica?"

"It is time to set up," she said, leaving without another word.

"Who was that?" Fin said.

"The band manager. She's kind of damp out in public, but a freak if you get her alone. She was trained as an opera singer. Imagine that kind of sucking and blowing power, if you know what I mean."

Fin turned red again and Lin winked at me.

"I'll find you on the break. You *have* to stay for both sets. O, promise you'll sing for me." She gave Fin's arm a squeeze and kissed his cheek. She leaned across the table and kissed me lightly on the mouth. "I missed your face."

Then she was gone. I turned back to Fin to assess the damage Lin might have done.

"Wow," Fin said, leaning back against the booth.

"She doesn't change."

"We *all* change."

Fin looked at me, clearly sizing me up, and I faltered. I wasn't sure where to start. I wanted to say everything, but a single thought wouldn't form in my mind. The diner took on soft edges, and the sounds around me dimmed.

"Why didn't you tell me Rose was sick?" I said after a minute, like the coward I was. The intensity of question surprised me. *Was I actually mad about this?*

"Why didn't you tell me about anything at all?"

"Seems like a big deal, Fin. You probably could have added it to your speech two days ago," I said. If I could distract him long enough, he might forget about me completely. Then I wouldn't have to own any of my shit.

"I don't think it would have been smart to tell drunk you that someone else in your life was dying." The harshness to Fin's tone seemed to surprise him as much as it did me. I watched his shoulders dip, embarrassment crossing his face.

"Orion, I—"

"No, you're right. Fair enough."

Fin looked at me awkwardly.

"I shouldn't have said that," he said, his voice small. I felt my heart stop. I sighed and rubbed the outside of my empty beer mug with my palms, the cool condensation soothing my skin.

"I'm sorry for...I just didn't know how to," I said. *Ask him what he is doing here with you. Ask him why he even bothered. Ask him.* "Why did you?"

"Why do I do anything?"

I was quiet for a minute because I understood him more than I understood myself. If I didn't say anything now, I wouldn't ever. "I've been doing odd jobs since I graduated. I got into some trouble after I found out Marge was dying. She told me to go and live my life. For me, that meant a year-long bender and five nights in detox. After that, I promised her and myself I'd be better. So, I thought a master's might do it. Nothing to show for it. None of that ever seemed worthy of an email, Fin."

See, Fin? A mess for you to clean up, like always.

Fin looked like he wanted to protest my last statement, but he didn't. Instead, he forked a French fry. "A master's in what?"

"Education is what I started with. Music therapy is in there too, but who knows?"

"And no luck?"

"Not really. Lin was right. I am kind of half-assing it. I'll be thirty soon and what...what does that even mean?"

"People do it, O. People do it all the time."

I shrugged.

"You ever think of traveling like Corv?"

"Naw. I can't manage it here. What would I do somewhere else? I'd have to have the damned U.S. embassy on speed dial. I don't know, Fin."

Fin knew when to back off and stop probing a subject before it became a sore spot. I knew he wouldn't let it go forever, if we had more than one evening together. The nice thing about Fin was he could just let things sit. Fin shifted in the booth and dusted the French fry salt from his hands. I watched him finish his beer. These moments were distracting, his big hands gripping his glass, his lips in warm, pink contrast with the gold liquid, me needing to get a fucking grip.

"Hey, I ordered a sundae," Fin said suddenly.

"I will get it. I was going to get another beer anyway. You want another?"

"Naw, I'll drive," Fin said, as if that had always been the plan. I didn't plan on being drunk another night, but I didn't say anything. I stood and crossed to the bar.

"Ms. Gra—"

"I know, I know. I said I don't need you tell me nothin', Orion."

She went to the kitchen and shouted orders at her staff. I slumped onto a bar stool and waited for her to come back. The bar was filling slowly with a lot of locals. I had kept my acquaintances to a minimum, so people didn't really pay me any attention, even if some of the faces rang distant bells in my memory. A few people approached Fin, but no one stuck around.

"I will never understand what it is that keep you out of that man's life." Grace sighed, put another beer on the bar, and came around to sit on a nearby stool. "I would tell you not to hurt him, but knowin' you like I do, you gonna let yourself get hurt first."

"What would you have me do, Grace? I'm here because my mother died, not to hook up. Shouldn't someone want to talk about that?"

"Do *you*?" she snapped back. Then she said softly, "That's real sad about your mama. But you livin'—barely, the way Lin tell it—and your mama ain't. Now, don't look at me like that, 'cause I know she'd be tellin' you the same thing. I know what I see, child. Saw it then, and I see it now. You still got something in here for that man."

"I don't see it," I said, sounding more like a liar than I expected. I didn't get it. My mom was dead less than a week, and here I was being told exactly to do what with my high school crush? Sure, I was the one who invited him out and whatever but still.

"Look at me," Grace ordered, her eyes intent.

I looked at her.

"Do I look Black to you?" she asked. I was taken aback by the question, I just squinted at her. "I said, do I look Black to you? Am I a person of color to you?"

"Yes ma'am," I said, feeling myself grin.

"So, you can see with your eyes that I have brown skin on me?"

"Yes, I can see that."

"Good." Grace smiled, tossing her towel onto the bar. "I was beginning to think you was having trouble seein' the obvious."

I laughed and shook my head. "Come on, Gracey."

Grace leaned toward me. "Listen, save your excuses for church. I can tell you this. Whatever stopped you then ain't around to stop you now."

I opened my mouth, but she said, "Like I said, I know what your mama would say, so don't *even* try that with me. She told me plenty when she came around—*Hunter is just so hard on himself.* Now, I agreed with her."

That pinched a little right in the chest, but I covered it up by rolling my eyes. "You do a pretty good impression of her."

"You a funny man."

Grace stomped off, and Lin's band started to warm up, soft chords vibrating through the room. I turned toward the band, pretending to be interested. I knew very well what kept me from a real effort at a relationship with Fin, both in high school and college, and it had nothing to do with my mother.

High school was the first lesson about the consequences of hanging out with Fin. I had been in the courtyard after school waiting for Fin to get out of soccer practice. I would meet up with him after work, and we would figure out how to spend the rest of the day. One day, I had been waiting and was ambushed by six guys from the soccer team. Four pinned me to the ground, one sat on my chest, and the last kept watch.

"What's the matter, fag? Not going to fight back?" one of them said.

I hadn't answered.

"Okay, fine. *I* came to *talk* to *you* anyway," the guy on my chest said. I felt myself tense even though I hadn't wanted to fight back. I could feel my body preparing for a fight.

"We know you're *friends* with Frank, but that's all you are *ever* going to be. See, Frank is someone we like, someone we need, and we can't have you fucking up everything we have going for him by being the sick, twisted fuck that you are. Do you understand?"

I fucking understood well enough. Every practical gay kid in the South with internet access understood. I still didn't respond. I could handle bullshit like that from people like them. The trick was holding still, giving them what they wanted. They didn't want a fight, either. They just wanted to scare me. The kid on my chest gave me a few quick hard slaps on the side of the face, then they freed me.

"Don't fuck up, Orion."

That incident usually wouldn't have fazed me. Fin and I went to Grace's for some fries and then back to Fin's so he could help me with summer homework. It wouldn't have fazed me *if* Fin's coach hadn't caught up to me the next day. He'd called to me after practice and had asked me to join him in his office.

"Come in, kid. Have a seat," Coach Jefferson said. *Kid.* They only ever called me that when they didn't know my name. "I see you and Franklin have become friends."

"Yes sir."

Coach Jefferson stood up from the desk. I sighed. The teenager sitting on my chest just the day before had been Alexander Jefferson, the coach's son. "I wanted to talk with you about that. See, Franklin and I have been working on getting him set up at a decent college. Now, with his life being the way it is, the only way he can get there is on some pretty hefty scholarships, mostly for soccer."

I waited.

"Now, given the way *your* life is, I just want you to think about what being your friend would mean to his chances with your juvenile record, being held back a grade, and other questionable activities."

Jefferson slurred the last words into a single accusation, but it still translated into gay activities. I didn't move. The fucks from the day before probably meant it when they said they didn't want me to be gay with Fin, like I was converting him. The coach meant so much more, though. He also meant don't be a criminal, don't be stupid, and *don't be brown.*

"I just want you to think about that, kid, before anything happens."

I stood and left, saying nothing. Despite everything else I had wanted, I mostly wanted Fin to have a great life. I wasn't going to be the one to mess it up. Between the coach and the team, the message was clear enough. I had messed enough shit up to force me and Mom to move to Painted Waters in the first place. Besides, I knew how the world worked. They could make it worse for me. So, I backed off, letting my crush be the best friendship I ever had. Till college when I seriously fucked that to hell.

"There's only two places I like to see ice cream, and neither's here meltin' on my bar," Grace said.

I jumped at the sound of her voice, memories scattering. I honestly lost track of what I was doing. The sundae was starting to drip, two small tracks of vanilla and chocolate working their way down the glass boat. I'd forgot. I considered both the dessert and Grace. She didn't look mad, her face more playful. I took up the dish and licked the edge where ice cream had melted over the side.

I laughed. "Where, then?"

"One is in the hands of my customers, the other involves a piano player from a band that passed through here once, but I'll tell you that story when you're older." She winked and walked away.

I slammed half the beer, then pushed the glass away. I didn't want any more booze for a while. The band was laying thick, greasy blues across the diner, and the waiters had finally gotten the lights down. The room took on soft edges again, as if it were a memory already. Haloed in a beam of light, Fin watched the band and didn't see me approach. I caught a easy look from Lin as she sang the final notes of a song. My heart had been slowing for so long: my brother moving, Mom being sick, and suppressing my feelings for Fin. Maybe even as far back as my dad leaving, if I thought about it too hard.

Lin had just sung a song I had written her, and I felt my heart rev as Fin turned and smiled at me. Fin had somehow made my heart beat faster when I thought my mother's death would stifle it for good. Lin and her music, too. And Grace and her watchfulness. And Rose and her warmth. It was like wheezing through a bad cold. I felt suddenly weird. Good, but weird.

Lin winked at me from the stage. "This song goes out to the man in the stars."

Fin cheered and looked at me over his shoulder. He smiled. "Song's for you, I guess."

Staring into Fin's face, I also felt my heart getting signals from farther south. Even my libido had been asleep for a long time. I did something just then that I had never done, surprising myself as much as I did him. For the first time since we'd known each other, I sat on the same side of the booth as Fin. As I moved over there, I could feel the distance between us become suddenly, indistinguishably small. I slid the ice cream along the table. The look of alarm and joy that crossed Fin's face was enough.

CHAPTER 9: FIN

I stared dumbfounded, eating the first spoonful of sundae. He was sitting by me and, like the ridiculous human I was, I was blushing. I wanted to shift so I could face him, but I didn't want him to think I was moving away. So, I just sat weirdly at his side. We were in physical contact, thigh to thigh. Sweet Jesus, nothing else mattered to me in that moment except what side of the booth Orion was sitting on. It was a small thing, a tiny gesture that closed a canyon between us. Orion was so close I could smell the beer and leather.

"Lin dedicated a song to you," I said clumsily.

"She always does whenever I come to a show."

"I remember. You kept in regular touch with her?"

An emotion I couldn't read crossed Orion's face, but he shrugged and returned to an easy smile quickly. Orion's shrug was a step in the wrong direction, his way of avoiding something.

I rushed to try to regain friendly ground. "I mean, that's good. I sort of kept in touch with her, too. She would find me around campus and sometimes she messaged me on social media when she was nearby. I think we both just needed someone familiar. I guess you know that much, though."

Orion took the spoon from me and helped himself to the sundae. "You keep in touch with anyone else?"

I had to swallow hard before answering. The ice cream already had me drooling, but the sight of Orion drawing a spoon between his lips doubled the effort. I gulped as he licked his bottom lip. He had great lips, dark reddish brown and— *Take a breath, Fin.* "Um…who… ah, kind of. The team, mostly. Some of the guys are still around, so I see them. Especially since I've been back."

"Are you back for your mom?"

I shifted this time, facing him. I had expected to talk about this at some point, but still wasn't sure I knew how. Rose had gotten sick after Orion's mom, and I figured it might be easier for him if he didn't know until his mom got better. Only she never got better. I knew Marge had known Rose was sick, but I couldn't figure out why she hadn't told him. It was like all of us knew that it would have to wait.

I propped an elbow on the table. "Mom has skin cancer."

Orion raised an eyebrow at me.

And of course, I started to babble. "I picked oncology to study before her diagnosis. She's been diagnosed for only three years. It was bad, but it's better. It was caught soon enough, so it hadn't yet metastasized, and the survival rates are high. It was the surgeries that—"

I forced myself to stop and take a breath, my brain flooded with medical jargon. I concluded simply, "Skin cancer, you know."

Orion offered me the spoon. I took it and jabbed at the ice cream, grateful to stop looking into his curious and sad face.

"That's your tattoo?" Orion said, referring to the black awareness ribbon tattooed on my chest.

I guess he got a good look at it while I was naked in the bathroom. It was linked with a yellow ribbon for my father. I nodded. We ate a minute in silence, trading the spoon and not looking at each other.

"People think being a doctor probably drives me crazy because I know all about it. But I think it helps. Her doctors start talking, and it can sound like gibberish, like she could have any illness in the world, but I know what's happening, and it keeps me from making up things. I mean, sure, I worry all the time, but…"

I had run out of thoughts on the matter. My voice always took on a childish sound when I tried to explain. I hated it. Sure, I could default to the jargon, but what would that tell anyone? It sure as hell had told me nothing about what my mother's life would actually be like. Orion didn't say anything, but I could feel his eyes on me. I became suddenly aware of our surroundings, the people and bar coming back into focus as the room applauded for Lin and the band.

"This song is for the redhead," Lin said after the applause had died.

"Oh, look a song for me," I said, perking up. It was a cover of one of my favorites, but I didn't mention it.

"Rose will be okay, Fin," Orion said quietly.

I didn't answer, just smiled and turned back to watch the band. We finished the ice cream in silence. A number of songs passed. Lin was approaching the break in her set, and I became aware of Orion shifting away from me, out of the booth.

"Where are you going?"

"Watch."

"It's about that time." Lin breathed into the mic as her band vamped in the background. "A lifetime ago, I met a young man. He charmed me like the Pied Piper. One song from this man, and I was hooked. He's here tonight, and this is my way of begging him to come up here. I know he has a song for all of us."

"That's my cue," Orion said.

I turned back to him, my heart racing with excitement. Orion just shrugged. I watched him cross the room as Lin urged the crowd to applaud. A roadie had a stool and a guitar ready to go.

"Take a break, boys, you don't know this one," Orion said to the band loud enough for the crowd to hear. It was part of the show, Orion's face taking on a practiced but pleasing grin. Lin was all smiles. She skipped off the stage and crammed against me in the booth. The rest of the band meandered away, leaving Orion alone under soft purple and yellow lights.

"If you didn't want to fuck him already, this would certainly do the trick," Lin said into my ear. I didn't say anything despite the heat that rose in my face. I just watched.

Orion was good looking. He perched lightly on the stool and started to strum. His hair had been loosely braided back, falling in temping whisps around his face. His leather pants had a distracting sheen under the stage lights, and he chewed on his lip as he strummed. I felt my mouth go dry.

"He might be hot, but he is not a ham. Close your mouth, Finny," Lin said.

When Orion looked back at the crowd, it was with the cool

cockiness of a guy who knew he was attractive and knew how to make the crowd sweat. He stopped playing a moment, the sound changing when he started again. His eyes had changed too and, for a brief instant, Orion looked vulnerable, his show face gone.

He cleared his throat once. "I ain't one for speeches, so here's a song."

Orion started to play a bluesy melody. It was the sort of simple, hungry sound that sank into people. I had heard Orion play and sing thousands of times, but something was different now. Everything was different. I would have been impressed with the guitar playing alone, but then he sang. His gravelly voice matched the sound of the guitar, and the intoxicating quality of the song was almost unsurvivable.

> *She watched him leave, he said he missed the fight*
> *He said missed the sand and stone, he said he missed the night*
> *She told him he could keep it, she knew the best part of the dark*
> *Was the stars that filled the sky and her two children's hearts*

I was suddenly in the Starrs' kitchen watching Orion and Marge have an argument, two sets of fiery eyes, their voices low. Then I was coming around the back of the house catching Marge and Orion in a rare hug, their voices soft, their laughs gentle and similar. Then I was clasping Marge's hand and cheering as Orion crossed the stage at graduation. And that hand taking mine again as Orion waved from a bus window. The two years of memories I had of Orion and his mother pooled in my brain. And tears filled my eyes.

I looked at Lin to find she was nearly as far gone as I was, wiping frantically at her wet eyes and running makeup. I looked back at Orion. His eyes were closed and his face a mix of things, so subtle that only someone who had spent time memorizing the way his face expressed emotions would know that any were there. His voice was steady and his hands sure. Orion sang on, exposed and perfect.

> *He left a watch and a glass of whisky on the nightstand*
> *Two sons who'd never know him and a woman's empty hands*
> *She went to their side that night knowing life had let them down*
> *She wondered how to face them, wondered what they'd do now*
> *She prayed*

Let them know I'm here, let me love them the best I can
I hope they can forgive me and grow to be good men
Love is not a fairy tale and life will get harder
But God please
Please don't let us drown in fear's tainted water
She watched them play, she watched them grow, and hoped they
understood
Their father left her not them and she'd done the best she could
Her oldest was like him, answering the call of foreign lands
Her youngest was like her, chasing love, chasing fire with both
hands
One day pain drove her young son to a demon she knew too well
His body soaked in whisky, his heart a burning hell
He left in search of a stranger, himself, his father, he didn't know
She stood on her front porch, knowing he had to go
She prayed
Let him know I'm here, let him know he can come home
I hope he can forgive me and know he's not alone
This life has not been easy and staying true will get harder
But God please
Please don't let him drown in hate's tainted water

I watched as tears rolled down Orion's face. The song was a prayer to his mother in response to everything she had ever wished for him. I felt it in every part of my soul. Lin's grip on my arm and her stillness let me know that she felt it, too. The relative silence of the entire state of Georgia let me know everyone was listening to Orion.

Orion played on as if he were entirely alone. He rolled over the melodies and harmonies building through the music, as if it were the only way he could be saved. While he played, Orion kept his eyes closed, held still. And the room held still with him. Then the bottom dropped out of the song and Orion continued almost a capella.

My mother fought her own monsters, and I have come to see
That she fought the monster that hunted my brother and me
My mother took the damage and gave us love that was real
But a heart can only fight so long before it won't heal
I pray

Let her know I love her. She loved me more than I was due
I hope she can forgive me for the hell I put her through
Her life was not easy, and I know I made it harder
But God please
Please pull her free of sorrow's tainted water
I pray
Let her know I love her. She loved me more than I was due
I hope she can forgive me for the hell I put her through
Her life was not easy, and I know I made it harder
But God please
Please pull her free of sorrow's tainted water

The bar was dead silent as the sound of Orion's song drifted away. Everyone was hanging on his performance. Then, as if the idea occurred to us all at once, the room detonated with applause. Orion stood, blinking like he had forgotten what planet he was on. Lin rushed to rescue him from the spotlight. She wrapped her arms around him and brushed the tears from his face with her thumbs. She wiped her own eyes on the back of her hands.

"Orion Starr, everyone," she said into the mic, reigniting the cheers.

Orion handed her the guitar and worked his way back to me. I watched him, people stopping him along the way to offer him praise. He accepted it shyly, like he always had. I wiped my face on the inside of my button-down, but couldn't get the tears to stop. Orion laughed as he sat.

"You are ridiculous," Orion said with more affection in his voice than anything else as he handed me a bar napkin.

"Well, you know me," I said with a sniff, feeling the blush burn my cheeks.

"I remember. We watched *Bridge to Terabithia*. I think you cried for three months."

"Damned creek."

"Fin," Orion said, scooting a bit closer. I met his eyes. Orion said nothing, but I knew what was there. His eyes were deep with concern and need. Orion needed me to tell him the song was great, that it wasn't too much, that he wasn't alone.

I flapped my hand at him helplessly and wiped my face again.

"No, I'm fine. It was a really great song, O. Here, let me out. I'm going to see if I can't find my composure, maybe in the bathroom."

I edged toward Orion, expecting him to back out of the booth. He didn't. Instead, he leaned toward me and pressed his lips gently against mine. My higher cognitive abilities died on the spot. The kiss wasn't short, but I didn't have time to process it, close my eyes, or even kiss back before Orion moved away. I stared as he stood up to let me out of the booth. My body took over and carried me out toward the bathroom. *The hell was that?*

I stood in the bathroom like a dope, shell-shocked and looking like I had never been in a bathroom before. I did the only thing that made sense and pulled out my phone. It was after ten but I chanced texting Mom. I felt like if I told someone it would be real.

Mom?

What is the matter, Fin?

Orion kissed ME!

Fin, I know we're close, but don't text me while you're making out with people.

Mom.

Are you happy about it?

Well, I had to think. My body was sure happy, because my heart started racing. And my dick sure remembered what kissing Orion could lead to. But was it weird now? Was it different? Was it anything? My head didn't really know what to do. If it was a vote between my heart, my head, and my dick, two out of three agreed.

Yes.

So what do you want, Fin?

Mom, what do I do?

Kiss him back. Marry him!

Mom!

Franklin Ian Ness, put your phone away and enjoy it. Don't let him make all the moves. Let me know if you aren't coming home.

I sighed. My phone buzzed again.

Or let me know if you are ;)

I laughed. *Maybe we are too close.*

Mom didn't text back. The kiss had been real, and I'd let it pass me by like a big loser.

"Leave the bathroom, Frank," I ordered myself, shoving my phone in a pocket. I turned on the tap, rubbed water over my face, and dried it. Then I washed my hands because, well, it was still a bathroom. I looked in the mirror, shrugged, and left. Orion was at the bar, and I sat on a stool just a little too close to be casual.

"Hey, you okay?" Orion said. I nodded.

I tried to find something to say, but I couldn't. All I could think about was Orion's golden eyes and dark hair. The smile that cracked his face was everything I needed. To my surprise, sitting at the bar so close to him after the brief kiss brought on feelings I had never had as a teenager or even at twenty-one. That young, I'd only had the impression of lust and attraction, the vague understanding you get from bad movies and shitty porn. A few boyfriends and as many years later, I had a real idea now. And all of that was focused on Orion. Plus, I felt something I couldn't name, something beyond admiration and awe. We just stared at each other through the rest of Lin's set.

I had almost figured out what to say, but I felt a gentle hand on my shoulder and I saw Orion's gaze shift from me to the person touching me. When I turned, Lin winked at me.

"Taking a break?" I asked.

"Just a bit." She practically slithered into the place between me and Orion, her soft arms brushing mine. She turned and smiled at me.

"I don't know why I torture myself," she sighed finally.

"What do you mean?" I asked.

She snuggled into me a little, leaning her hip against the inside of my thigh. She was making it very clear that she only intended to talk to me. She continued. "I don't know why I let him onstage, Finny. One song and he's all anyone will remember. I sing twenty and what do I get?"

"I think he pays them off," I said, trying not to laugh.

"Really?"

"Hey—"

"I mean, you know how he got me to be his friend, right?" I said to her, ignoring Orion.

"How?" she asked, though she really did know. She knew everything.

"Cake. He bribed me with a cake."

Lin laughed. "I see. Well, I guess I'm the luckier one."

"Hi. I'm right here," Orion said, putting his arms around Lin.

"How's that?" I continued ignoring him.

"He gave *me* cash," Lin said with a laugh. That was true. He'd offered her a twenty to say he had been with her during a mandatory school assembly and not out joyriding on his bike. She did, it didn't work, and they both got detention.

"It's not like it helped," Orion said.

"Shit, I think I need to up my price," I said.

"Fuck the *both* of you."

"Promise?" Lin and I said together. It was Orion's turn to be embarrassed. He looked away, his grin going from gentle annoyance to embarrassed annoyance.

"Don't you have a show to do?" he said to Lin. She winked at me, slithered out from between us, and sashayed away.

"O—"

Orion put his hands up, surrendering.

I couldn't say anything more after that. I just watched him as he watched the band. We stayed at the bar, listening to Lin for a few more songs. I was engrossed by the drummer, his hands flying, feet pounding away, and he didn't even look winded, when I felt a slight pull on the cuff of my button-down. My skin flushed at the contact. I looked at Orion. I tried not to make a big deal out of it. Orion never seemed to notice when he was doing it, but he always found something—buttons, hood cords, sleeve hems—to touch on me. This time it was a gentle pull at the fold of my sleeve where it met my forearm. His eyes were on the band, but the back of his hand brushed softly over my skin. I thrilled at the familiar, distracted gesture.

Orion sighed and finally turned to me. "I hate to do this, but we should go. I have appraisers coming to the house in the morning, and you know me."

I nodded.

"Is that okay?" he said, scanning my face.

"Sure, O. Do what you gotta do."

"Let's go, then," he said, sliding off his stool into the space that had been between us. It was narrow and almost brought us chest to chest.

I took a breath. "We have to pay."

"I already did." And the fucker had the audacity to wink at me.

Orion left a note for Lin at the bar. I signed it too and left my phone number at the bottom. Willy hugged Orion like she would never see him again, and it occurred to me that was a possibility. Orion was there for his mother's funeral. A fucking funeral, and what was I expecting? To go to bed with the guy? Then what?

I was still mulling these questions over as we walked out to the car. Rose had been right about the rain, the red dust turned to red mud in the parking lot. I kicked a rock into a puddle, feeling irritated.

"Fin, how about you just drop me off at home. Then I can just walk over tomorrow after everything." Orion's voice lingered just at my back as we crossed to the car.

"For your bike?" I murmured offhandedly, searching my pockets for the keys.

"For you."

"Get in the car, O."

That sent my guts rolling like I was jumping off a cliff. *Hell.* I was in it now. He was actually flirting with me—and kissing me. It was amazing how dangerous Orion could be with only a few words. *What will you do to me this time?*

❖

I hadn't been the only one thinking of Orion's mom, apparently. The closer we got to Orion's house, the more anxious he became. He was trying not to let me see, but I noticed him doing anxious things like playing with the zipper on his vest or pulling his hair out of its braid, then scrunching it up into a messy ponytail. I resisted the urge to reach out and take his hand. I wanted to, but I didn't know if I could, if I should. I was also at a loss of words. He didn't like to be left alone with his feelings. *I could probably give him that*, and I kept silent until we were in his driveway.

"O," I said, staring into the dashboard. "You don't have to be here alone. I can stay. I…"

I forced myself to stop talking. I wasn't going to beg to stay with Orion. I didn't look at him, either. A nod or a shrug wasn't going to cut it. If Orion wanted me to stay, he would have to say it.

Orion's voice was barely a sigh. "I would like that."

We went into the house, and he led us straight to his room. He found a pair of pajama pants for me that turned into a pair of pajama capris with our height difference. He also found a set of pillows and another blanket. As Orion moved around, he became even more unsettled. It was as if he was trying to keep a certain distance between himself and everything else in the room, standing too far from the bed, or me, or the dresser for it to make sense. I tried not to let my own thoughts in. I had many. For example, we had never shared a bed, so I wondered if I should offer to sleep on the floor. We had never stayed together in Orion's room, so should I sleep on the couch? I dropped the questions as quick as they came. Orion would tell me what he wanted. I watched him pace.

"Did your mom ever hear that song?" I said, trying to keep it light as I texted Rose I wouldn't be home. I set my phone on the desk. I knew Marge was bothering him, so I figured we might as well get it out in the open.

"Yeah, she did. Why?" Orion said, pulling on pajamas of his own. I tried not to watch him change.

"It says a lot about you...about her. I don't know."

"Well, it's just a song. Doesn't matter now." I didn't like the sound of his comment. I watched him.

"Are you just going to stare at me?" he snapped, tossing the words over his shoulder.

"Yup."

"Fin!" Orion faced me, looking lost for words momentarily. "Maybe this was a bad idea."

"Maybe."

Orion groaned and rolled his eyes. "You know what—"

I crossed the room in only a few strides, not really knowing what I was going to do until I was there. I wrapped my arms around Orion and hugged him hard. He didn't move at first. He just stood still, probably from the shock of being touched at all. Then his hands came up and settled first on my hips, then hard around my back. As he let me pull him closer, I noticed the ragged breathing that meant tears. I didn't say anything. I didn't move. I just held on and let Orion hold on, too. And because I was me, I cried with him. I hadn't thought touching him would work. *Why hadn't I thought that?*

Eventually Orion was spent, sitting then lying on the bed like a wounded man. I turned out the lights and hovered for a minute somewhere on the side of the room before I crawled into bed with him.

We lay facing each other, the blankets puddled somewhere at the foot of the bed. I had my eyes closed to it all. It was familiar, and I remembered falling asleep with him in that hotel room. He hadn't slept, I knew that much. He had waited until I was asleep before he left.

I thought the memories of that night might come spilling out of my mouth the way most of my thoughts did, but everything stalled out when Orion slipped his fingers over mine. His hand settled on mine, palms together in a way that was more like a handshake. We stayed like that, quiet and still, then I heard Orion's breath change.

I knew what he sounded like asleep, so I wasn't surprised to find his eyes closed when I opened mine. I shifted slightly, feeling a weird sense of relief. This already was different from college and the night he left me. He was asleep, and he was going to stay with me, at least for a while. Maybe a long while, I thought as he shifted to be closer to me. I hadn't moved away exactly but just flipped from my side to my back. He must have sensed it and scrunched closer, pulling his arms up against his chest and snuggling into my side. All I could do was put my arm around him. It was so comfortable.

I had to fish the blanket up with my foot before I could reach it, then I let it fall around us. And I fell asleep. Sometime later, Orion jumped awake, his entire body rigid with panic.

"Nightmare?" I was a light enough sleeper to have been woken by it.

"I don't know. I just I wasn't here when she died," Orion murmured after many silent moments. I had almost fallen back asleep.

"I know," I said gently.

"Was that the right thing to do?" Orion said, lying back where he had been under my arm.

I ran my hand over his hair and down his back. "It's what she wanted, wasn't it?"

"Yeah, but fuck, Fin, who lets their mother die alone?"

"She had her reasons."

"The wrong reasons," Orion said into my shoulder, his voice misty.

"The *best* of the wrong reasons, I'm sure. We both know how stubborn she was, and it was always going to be her way."

It didn't seem like enough, so I kept talking. "My dad chose to go on his last deployment. He wanted to. I used to ask a lot of questions about it and never once got any answers. What I hold on to is that my dad thought he was doing the right thing for us. Right or wrong, who knows? The best he could? Yes. People only die once, O. There's not really enough time to figure out if you're doing it right."

Orion didn't say anything, just pulled himself in closer and sighed. I pressed my lips softly to his forehead and ran my hand over his hair. He fell asleep again with my arms around him.

CHAPTER 10: ORION

I watched Fin sleep. I was surprised at how easy it was to sleep with him, and I was even more surprised at how easy it was to wake up with him. I had fallen asleep with his arm around me and now mine was around him. He was stretched out on his stomach, taking up most of the bed.

I had woken up with people before and had always had the urge to run. Fuck, I had even left *him* once, running being better than facing the consequences of sticking around. Watching him, however, I was suddenly afraid he would want to leave. After everything I'd done to him, why would he stay?

Mr. Starr, this is our ten thousandth attempt to reach you. You are trying to draw on an account that no longer exists—

Wasn't that old news? Fin couldn't possibly feel anything but sorry for me, and I was doing nothing but trying to drown in the guy for a while. Mature. *Drowning in you*, wasn't that the most clichéd lyric? I blinked. He had more freckles now. He wasn't picture perfect asleep, his hair a mess, mouth open, unflattering sounds escaping him. I felt myself smile.

I knew it had been the song, the energy of the crowd, Wilhemina Grace's stupid words. Singing that song last night had given me a sense of bravery I wasn't used to having. I was suddenly and temporarily guiltless, shameless, and free. And the first thing I'd wanted to do with that feeling was kiss Fin. I wanted to kiss him awake. But the feeling from the night before was gone. I was afraid again. *I would kiss you awake, drown in your eyes, take a deep breath and confess all my lies/but I can't I'm all out of bravery/too scared to accept you and me.* Accept? Pursue? Another work in progress.

The alarm on my phone sent music screeching into the quiet. I'd forgotten I'd set the alarm. I groaned and scrambled after the phone somewhere on the floor.

"Damn it," I groaned, straining to reach it and cut it off. I could hear Fin snicker a little when I finally managed to kill it. I sighed and flopped back on the bed.

"Oh, no! Darth Vader, no," Fin said in a high-pitched voice. He knew my ring tone was from *Star Wars*. "Someone help us. Luke, save Abba-Dabba."

I growled, trying not to be amused. "You know the name of the planet, Fin. And don't start."

Fin wasn't done. He switched the tone of his voice to something as close to mine as he could manage. "I'm Orion. I am a cool, moody biker who can sing 'cause I'm a rebel, but I go home and jerk it to pictures of Luke Skywalker."

I laughed and jumped on him, pinning a pillow over his face. Fin laughed and easily flipped me off him, his long-armed strength working to his advantage. He propped himself up on his elbows.

"Come on, we have to get up. Appraisers are coming," I said, trying to avoid his fucking amazing smile.

Fin sat up all the way and looked intently at me. "Do you want me to leave?"

I shook my head. "No, but it's probably rude to leave a guy sleeping in your bed while someone wanders through your shit figuring out if the hardwood brings up the value of the house."

Fin grinned and blushed. I stood, pocketed my phone, and started for the door.

"I can't believe that's still your ringtone," he called after me.

"The Rebellion is eternal. You know where shit is."

I was halfway down the hall when I heard Fin shout, "Were you watching me sleep?"

I felt myself warm with a flash of embarrassment. I *had* been watching Fin sleep. Then again, I didn't exactly have to own up to it. I hadn't *just* been watching him sleep.

"I wouldn't say *watching*," I called. I heard Fin scoff before I continued down the hall. I couldn't get the smile on my face to go away.

I got Fin some fresh towels and let him have the hall bath. I showered in Mom's bathroom. I felt suddenly shy, as if Fin could see the pockets of light he was creating inside me. But that was okay, because he was smiling at me, so he must like whatever it was he saw.

Clean and dressed, I peeled the too-old contacts out of my eyes and got my glasses out of my backpack. The appraiser was set to arrive at eight, and it was seven fifty-something by the time I made it downstairs. I slipped on some sandals and tried to look like a capable person. Jeans and a T-shirt, no leather, no piercings, no sign of the me that people usually judged.

I scrolled through assorted notifications on my tablet, ignoring all of them, including an email from Corvus and a string of angry texts from Lin. I found a game to play and waited, trying to look around as little as possible. *Mom's stuff...my stuff...Mom's stuff...my stuff.* All of my resolve and whatever I had found yesterday was gone.

I heard Fin's shower cut off as the appraiser's car pulled into view. The house was set back from the road, but he parked on the street instead of coming up the drive, which gave him a decent walk up to the house. I watched from the formal living room as the man got out of the van, satchel over one shoulder. I silently debated whether I should let the guy ring the doorbell or meet him on the porch. The sound of Fin stubbing his toe and cussing made the decision for me.

I sprinted out from the porch as he approached, clad in a blue polo, matching blue hat, and khaki slacks. He was a big guy, like a former pro wrestler, arms thick in his shirt, gut just starting to stretch his belt. He walked the whole way looking at a clipboard, climbed the stairs, then he looked at me. *Holy Hot Jesus.* Alexander Jefferson, the coach's son. Shock and rage filled me so fast, it hurt. I schooled my face back to calm as fast as I could, but my internal defenses were all blaring alarms and red lights.

"Orion. It's been a while," he said with a sincere shyness, extending his hand. He hadn't been surprised at all. Against gut instinct, I accepted the handshake.

"Um...yeah. So, you're here to do the...?" I wasn't sure how to continue. I swallowed and blinked and never managed to find the right words.

Fin—God bless him—practically skipped onto the porch, a happy smile on his face. I nearly passed out. *Fuck, FIN!* Fin was the whole reason that guy had come after me in the first place. And here I was back with him. Fin didn't seem to notice anything, though. He had on last night's jeans and an old Darth Vader shirt of mine, probably just to be funny. He had also managed to find a ball cap, which made him look slightly closer to the teenager I had known.

"Hey ya, Al," Fin said with a grin, his accent getting slightly more Southern.

"Frank!" Al cried. Al's face contorted into a surprised, horrified look.

"When Orion said an appraiser was coming, I didn't think it was you," Fin said casually. Fin kept his eyes on Al, but spoke to me. "This is one of the guys from the team who are back in town. Al had been at college on scholarship, but he got hurt. Now he runs his grandfather's land appraisal business."

"Marge placed a call, and I'm the guy who answered. I am sorry for your loss, Orion."

"Sure." I crammed my glasses back on my face and leaned on a stair rail so I could look at my feet and not at Al.

I could feel Fin look between Al and me. I knew he was trying to figure out what was going on with us. It was no secret the team and I hadn't liked each other, but I'd never gotten around to telling Fin about the attack.

Apparently ready to move on, Fin put a hand on my shoulder and gave me an intimate but chaste hug. "Well, O, I'm gonna stop by Mom's and then, since there is no food in your house, I'll grab some breakfast and be back. What do you want? Bagel? Burrito?"

"Sure, and coffee," I mumbled. I wanted Fin to stay. I wanted Fin to do this for me. I wanted to go with him and never see Al again. But that wasn't what was happening. I was happy to know he would be back. I also had to fight the urge to kiss Fin goodbye just to spite Al. Not the right reason to kiss someone.

Fin rolled his eyes at my indifference and turned back to Al. "If I don't see you before you're done, it's been something."

"Same," Al said, shaking Fin's hand. Fin patted me on the shoulder and jumped off the porch. Al and I watched him leave, staring into the empty street for a few seconds after the car was out of view. *Thanks a lot, Midge.*

"Should we do the thing?" I wanted to get this over with. Al was still looking down the road before turning to me. He looked like he wanted to run away.

"Sure. I've got your property lines here. We'll walk the place first. I'll get some history from you and do a preliminary evaluation of the property. Then if you wanna continue, I'll take this back to my office and bring a team in on Monday to do a final walkthrough and get you a formal appraisal."

"If I want to continue?"

His face went a little red and he let out a nervous breath. "I mean, sure. There are a few other companies around who could get this job done. It doesn't have to be me."

Well, isn't that something? Part of me wanted to tell him to go away. But this wasn't my deal, it was Mom's. She would have done the work to find the best person to do the job, and if that was Al, then that was Al.

"Fair enough. Let's go."

Al looked at me, a little relieved, and we started down the porch toward the western corner of the yard. The ground was wet and soft from the dew, and the whole atmosphere was a swamp. He was doing a decent job of hiding it, but I could tell he was uncomfortable. I was too, but I guess finding your high school best friend with the one guy you never wanted him around ten years later was somehow worse than anything I was feeling. *Maybe?* I thought it was good either way. I wanted him to be uncomfortable. And that was about as spiteful as I got. We didn't say anything as we walked, which I thought was counterproductive, but it wasn't my job. I wasn't even sure what a land appraiser would be looking for. I waited.

Suddenly, Al stopped walking. I glanced over my shoulder, went to continue walking, then stopped too. Al looked like he was about to vomit. He adjusted the blue cap for no reason and looked at me. Then he just spewed a bunch of words. "Orion, I'm sorry for everythin' I said back then. I had the wrong idea about you and Frank. I have plenty of excuses for that moment, but it really is that I was a shit to you, and you didn't deserve that. I am glad you and Frank have reconnected. I just didn't want to lose my friend."

I was surprised, and I could recognize the sincerity. The truth was, I hadn't held any grudges. I might dislike the guy, but whatever. People were people, and people did shitty things. I could see the energy it was taking for him to apologize after all this time. I cocked an eyebrow but didn't answer.

"I mean, it wasn't even about you being queer," Al shouted. "I mean, yeah, I *didn't* get that either, but mostly I just didn't like that Frank was spendin' all his time with you. Before you turned up, I was his best friend. Well, I am sorry."

I wanted to ask. I heard something in the way Al said *I didn't get that* as if he *did* get it now. And there was something in the way he had said *all his time with you*, the *you* sharp, accusatory, and oddly forgiving. I thought Al might just confess to having been in love with Fin himself if I let him talk long enough.

Al looked like he was waiting for me to answer or react. I shoved my glasses higher on my nose and flipped hair out of my face. I could tell by the way he was looking at me that he couldn't read my expression. I considered staring for as long as he would let me, just to mess with him. But I didn't really have the energy.

"It's okay. Apology accepted or whatever. Don't worry about it."

Who was I to hold something that old against Al? I had my past follow me well into adulthood. I hoped I was different from that angry kid I had been then. Maybe I wasn't better, but I was at least different. Al could be different, too. I could forgive Al, if not for any other reason than just to have some baggage to let go of.

"That easy?" he said, looking surprised.

I shrugged. "Yup."

Al nodded and started walking again, apparently content with my minimal response. "I always sorta wondered what happened to you. Every time Frank would call me up, I thought he would chew me out for what I did. It's been so long. I don't know why he never said anything."

"When did you tell him?" I said, chewing my fingernails and stumbling over a stick.

"I never...You mean you never told him?" Al cried, his voice rising.

"Of course not."

Al let out a frustrated growl and shifted his notes from one hand to the other. "Why not? We were all sure you would say something soon as you could."

I was surprised by his excitement. I cocked my eyebrow again. "What good would it have done?"

Al stared at me, open mouthed.

"Soccer was important to him," I said. "I wasn't going to ruin it. I didn't want him to lose his friends either."

Al just shook his head, speechless.

"Why didn't *you* ever tell him?"

Al laughed. "Are you nuts? Even then I knew we were wrong. I'd never hear the end of it now."

"When did you come out?"

Al opened his mouth like a fish out of water, staring wide-eyed. I grinned as the time lengthened. Reaction time to that question said a lot about the nature of someone's closet.

"Bi only. Not many people know."

"Fin know?"

"Of course."

I knew my expression was getting smug. A part of me was proud, in the way that people can be for others who come out. My ego was bolstered by the idea Fin chose me and not Al.

"Get over yourself, Orion. That was a long time ago."

We stared at each other for a second, then shared a laugh. Neither of us had anything more to say on the matter, so we didn't. We let it go.

"Look, man, we're gonna have to start over. I haven't been paying attention."

"You're fired."

"I don't think I am."

He wasn't. I led the way back to the house. The rest of the meeting proceeded in a very professional, but much less tense manner. We had walked the whole place before Fin returned. I escorted Al back to his car.

"This is some great land. I think you will be pleased with the results," Al said in a rehearsed way.

I wasn't really done with him, though. "Alexan—"

"Call me Al. Or Alex."

"Al, you met Midge? Mom?"

Al shrugged and carefully put his supplies back into his van. He shut the door. Facing me, he nodded.

"When?" I was on high alert. I couldn't bring myself to meet his eyes. I couldn't physically stand the question I was asking, I couldn't understand why, of all people, I was asking him, but my mouth wouldn't stop moving.

"About two weeks before she passed. She looked good, Orion. Peaceful, strong. She didn't look like she was suffering."

I was almost relieved and definitely embarrassed. Fin pulled up just then, beeped the car horn twice, and went up to the house. Al and I waved and watched silently as he pulled a surprising number of bags out of the car.

"Orion, I don't know what you plan to do with this place, but if you're gonna put it up for rent, me and my girls would really like a place like this."

"Got kids?"

Al laughed and pulled out his personal phone, scrolling through picture after picture of an assortment of small blondes and brunettes, and one beautiful, dark-haired woman. "I have seven."

"Seven?"

"Seven girls, not counting the wife." I happily looked at the school pictures of the elder Jefferson girls and the baby pictures of the rest.

"One a year since I was injured."

"Damn."

"You might like this one here," Al said, landing on a photo of a little brown-haired girl with green paint on her upturned hands and a coach's whistle in her mouth. "This one is Ursa."

"Ah, a fellow constellation."

"We needed a U name, but Ursula wasn't gonna happen."

"A U name?"

"Yup. From top to bottom you have Zara, Ysabel, Xander, Winnifred, Victory, Ursa, and Tessalee. The wife is Kelley."

"Damn," I said again.

"Well," Al concluded. He put the phone away quickly, like he was embarrassed for sharing so much with me.

"I'll see ya Monday."

CHAPTER 11: FIN

I almost didn't see Orion come into the kitchen. My phone had chirped, letting me know Lin's band had posted Onion's video to their YouTube channel. I started following them nearly four years ago, probably hoping Orion would show up. He did. Of course, the Leather and Lace audience loved him. I was about halfway through the video when he came up beside me. Something about Orion coming into the room suddenly embarrassed me, but I couldn't look away from the video.

"Hey," Orion said. He looked disinterestedly at the bags of food. "Are these groceries?"

"Uh, yeah. You don't have any food. Sorry, Lin just posted on YouTube," I said, engrossed. Orion hopped onto the counter behind me, his thigh brushing my hip as he leaned over me to see the video. We watched in silence. When it was over, I sighed and tossed the phone onto the counter. "You are really talented."

Orion didn't respond. I turned to face him and found myself impossibly close. Orion was balled up on the counter, his chin resting on his fists on his knee, a happy grin on his face. I was embarrassed by my secret four-year relationship with YouTube Orion, curiosity drawing me again and again to his videos. Finding myself so close to Orion in real life made me forget how to speak.

"It was a good show," I said slowly, hearing the gulp in my own voice.

He looked at me. He looked into me. Some feeling crossed his face and disquieted his expression. I knew what he was going to say before he said it.

"Fin, about the—"

"O, I swear to the almighty Lord, if you apologize for kissing me, I will drive us both off a bridge."

"How about I just say I'm sorry for not asking first?"

"Accepted." I realized then I had somehow managed to get closer to him. Not only that, my hand was on his thigh. I looked at him, searching for some sign he didn't want me so close. I waited. He waited, his eyes wide, the way a gazer looks for a shooting star.

"It could happen again," I whispered. He slipped his hand over mine, sending small tingles all over my body.

"Any time," he said.

Well, hot damn. I stepped in closer and leaned forward until our lips met. It was like a sunny day. Warmth pooled inside me, dripping like honey into my guts. I half expected the kiss to be timid and one sided, like the night before, but Orion was reciprocating, pressing tentatively back. Unable to resist and unwilling to miss another chance, I drew him closer, clasping his arm and hip, and pressing my lips harder against his. I felt Orion smile as we kissed, but he remained coolly still, letting me do the driving. I pulled us a little deeper. I couldn't suppress my moan as Orion's lips parted for me. His mouth was giving, warm and soft and welcoming. I wanted more, but I wondered how much he would let me have.

We jumped apart as my phone buzzed against the counter and emitted its stupid chirping. I laughed and backed away, my skin burning. I picked up the phone as I retreated. It was a text from Rose. *Fay says hi.*

"Coffee?" I said to Orion, turning to the semi-forgotten breakfast. Orion didn't say anything, just curled around himself a bit more on the counter, like a shaggy cat.

"I got groceries, like bread and stuff. Also stuff to eat now. So here, just whatever." I handed one of the two paper bags to Orion along with a coffee. I was flustered by the sudden loss of the kiss and by how turned on I was by only a few seconds of contact. Orion peered into the bag and discarded it in favor of the drink. He popped off the plastic lid and seemed pleased with what was inside. He sipped. I retrieved a donut for myself and started pulling the groceries out of the bags.

"You didn't have to do that," Orion said, his voice cold.

"I wanted to." I could have told Orion about the piles of food people brought when my father died and when my grandparents died. I didn't explain, though. I didn't want to make him feel like the only reason I was there was because his mother died. I was there for so much more.

"How did things go with Al?" I asked after a while around a mouthful of bear claw. By then I had gotten everything out of the bags, piled on the island, and had the bags stuffed inside themselves into a single, fat, plastic ball. I picked up the cold stuff and moved to the fridge.

"Good, I guess. He offered to rent the place." Orion seemed lost in his coffee, running his fingers temptingly through his hair.

"Yeah, that man is one girl shy of a baseball team. Was it as weird as it felt? I mean, you two seemed pretty hostile when I left. I was worried what I might come back to."

"It was, but it got better after he apologized."

"Apologized?" I said, suspicion growing inside me.

To my surprise, Orion growled, a low, pained sound. I knew a confession was pending. I had never suspected of Orion keeping secrets from me, but I guess I shouldn't be surprised. If you asked him directly, Orion wouldn't lie. That being said, you needed to know what to ask him. My best friend Al wouldn't keep secrets. I knew—*what* did I know? *You don't even know what happened.* I took a steadying breath, I crossed back to the groceries, and waited. Orion resolutely put the lid back on his coffee and set the cup away from himself on the counter.

"So," Orion said.

He explained his run-in with the team and then with the coach. I listened, anger starting to color my vision. I was definitely going to throttle Al when I saw him again. A part of me wanted to throttle Orion for not telling me. It was fucking about me, and no one thought I would want to know? Damn Orion and damn Al for thinking I needed protection.

"Al apologized today. He said he'd been wrong, and I didn't deserve to be treated that way."

Orion looked down at the floor, waiting for me to react. I didn't do anything. I tried to retreat into my own mind, give myself space to think about it. But all I could remember was those guys in the bar talking shit about Orion. I had confronted them. I would have confronted anyone who spoke the way they did about someone, let alone him. But that had driven Orion away. The events were so similar. Some always hating that I wanted to be with him and him with me.

But apparently no matter what I did, Orion was never gonna fucking be with me. And that was a hell of a thought considering I had no idea if that was even what I wanted now. I wanted the chance to fucking decide for myself. Now I know why he backed off in high school, and he in left college for the same reason. Right, okay, so whether I act or not, Orion still thought…

I didn't actually know what Orion thought. He had never explained that night in the hotel, and he hadn't really explained his thinking about the events in high school, just relayed the facts. I had beef with that for fucking sure. And Orion needed to hear it.

"Look, Orion—" I started, but then I stopped. I knew better than to scold him or let my anger speak for me. I sighed. What was I going to say? It's not like we were dating or whatever now, anyway. This was probably as informal as any other point in our lives. "Al was right."

"About?"

"You didn't deserve that."

He half rolled his eyes and looked back at the floor. "It's over now, right?"

That sounded like an out. It sounded like a way to talk about all of this later or never, *some* other time. And I considered taking it since I knew I wouldn't be able to get through the conversation at that moment. I was fucking speechless. Usually I deferred to the majority, but my head and my heart were in two very different places over this, and my dick was out of commission. So what now?

"Fin, I'm sorry that it happened, and I'm sorry I just now told you about it," Orion said, interrupting my train of thought.

I just grunted.

He sighed and opened his arms. "What do you want me to do? Sing it?"

Well, fine. Since I didn't know how to talk about it any more than he did, I guess I was going to ignore it, too. For now. I squinted at him and shrugged. "Yeah. Sing it."

He glared at me, thinking, then started in a cheesy voice, to the tune of "F.U.N." from *SpongeBob SquarePants*. "F is for friends who hung out together, I is for I acted really dumb, N is for nobody wanted us to be gay to—ge—ther, down here in the fucking South."

I laughed. I hadn't expected that. Once I was able to get it together, I shrugged. "You didn't actually say you were sorry."

He growled and flashed me a middle finger. I just smiled and gathered more groceries. I passed by him and felt his hand close around my upper arm. His gaze was intense and deep, like looking into dark rolling waves. I searched for the meaning behind them.

"What is it?" I asked.

"I don't know what I'm doing," he said. He let go and ran a hand through his beautiful messy hair. At that, my dick and my heart snapped back into agreement. And I had to know what it was that he wanted.

"Just tell me what you want," I said, putting aside what I had in my hands. We were almost eye to eye with him sitting on the counter. His eyes were so gold. I took a breath. "Tell me what you want right now."

"Kiss me," he said as if he was embarrassed even to ask. And maybe he was. Maybe he had a need and didn't know how to get it filled, like the night before when he needed me to stay and didn't know how to ask.

Well, I sure as hell wasn't going to say no to that. Orion let me kiss him and kissed back. I could feel the restraint in him, his muscles tense but his mouth desperate. Some barrier needed breaking. I took a step in, forcing more of myself into his space. I was met with a gentle sigh and a little relief in his body.

"Orion."

"More. Anything. Please." His breath was warm against my lips.

Damn. Hearing that did a world of good things to my body and senses. I kissed him hard, his head nearly falling back against the cabinets. I steadied him with one arm, pulling him against my body. I also managed to pull back my own intensity a little. I kissed him, then I pulled back.

He watched me as I slipped his glasses off and put them on the counter. He pulled the ball cap off my head, flinging it behind me. I felt a surge of giddiness. His arms were gentle and warm, and I ran my hands over them from wrist to shoulder. I wanted to undress him, but that felt like too much, too busy. I traced my hands to his neck, and he closed his eyes and relaxed a little more.

"Damn," I said. He was so beautiful. His stubble made his jawline look sharp and kissable, the black hair making his skin stand out. He looked rested today, better than when he had first showed up in town.

"What?"

"Nothing, I just like looking at you."

I kissed him with a little more care, a little more thoroughness, letting my lips and tongue barely caress his mouth, biting softly at his lips. I finally ran my hands through his mess of black hair. It was so fucking soft and long and grabbable. He moaned at that, the sound muffled by my mouth pressed against his.

I didn't notice his hands on my body until he trailed his fingers down my ribs and sides to my hips. That sent jolts of arousal all over my torso. I liked that a little too much, rocking into him, my thighs bumping the counter. That was definitely a hot spot for me. Finding it seemed to make him happy. I just laughed and let myself have a little more of his mouth, my tongue pressing against his. I pulled him closer to the edge of the counter.

I was tall enough to rest my balls on most people's kitchen counters, which was probably unwelcome. But as Orion spread his legs, I was pleased to find my dick aligned with his perfectly.

Sweet Jesus, why did he have to have on sweats? I could feel the hardness of his dick against mine, prominent in the loose fabric of his pants. The only thing I could do was rock against it, feeling him against my own hard-on. He growled into my mouth as I rocked again and pushed his hands around my back, pulling me against him. His hands were hot and hard, pulling at my skin, massaging my muscles. I couldn't kiss and breathe with him doing that, so I pulled my mouth away and rested my forehead against his.

"God, your body is fucking amazing," he moaned, his hands tracing back around to run over my abs.

"Your mouth is fucking amazing."

I ran my hands up his thighs, and he hissed softly. I kissed his neck while I massaged the tight muscles in his thighs. I wanted permission so badly to touch his dick. Using the belt loops on my jeans, he pulled my hips closer and kept exploring my back, sides, and arms. I turned into a gasping mess. I let my head fall back, and he kissed and sucked and bit my neck. I moaned and rocked against him. He kissed and massaged me for long, agonizingly delicious moments, and I tried to give him the space to explore, kissing his mouth when he wanted it, letting him kiss whatever he wanted on me, running my fingers through his hair.

"Fuck, Fin," he said after who knows how long.

"Yeah?"

He stilled my body with his strong hands and looked at me. I looked drunkenly back, unsure how my efforts to give him what he needed turned into getting myself worked up.

"If you're going to keep rubbing against my dick like that, you might as well touch it." His eyes were bright with humor, edged in shyness.

I smiled and went back to kissing him. I outlined his thigh and ran my thumbs along the length of his dick through his sweats. He grunted against my mouth and squirmed under my touch. He was so hard and so responsive. Despite our past, I hadn't actually gotten my hands on his dick. I pulled his sweats away from his hips enough to free him. I wasn't in any kind of hurry. I wanted to memorize the damn thing. I wrapped my hand around the base and rubbed my thumb along the length, caressing the dripping tip. And the damned thing was fucking amazing, soft in the right places, hard in the best way, veined and thick and—

"Fucking fuck, Fin."

"I know."

I stroked his dick, testing to see what he liked. He was only breathing, so I changed my grip and did it again, and he moaned. I liked the sound of that. I did it again, slowly, feeling his hips rock toward me. Panting, he shivered, and I felt trusted and wanted. He muttered cuss words and moaned. It sounded like sexy, out-of-control music.

"Shit, you feel so fucking good," I mumbled as he dug his hands into my hips and thrust his dick into my fist.

"I want to feel you," he said.

I didn't have enough blood left in my brain to understand what he meant. He slipped a hand between us and popped the fly on my jeans. I think I blacked out from the excitement. I braced my free hand against the counter and anticipated the warmth of his hand on my cock.

"Is this okay?" he asked, stopping short of releasing my dick from my briefs. I had the sudden urge to flip a table.

"Holy fucking Jesus, yes, damn it," I babbled, pressing myself against his palm. He smiled and slipped my briefs down enough to free my dick, the rush of air on it making me gasp. But still I didn't feel his hands. Instead he put them back on my hips.

"Take us both."

His words surprised me. I stared at him. His hair fell in loose loops and waves around his face like a wild aura, his jaw unshaven and his bright, gold eyes deep and intense. That. That was exactly what I wanted. I pressed forward, lining us up, wrapping my hand around both our dicks. The length of him was like fire against me. I stroked gently, up our shafts and over our cockheads, his leaking more precum. I couldn't help but buck against him, slipping myself over him with both hand and dick.

"Holy fuck, yes like that," he breathed. "Fuck, Fin. You feel so fucking good."

His voice mixed with the molten feeling in my guts, focusing all of my energy into a building orgasm. It felt so exact, like the perfect combination of things. I tried to breathe and tell him I was close, but I don't think I managed to do more than grunt and vibrate with pleasure.

"God, I am—" I heard him say.

Then he took my hand, completing the hot circle of friction around us. And I came. Hard. All over our hands and shirts. The blackness behind my eyes burst apart with white sparks of satisfaction. A frantic stroke later, Orion was coming, my dick and hand washed again by a gentle warmth. I am not sure how I remained standing. And he didn't let me move away. He kissed me softly, his lips relaxing the sharp spark of orgasm into a hazy hum of gratification.

The world was suddenly silent without him moaning and gasping in my ear. But I could hear his heart, or feel it pulsing blood where we were still in contact, and I could feel him breathing.

"Damn," he said, slipping his hand out from between us. I did the same, trying not to touch anything. We were still in his kitchen, after all.

"You got jizz on Darth Vader," I said.

Orion broke into a crazy laugh. I laughed, too, overcome by a giddy feeling.

"It wouldn't be the first time," he said after a moment, hopping to the floor, still close too me. We adjusted ourselves as best we could, shirts, hands, and pants sticky with cum.

"Do I want to know?" I laughed.

"You might not."

CHAPTER 12: ORION

I was grateful Fin hung around for the rest of the day. I didn't know what I would do otherwise. I let him lead me around, first to a movie, then to Grace's for burgers. We went back to his place and just spent the night kissing. I think he talked nonstop for twelve hours. But it was great. Saturday became Sunday and Sunday became Monday. All the days were tinted miraculous colors, and Fin was the source.

I didn't give much thought to guilt, to Mom. I hadn't expected Fin to stick around, and I hadn't expected to see Rose or Grace or Al or anyone else again. But they all marched through my weekend and the early part of the week like a perfect parade. Monday, Fin was waiting on my porch when Al came back. Fin yelled at Al right then and there. And it made me feel weird, because he hadn't yelled at me. Al ended up buying us lunch as penance. It was unsettling that I could hold a conversation with the guy. But I could. I actually liked Al.

Lin found us again, too, taking most of Tuesday for herself. She had me look at the bus, then loaded up the crew and took us all two towns over to play a show in a seedy bar. While the drummer of the band showed Fin how to manage a kit, I updated Lin. She nearly shit herself when I told her what happened in my kitchen. She didn't bring up the elephant in the room, the fact that I had ghosted Fin years ago.

I had expected to hole up in my house, waiting for my mother's ashes. I knew at some point I would be alone again, more alone than ever without Mom, so a selfish part of me insisted I take what I could get while it was being offered. But I already knew it wouldn't last. I could see that reality lurking.

I woke up Wednesday morning, my heart pounding a little too hard in my chest. That had been my first real night alone. I'd had a nightmare, but with my eyes open it was already gone. Fin was gone too, sleeping at his own house. I felt something at his absence but I shoved it down. I knew I wasn't entitled to or even worth his time, so what was the point?

I stared up at the ceiling, trying to figure out what to do. The day already felt empty. I was considering staying in bed when my phone rang. I looked hard at the unknown number on the screen before I decided to answer.

"Hello?"

"Orion Starr?"

"Yes, that's me," I said, not liking the official-sounding tone of the man on the line.

"Hello, I'm with Georgia Cremation."

I sat up so fast I almost dropped the phone. I scrubbed my face with my hand. "Oh, um, what's up?"

I rolled my eyes at my stupid inability to be on the phone.

"I have some news about your mother's remains."

"Okay."

"We have had to delay the completion of her procedure," the man said tonelessly.

I couldn't tell if the dial tone sound was coming from the phone or just ringing in my head. My mouth went dry, and I couldn't see for a minute. "I don't know what that means."

"It will take some time before her remains become available. There has been a complication with the paperwork from the hospital where she passed, and we'll have to delay the completion of her procedure until the forms are corrected."

"You are saying you can't cook my mom till you get papers from her...who? Doctors?"

The man on the phone took a loud breath. I could almost hear him nod. "More or less. The document must then be sent to the proper authorities before the procedure can happen."

"How long? I mean, it has already been a week since her funeral, two since she died."

"That is why we are calling. The copy of the form has your

signature on it, but we need the signature of the person with the power of attorney."

"Me," I insisted. Shively had the forms. They even had the stupid notary stamp or whatever it was on it.

"A Mr. Corvus Starr. If he could just come to our—"

"Fuck that. He's not even in the country," I growled, flopping back onto the bed.

"Mister—"

"Look, I am going to give you a phone number, it's for a lawyer called Shively. Tell him. I'll tell him to expect your call." I didn't recognize my voice. I couldn't even really tell if I was talking out loud.

"Sir—"

"No."

"Excuse me?"

"Talk to Shively. He's our lawyer, and he has the paperwork. He knows how best to contact me. Corvus can't even be reached right now."

"Okay sir. We can do that." The employee on the other line sounded as done as I felt. I imagined he was a resting bitch face type of guy. I gave him the number and hung up. I sent Shively a text telling him what happened. Then I tossed my phone somewhere else and went back to staring at the ceiling.

Hours later, I tipped myself out of bed, desperate for something to ease my rising panic. Any life I wanted depended on these days ending, and that depended on getting Mom's ashes. I felt like I would never get her remains, which meant never leaving Georgia, which meant I was trapped. Trapped was bad, always.

I went in search of something to take the edge off. There hadn't been alcohol in the house since Mom quit, and the hardest drug was migraine pills. I took some of those. Then I started the coffee pot. I went back upstairs to find my glasses and my phone. There was a message from Shively. I wasn't in the mood to read it, but I thumbed the screen anyway.

Orion, I'm sorry about the delay in being able to lay your mother to rest. I will get it taken care of. The person I spoke with on the phone said you spoke highly of me! Thank you for your faith.

Sure. I tossed the phone back on the bed and took my coffee out to the porch. There were heavy clouds and a sporadic breeze. *When you left, you took the colors with you. Let me tell you what, dear, gray is a lonely hue.* Naw, that song sucked.

❖

The rest of the next week passed with the emotional chaos of a Tarantino movie, the feelings of being freed by Fin and trapped by Mom pulling me apart. More people came to the house, and things with the estate settled quickly, despite the continued delay in getting *her* settled. The days were a roller coaster of highs and lows, high colorful events, and lows in between full of intangible emptiness: Fin at Grace's, me alone in bed, Rose at the hospital, me alone on my bike. By Saturday, the summer weather gave rise to a static-heavy thunderstorm.

I was sitting on the porch watching lightning flash over the trees when Fin pulled into the drive. As he came up, his hard scowl matched the storm.

"Hey," I said, annoyed and sticky in the humid heat. I clicked the lock button on my phone, the screen blinking out, taking the game I had been playing with it. I expected Fin to speak, to go off on a rant that would convince me to go to the store, to the city, to do something. Thunder tumbled out of the clouds and landed heavily on the damp atmosphere around us.

"'Sup?" And that was all he said. He just flopped on the stairs a few steps below me.

"What's going on?" I didn't know what to do with grouchy Fin.

"Rose and Fay went someplace again. I think they're going to the bakery, but who knows?"

I tried to figure out a way to ask him why he was mad about that, but I couldn't think of one. So that was the extent of the conversation. We just sat, brooding.

My mood for the day had resolved itself early that morning. *I miss my family.* I'd gotten around to reading Corvus's emails and had been told to expect a phone call either that coming Monday or Tuesday. I hadn't spoken to him since the day before the funeral. After reading the email, I got a homesick feeling for my brother added to the mountain of things I felt for my mom. I had wondered what it would mean to lose him, too, someday. I wondered if it was possible to preemptively grieve for someone. *You're alive but I'm still grieving, everything is fine but I know you're leaving. I can't wake up from this dream cuz I know there'll be a someday without you.* I couldn't write that one.

Fin's arrival offered some hope, even if he was as pissy as me. What I had in mind could probably help us both. I slipped down the stairs, sitting closer to Fin. He looked at me, his expression becoming neutral. Slowly but forcefully, I leaned over and kissed him. Caught off guard, Fin paused only for a moment before he welcomed me. He met my force and pushed into my mouth, tonguing deep. Our kissing was a clashing of teeth and lips. He dominated me, forcing me back against the stairs. There was nothing gentle about it, and that was exactly what I wanted. But I had plans way beyond kissing, so I pushed him away. Wordlessly, I stood and gestured for him to follow.

I was always nervous when it came to him. Our intimacy so far had left me with a lot of doubt. How could he want me like this? How after all these years? I wondered if he thought that, too. I wondered if this was just a convenient way for him to pass the time in this fucking town. Every moment with Fin was so different, incomparable to any other lover I had ever had.

Fin followed silently. Lightning cracked as we entered the room, a thunderous peal setting the windows rattling. I stopped short of the bed, facing into the room with Fin at my back. I could feel Fin's eyes on me as I carefully put my glasses on the desk. I tried to find some confidence I didn't feel, breathing. I turned to Fin.

Fin was so there. He ran one hand through my hair and slipped his other around my back. His hands were hard, bruising. I could tell he wanted to knock me down, find release as quickly and roughly as we could. It already felt too intense, like something we shouldn't be doing. Instead of listening to that idea, I practically flipped him onto the bed, trapping him beneath my body.

I kissed him, holding myself up on my elbows. He slipped his hands up my shirt. I loved the feeling of Fin's hands on my body. I pressed into him to feel his hard dick against me again. His hands, his mouth, his cock. He wanted me with a surety I could only understand physically. I wanted him. I wanted to fuck him—

"What the hell?" I heard myself shout. For a second, I was pretty sure one of us had broken something. I jumped off him with surprise as something vibrated between us, the soft hum of the ringtone muffled by our bodies. It was just Fin's fucking phone. Groaning, Fin fished it from his jeans.

"I'm starting to hate this thing," Fin said, embarrassed and out of breath. His hair was a mess, his face pink, and I could see the start of a hickey just at the base of his neck. All of that sent a fresh wave of arousal to my dick. Fin sent the unknown number to voicemail and discarded the phone nearby.

Fin took advantage of my position and, in a quick maneuver, he had me pinned beneath him. He pressed his whole body against me and kissed hard. I didn't waste time getting my hands under his shirt. I managed somehow to get it off him, even with him kissing me everywhere he could. Fin seemed busy, distracted by my lips and neck, so I focused my attention lower. I traced the curve of his hip, fingers grazing over his hard cock until my hand cupped it through his jeans. Fin moaned and panted, rocking down for more contact, for some friction—

Then he stilled so fast that, for a second, I think he even stopped breathing. It wasn't until there was a break in the thunder that I heard the phone ringing again. The vibration was muted on the bed, but the ringtone was loud and different from the first call.

"What happened?" I asked. I don't know how I sounded to Fin but I hoped it was concerned and not frustrated. Fin looked like he was in shock.

"That. Was. Lucas. Hospital. Ring. Tone," Fin croaked before the phone went off a third time.

Understanding, I gently forced Fin to move off me and answered the phone myself. "Lucas?"

"Frank?"

"No, it's Orion, Fin is right here, though." I stared at Fin, who stared back, his hazel eyes looking close to gray in the dim daylight.

"Fuck, I told them to let me call first. Is he all right? I've been trying to call but—"

"He didn't answer the first call. Who was it?"

"The hospital. I bet Fin is whiter than the Republican convention right now."

I couldn't disagree with that. I didn't answer, though. I listened to Lucas growl a response to someone else before returning to our conversation.

"Look, Orion, tell him Rose is fine."

"He says Rose is fine."

"She caught a sack of flour wrong down at the bakery and cracked a bone in her wrist. Fay brought her here, and since Fin is her emergency contact, they called him. I told them to let me call, all things considered, but you know how these fucking things can be. Tell him they're going to do X-rays soon, and then they will wrap it. There is time to get down here if he wants, room 108B."

"Yeah, we'll be there."

Lucas started barking orders at people around him and ended the call without a goodbye. I slid over to where Fin sat at the edge of the bed. He was still watching me, but I don't think he was saw me. I calmly relayed the message and gently urged him to find his shirt.

I could see Fin getting angrier as we drove to the hospital. Fin looked like he was ready to punch through a wall. He seethed with rage in the passenger's seat. The emotion was oppressive. I tried to breathe and focus, but my space filled with Fin's sorrow, rage, and frustration. I had no idea what to do about it.

My head was a mess on its own, a combination of guilt and regret. I remembered thinking we shouldn't have started that. The bill collectors started calling in, wondering why I was still damaging Fin. I tried to shut them out, but one question was on a loop in my head. *What if he hadn't been with me?* Marge had died. Rose was fine. And Fin was livid.

I wanted to tuck and roll out of the car away from him, and that was pretty fucked up considering all the guy had done for me. Sure, I could have real, deep, true feelings for Fin, but where were they when Fin seemed to need me? I couldn't offer him anything, not even comfort. So I just drove.

Fin practically ran across the parking lot and barreled through the doors of the ER, nearly knocking over a nurse. He barked at the desk clerk and elbowed his way back to the exam room area. I was caught off guard and maybe a little impressed by the uncharacteristic force Fin was using. I remembered Fin's temper as a teenager, but Fin grown was scary.

"Sir," the desk clerk said to me, "I can only let family back there."

I sighed and flapped my arms helplessly. I very obviously stood out compared to the pale, fair-haired family.

"Can you at least tell them I have to stay out here?" I pleaded in as kind a voice as I could muster.

"I'll send a message back."

I was turning to go back to the waiting area when I had a thought. I turned back to the woman behind the desk. "Is a nurse named Lucas working? Big dude, green hair?"

She tapped some keys at her computer. "We're not allowed to say."

"That's all right, thanks."

Feeling thwarted, I found a *Time* magazine from 2003 and a wide waiting room chair to sit in. Thunder shook the windows behind my head. Sitting made me aware of how burdened I felt. Fin's emotions were still clinging to me. I felt the negativity seep into my blood.

There were two cures. One was a drink, and I didn't want that. The other was escape. I instinctively looked back toward the entrance of the hospital. I could easily leave. I could toss Fin's car keys to the clerk, summon an Uber, and leave. Leave the hospital. Town even. *Mom.* Somehow staying for her meant staying for Fin.

"Fuck." I flapped the magazine in my hands.

I had settled in, expecting to wait for a while, so I was surprised to see Fin practically kick through the doors only a few minutes later. I jumped to my feet and crossed to him. Fin was moving in on the desk clerk as if she was prey. He scowled at the woman, not giving any sign of having seen me.

"I need to check Rose Ness out."

"Yes sir, give me just one second—" the desk clerk said, the phone starting to ring.

"All the fucking phones—you have to wonder how anyone survives this hospital."

I had never heard Fin sound like that. I cleared my throat. "Fin?"

Fin turned, looking like he was ready to attack. But he didn't. His eyes flashed with a hint of recognition before he turned back to the clerk.

"It takes one second." The clerk rolled her chair back a few inches before holding up a finger to signal that she planned to continue her call. Fin screeched, "It takes one *second*!"

I moved between them, feeling like he was about to climb the desk. People were staring. I shoved him toward the entrance of the hospital, out into the space between the first and second set of sliding doors. Fin growled and thunder poured through the door. He did a lap around the space before sitting heavily in a discarded wheelchair.

"What is going on? How is Rose?"

"You would know if you had gone back with me."

"They wouldn't let me," I said. "Family only."

Fin just scoffed.

"Well, since you were trying to check her out, she must be fine."

Fin shot out of the chair like it was on fire. "I should finish doing that."

I stopped him, placing a gentle but firm hand on his shoulder, "Take a breather, man—"

Fin ripped his arm from my grasp. "Don't start with me, Orion. You couldn't possibly understand!"

I hadn't intended to make a huffing noise, but I did. "How could I not—"

Fin turned on me, his height giving him power, the red of his hair and face making him ferocious. "How! How *could* you? You weren't even with her, Orion. Your mom got sick and you went on with your fucking life. I am *here* every day watching mine die. You took the easy way out. Not all of us are like you. I swear—"

Fin paused and covered his face with his hands, his accent breaking through his cool Northeastern overlay. "I should've never gone to your house. I should've gone with her. What a fucking mess."

At this point, I wasn't even sure Fin knew I was still in the room. I didn't say anything. What could I have said? The force of Fin's words passed through me like a spray of arrows. I backed against the wall, put my hands in my pockets, and kept still.

"Frank?" Fay called, coming into the now silent passage.

"Oh yeah, sorry," Fin said, jumping, nearly running back.

"Hey, Fay?" I said. She stopped and offered me a sweet smile. "We brought Fin's car. If you're going back home, maybe I could ride with you, and Fin can take Rose?"

"You sure you don't wanna go with 'em?" Fay said, giving me a side glance. She had hair the color of a blood orange and all the features of the Ness lineage, only softened by a gentle nature. She was tall but not imposing.

"Naw, I will go by later or something, I have someone coming by the house."

I could lie to Fay.

"You and me then, kiddo."

Not much was said as it came time to leave the ER. Fin and I didn't say goodbye. Fin said goodbye to his aunt, and I said goodbye to Rose. I couldn't even look at him before we parted. Fay didn't seem to know what to do with me. She tried small talk, but she eventually gave up.

As I went into my house, tears burned my eyes, but I didn't let them out. I went up to my room. I before I shut down completely, I registered two things. The first and least painful was that I had been right. It *was* shitty that I hadn't been with Mom as she died. Fin had screamed it at me.

The second thing hurt just a bit more. Fin had lied to me about it. That night Fin had told me it was okay, and it clearly wasn't. I could handle the confirmation of things I hated about myself, but I couldn't handle learning someone I loved lied to me about it. *Maybe loved.*

I changed into sweatpants and a tank and sat in the living room. The rest of the weekend and the start of the next week passed in silence. I found a place on the couch and stayed in it, time slipping by. For me, the safest state was nonexistence.

CHAPTER 13: FIN

I had been a rage ball from the minute I got into the car with Orion until the minute I got into the car with my mom. I could feel her staring at me as I drove, barely seeing the road, barely noticing the rain. I didn't want to talk. And she didn't ask. Anyone, *anyone*, could recognize the natural disaster that was my temper.

I felt the tears on my face almost before I made it into the house. I let us in and went straight to my room. Man, if they were handing out medals for being a shitty person, I would get a third for yelling at mom, a second for yelling at my aunt, and a first for—

I almost couldn't think of the awful things I had said to Orion. I flopped on my bed and replayed those moments in my head. I could see the hurt on his face and the grim set of his jaw as he took my words for the truth. I would have to talk to him, try and explain.

He had been perfect. I shut down as soon as I heard Lucas's ring tone, but somehow Orion—the man who never answers the phone— answered it. He looked like he knew what he was doing. It felt like he knew what he was doing. He helped me, got me to the car, got me to my Mom when all I could do was stop breathing.

Selfishly, stupidly I had taken that personally. Instead of feeling proud and grateful and for lack of a better word, loved, I resented it all. That actually summed up my mood for the whole day. I resented Rose and Fay and then, at the end, Orion.

I had offered to spend the day with Rose but she turned me down, explaining she was going somewhere with Fay. That felt painfully like the old pre-cancer days. Mom and Fay had been attached at the hip since my dad first introduced them. I was closer in age to Fay than she was to Mom, but my grandparents used to say that Fay was Mom's shadow even though she was my father's sister. So, before the cancer it was Fay and Mom, and that was the end of the story.

I hadn't noticed how much of Rose's attention I had siphoned back from Fay. Finding the source of my jealousy that morning was simple: I missed my mom. The irony of it all was that I still would have wanted to be with Orion, even if Rose had said yes to our day together. And that was a fucked-up place to be in. Spending time with Orion had been seven kinds of perfect. But I felt guilty, like I shouldn't be with him but with my healing mother. But she didn't want to be with me. Two problems for the price of one.

It got both better and worse when Orion climbed on top of me. He had seemed to know what we both needed. He felt so right in my arms, and I felt so right on his bed, under his body. But getting that phone call was like the universe saying, *hey, shouldn't you be with your mother?* My whole world collapsed in on itself. I honestly thought she was dead. I thought the worst thing in the world had happened, and it was my fault for not having been with her. For not trading every spare moment I had in my life to her. How dare I trade her time for time in the bed of a man I barely knew? How could I have made any choice over her?

But then I noticed Orion's concern and care toward me. And he told me she was fine. Instead of being relieved, I was suddenly pissed at her. She had interrupted what was probably would have been fantastic sex. It was completely exhausting to be rock hard and panicked. I also didn't understand why anyone had to call at all. They could have texted, *Hey, son, I got hurt. Carry on humping your boyfriend and I will see you at home.* Not that Orion was my boyfriend.

Getting to the hospital, getting back to the rooms was a blur. I didn't register anything along the way. I barely noticed when Orion had been with me, then suddenly he wasn't there. I was alone, practically running down the hall to Rose's exam room. That made me resent Orion more.

"*Mom!*" I heard myself shout, practically kicking down the door.

"Fin!" Rose and Fay cried in unison. I rushed past my aunt and went to my mother. I asked her every question I could, not only as a medical professional but as her scared, angry, tired son. She ended up shoving me away.

"Franklin!" she shouted. I backed off, alarmed at her voice. "I'm okay. They said it was a minor crack, it'll heal."

"What happened?"

"They were moving sacks of flour at the bakery and one of the wheels on the dolly popped off. The whole stack nearly crashed down on the cupcake kid, but I managed to save him," Rose said, sounding very proud of herself.

I didn't share her humor. I paced a semicircle around her bed as she talked, all the while pulling at the buttons on my shirt. "You shouldn't have been doing things like that. You need—"

"Frank, don't—" Fay started, her voice lightly scolding but kind. Well, Fay just put herself at the top of my rage list with those two words.

"Don't start with me, Fay. Of all people, you should know—"

"Franklin Ian Ness."

Rose saying my name like that meant only one thing. I was in trouble. I looked at the floor. I didn't miss her nod to Fay, who just shrugged—their code for *can you believe this child*. I bet they couldn't. I couldn't. I felt like Fin had gone on vacation and Hyde had shown up.

"I am your mother, not your daughter. I have cancer, but I'm not helpless. It'll be a cold day in hell before I let you talk to your aunt or anyone else that way. Do you understand?"

"Yes," I said, purposefully not adding "ma'am" because I wasn't six.

"Fine. The doctor was here, and I'm ready to go. Go sign me out," she said, swinging her legs to the edge of the bed.

"Mom, I—"

"After the show you just put on, I think we have had enough of you right now, son." I'd heard that sentence a lot in my life and understood I should do as I was told. I left the room.

I couldn't think about that happened next. I knew I was out of control as soon as I crossed into the breezeway with Orion. I was disappointed in myself. I could see Orion in my memory, the hurt in his eyes, the way he backed up like an animal in danger. None of it made sense. It didn't need to. I had just been angry, and I wanted to be mean. How do you recover from that?

It was close to dinner time before I came out of my room. I found Mom in the kitchen reading a bread magazine. I just sat at the table with her. She offered me a smile and limply tried to turn the page with her wrapped hand. We ended up ordering a pizza, and I ate some of it while she read. When she moved to the living room, I followed and continued my silent vigil. I tried to tell myself I was following her around to see if she had anything to say to me. Really, I just couldn't stand my own company. When she went to bed, I had no other choice but go to my room and pretend to sleep. I quietly lay looking over to where Orion's blanket and pillow were sitting on a chair, laying in reserve. The storm raged on through the night.

The whole weekend passed, and I couldn't get Orion to answer my calls or return my texts. I didn't want to just go over there, especially if he wasn't ready. But I would if his silence kept up. Monday evening, I found myself sitting on the front step of my house watching Rose read a different bread magazine. She sat in the swing. I had a book in my hands, but I hadn't turned a page in forty minutes.

The fear that for the third time in my life Orion was just simply gone was making me anxious and jumpy. This time, it would serve me right. And it was not like I could do anything about it. We weren't dating. He wasn't my boyfriend, and the days we had spent together didn't make him that. He was probably just biding his time with me anyway, waiting for the chance to get his mom's ashes and leave. And why shouldn't he?

Rose shuffling on the swing set off my nerves. I jumped to my feet. "Need something? Are you chilly? Want a drink?"

Rose laughed. "Son, what the hell is wrong with you?" She shut her magazine and looked at me. "Why don't you get out of the house? Go do something? I haven't seen much of Orion since Saturday, and you two were practically climbing each other."

"Rosey," I said, sitting by her. Everything I had been feeling and everything I said to Orion poured out of me like a fucking flash flood. I couldn't even look my mom in the eye.

"You said all that?"

I nodded.

Rose sighed. "You fucked up, son."

I jumped up to pace. "Mom, that doesn't help."

"Go talk to him, you know how he is."

"I tried calling."

"Calling? You need to grovel in person, Franklin."

"I know that. I was trying to see if he was home. He usually finds some way to go somewhere else."

Rose shook her head and settled into the swing some more, rocking herself with the few toes that could reach the ground. "He's in town."

I sat heavily, jostling the wooden structure. I slumped, letting my limbs hang off in all directions. "How do you know?"

"He can't abandon his mother," Rose said. I knew that. And I knew he had a history of leaving. Waiting for your mother's ashes sounded way more important that leaving town because the guy you were fooling around with was a douchebag.

"I am the biggest ass," I said.

"No use stating the obvious." Rose sat up and turned to face me. "Now, let's talk about something you don't seem to know."

I waited.

"Do you know why I asked you to come home last year?"

I looked at her, feeling patronized. "Your cancer got worse."

"So?"

"So, you wanted me to help out and to just be around."

"Right. Now, do you know what you're *not* here to do?"

I didn't have an answer.

Rose took my face in her hands and made me look at her. "You are *not* here to save me, Fin."

That felt confusing. Rose looped an arm around me. "I will die someday, Fin. There's nothing you can do to change that. Now, when someone gets sick, you should do what you can to help them feel better. But I would never ask that of you if it meant you had to destroy yourself to do it. I asked you to leave school for a little while, but I never meant for you to abandon everything. Son, I wanted to spend as much time with you as I could."

"Now you don't want to spend time with me?"

"Don't be a baby." We both laughed. "You've always been jealous of Fay. Even as a baby. When you started to walk, you'd always force yourself between us instead of walking on my other side."

I felt my face warm.

"You're a big, jealous mama's boy," she said sweetly, "and no one can change that but you."

I didn't answer. I had actually done a pretty good job of trying to change over the last few years. I even went to counseling my freshman year. It helped, but I apparently I had a long way to go as far as anger and jealousy were concerned. She was silent for a while.

"I was that way when I was a young, too," she said. "Jealous, I mean."

"How did you change it?"

"Your father said something one day that made me think about things differently."

"How?"

"One day, he said, 'Rosey, you have the privilege of my company, not the right to it.'"

"Damn." That was it in a nutshell, wasn't it?

"I try and keep that in mind when I get worked up. Now, let me tell you something else. Before she passed, I had a talk with Marge Starr. I asked her how she was feeling and how her sons were doing. Which of her two answers do you think was the longest? That woman's whole life was her sons, and my whole life is you. We just happen to be sick, too. Now, you said he had it easy not being around, but let me put it to you this way. How hard was it for you to be in Rhode Island those first few years? Look at how hard it has been to have your own life even now and to actually live it."

Rose paused and looked to make sure I was listening. "Son, in these things there is no hard or easy. When someone you love is in pain, there is only guilt and rage. For the lucky ones, there's hope. You tend to run high on the hope, which makes your guilt feel like the biggest weight in the world. Orion runs high on the guilt, but how truly valuable do you think hope is to him? How valuable do you think you are?"

"I give him hope?"

"You did till you threw a tantrum."

"Right, Rosey. I get it, I know all of that. I told him as much about his mom, anyway. How do I fix it?" I pulled her into a hug. We were silent for a few minutes. Then I laughed, turning a light pink, "Also, I think I was *also* mad at you. Your accident was sort of a cockblock."

Rose stared at me for a heartbeat, then laughed herself to tears. "Well, I'd be mad about that, too, I guess."

I had enjoyed watching her laugh. She looked so warm, so young. "What do I do?"

"Beg. Take the car. I'm not going anywhere," Rose said, pushing me away.

"What the hell am I going to say?" I mumbled as I trotted to the garage, car keys already in my pocket.

I drove around for nearly two hours, specifically avoiding the part of town Orion lived in. I couldn't figure out what to say. I racked my brain for any genuine, meaningful words. Orion was not the best at accepting apologies, and I needed a good one. As I filled the tank of the car, I decided to call it quits. I was three blocks from Orion's and headed for home.

"How did it go?" Rose called. She was still with her magazines, this time curled into a chair in the living room.

"Terrible. I didn't even go over there. Rosey, I have no idea what I am going to say."

Rose didn't answer. I just dropped the keys into the bowl on the coffee table and wandered, defeated, to my room.

CHAPTER 14: ORION

I had managed to shower, find a clean shirt, and get my glasses on my face before my phone started ringing. I was expecting the call from my brother, but that didn't mean I was ready for it. I answered the video app, fumbling to get the earbuds into the jack.

"*Hunter!*" Corvus cried. The nickname sent a pang of sadness through me. It was the first time I had heard it out loud in a while. My brother looked like our mother. They had the same dark eyes and pale skin. He looked like a hipster, his hair trim and neat, beard full and kept, rimless glasses perched on his stupid nose. I was fucking happy to see him. But I tried not to look happy.

"Hey, Crow," I said weakly, landing on the couch.

I watched as Corvus surveyed me. He came to some sort of conclusion. "What's happened?"

"What do you mean?" I could have told my brother everything. Maybe should have? But I didn't really want to.

"You showered, like this morning," Corvus said, his voice growing deeper with suspicion. He even had the nerve to lean into the camera, as if to see me closer.

"So?"

"So, it's noon there on a Tuesday. If you were in a good mood, you would've said fuck it and answered the phone looking like the slob you are. You went out of your way to look put together." As he spoke, Crorvus shuffled pages on his desk. He then took off his glasses and looked calmly at me. "What's wrong?"

"What else?" I said, implying only one thing could be wrong—our dead mother. I hated it when he read me like that.

"This isn't about Midge."

"Ain't it?"

"Nope. I know you and Midge had a deal, no guilt. Who are they?"

"There is no *they*."

"Okay, who is *he*?"

"What makes you jump from *they* to *he*? There is nothing," I cried, fighting the urge to just hang up. Corvus stared. I stared. We were silent for nearly two minutes. I had always been better at silence than my brother, so I knew he would break eventually. Crow looked around me.

"You still in GA?"

"Duh. Isn't that why you called? I don't know if you talked to Shively, but—"

"I know. He sends me emails. Have you been there since the funeral?" Crow continued casually, sipping whatever was in the mug on his desk.

"Where else would I be?"

"How is Fin?"

"I wouldn't know."

"What happened? Did he hurt your feelings?" Crow said, almost mocking.

"No, there is no Fin."

"Fine, the post of you two on YouTube must be fake. Whatever it is, I'm sure you'll beat yourself up for it for the next year if it's shower-just-in-time-to-answer-Crow's-call bad."

"Go fuck yourself."

Corvus was about to retort when the doorbell rang. I leaned forward enough to look out the glass. I could see Fin, shuffling on the front porch. I snapped back out of sight.

"Was that him? Go answer—let me listen!"

"What? No to both."

"Hunter! How can it be no to both? Damn it, Orion. Answer the goddamned door," Crow screamed into his computer, shaking it. He grinned as the doorbell rang again. "He knows you're here!"

"Where else would I be?"

"So, will he go away?"

"Probably not."

"*Then answer the door!*"

I looked at the door again. I sighed. Damn it, I wanted to see him. I wanted to not dislike him. It wasn't the first time I had been on the lethal end of Fin's temper. It just hit a little closer to home than it used to. I knew if I went out there, Fin would apologize, and I would forgive him.

He had been so different from when we were young. Young Fin would have never demanded I give him the bike keys, young Fin would have never thought to fill my house with food or hold his temper about the secret I'd kept with Al. But the hospital was a lot more like the teenager I had known. Maybe hometowns and ex-crushes did that to a person, reverted them. I sure as hell felt it. I crossed the hall slowly and took a few breaths as I pulled the door open.

Fin, who had been facing out into the yard, spun to look at me. We stared a moment. Fin put a hand to his chest and clutched at the fabric there. I tried to look casual, slipping my phone, and essentially my brother, into my pocket. I pulled the earbuds out of my ears and tucked them into the collar of my T-shirt. I waited, arms crossed.

Fin did a slight lap around the porch before he said anything. "Hey, I know I said some pretty fucked-up things the other day and I'm probably the last person you want to see right now, but I wanted to explain before..."

He sat down on the top step of the porch. Looking at him only made me want to comfort him, but we both needed to let him say what he needed to. I sat, too, leaning against the handrail.

"First, I wanted to say I was wrong and an asshole. I was feeling mad and jealous and confused. And I said all the things I said because I was looking for a fight. I honestly don't believe the things I said. I just wanted someone to understand how I was feeling, and the only way I could do that was to make someone else feel as bad.

"Jesus, Orion, it's been so long since I felt that way. Hell, it's been so long since I felt a lot of things I have been feeling lately. I tried getting a rise out of Rose and Fay, but they weren't biting, and neither were you." He paused, wiped his palms on his jeans, and used the inside of his overshirt to wipe his face.

I didn't move. That much I already knew. Because I knew him. Just like he'd known I was likely to drink myself into trouble the evening of the funeral. Those were the parts of each other I think we had been expecting. The rest was something different.

"Rose and I had a chat," he continued casually. "She set me straight. I know firsthand how hard it is being here watching her be sick, and I've been doing it so long, I forgot how hard it was when I was away. No matter what you want, you'll do what you think is best for others. What was best for Marge was for you and Corvus to be happy and live your lives. That sure as hell couldn't have been easy. The easy way out is making everything about yourself, which is exactly what I was trying to do at the hospital. I am sorry for saying any of what I said."

"Thanks for the apology," I said. It wasn't a welcome back into my arms, but it was a start. Fin seemed to notice and accepted the small step.

"I know you won't let me get away with simply saying I was wrong, but being alone and being lonely are not the same. I used to think about how lonely life would be without Rose, then life sort of got lonely anyway.

"For the past few weeks, though, it felt way *less* lonely. I want that for myself. And I want that for you. Because despite the fact I can be a real dick, I am here for you. Plus, there is Lin and Mrs. Grace and Corvus and Fay, who I should also probably apologize to." Fin sighed and had to regroup.

That was unexpected. It did something to me that I made Fin feel less lonely. Fin was handsome, fun, and smart. He could talk to anyone, go anywhere, do anything—even something as hard as apologizing to me. And I made him feel less lonely. *Damn.*

"Finally, I said I should have never gone to your house and that I should have gone with Rose. I know either way the accident would have happened, so saying shit like that is just a jerk move. What really happened was when we got interrupted, I was pissed with myself because you were the only person I *wanted* to be with. I felt guilty for wanting you, for picking you over her. But I also recognize that's not how things work. So, I'm sorry. Everything I said was out of anger, and I am sorry I took it all out on you."

Fin seemed so light, so ethereal. He didn't have debt collectors calling him. Were apologies so freeing? But could that really heal everything, even the worst of it? *If forgiveness were enough, I'd ask for it*, my brain hummed. *I'd make it the feathers in my wings.*

Fin's words did stir something inside me. I wanted to smile at him, but I didn't. I stayed silent. *And I'd fly us away from the painful things on to better things.*

Fin stood and faced me. "I don't want to stop seeing you, O. And the only way that can happen is if you want it, too. I'm not asking you to decide anything, but I want you to know I want it."

Fin waited, but I didn't move. He sighed, offered me a sad smile, and started slowly down the steps. I watched him leave and put the earbuds back in my ear.

"Crow?" I said, my voice sounding not like my own.

"Is he still there? Go after him, don't let him leave!"

I just scoffed.

"Hey, take me out of your damn pocket!" Crow screamed in my ear. In a bit of a daze, I did as he said, propping the phone on a porch step.

"That was a damned good speech." Crow sighed, looking me over.

"Seemed rehearsed," I said just to have something to say.

Crow laughed for a second, "Of course it was. Anything anyone says to you pretty much has to be."

"What does that mean?"

"You tend to take people at their word, and you lose faith in people who say one thing and do another. That kid seems to know that. He maybe said some hurtful things but acted like he doesn't want to hurt you. He owned his shit. What he said at the hospital was the mistake. The rest? Ah hell, give me his number. I'll call him. His speech fucking worked on me, man, and he didn't even know I was listening."

I let a grin slip for an instant. "I forgave him before he started talking."

"Both of you have it so bad. That's precious."

"Fuck off, Crow."

"Fine, but I don't think gay marriage is legal in GA, so—"

"I'm not having this conversation with you."

"Why won't you make me a grandpa?"

I just laughed. There was a moment of silence, and Crow shuffled his pages again. He looked at me carefully for a moment.

"Hunter?"

"Crow?"

"You okay? You don't have any plans to hurt yourself or do anything else stupid?"

I blinked at him. I wasn't surprised he asked. It wouldn't have been the first time I got a little too depressed for Crow's liking. I held up my hands, surrendering. "Not personally."

That caused him to grin and pat the pages on his desk. "So, is his hair red all over?"

"Fuck, Crow. Seriously?"

Corvus just laughed. After that, our conversation was light and great. Corvus made me write down his itinerary for the holidays. He planned to be in the country and wanted to spend a few days with me. As I closed the video app and stared at the sticky note of dates, I realized I was happy to have something to look forward to, and it wasn't all Corvus either.

The couch claimed me for a few hours, but I was restless by the afternoon. I was still too submerged to think much about Fin. There were no updates on Mom, but her remains would be ready someday, and I would have to do something with them. The only thing Mom said was that she trusted me and I'd know the spot when I saw it. So far, I hadn't seen it.

I needed something to help me feel better. I went searching through Mom's stuff, looking for something in particular. Amongst the shit on the dresser was the silver key with a tiny keychain photo of me. I couldn't have been more than eight years old in the picture. I had no context for the photo, but I sure as hell knew the key. I went out to the garage and flipped the tarp off the white, ragtop Mustang. The muscle car had been hers since she was a teenager, and Midge spent a lot of time and money keeping it pristine. I ran my hands over the glittering paint and soft leather. *It was mine*. I had always wanted it.

While musing over the car, my phone buzzed. I almost didn't answer, but I knew I had to. Colonel Sanders's voice came to me as if he was underwater. He told me my mother's cremation was now delayed because of a mechanical malfunction. It made me feel like I was living in a reality I didn't belong in. The news sent me back into the house.

Sometime after dark, my phone buzzed again. I was so tired of the phone. It was a sad face from Lin. Six more sad faces later, she sent a picture of Fin alone at our booth at Grace's. She then sent the lyrics to a sad country song about being alone. I didn't know how she knew he was down about me.

In order to keep from lingering on the photo and my own feelings, I looked up the chords for the song Lin had sent. I spent most of the night mastering the song, then recorded a video of myself singing and sent it to Lin. Then I played every song I could think of and even looked up some new ones. I played and sang until I was too tired to place my fingers, too tired to think, too tired to feel.

CHAPTER 15: ORION

I woke to bloody fingertips, aching wrists, and a sore voice. The music lingered. It was late in the day. I felt a little more returned. The pain in my body, the songs in my head, and the words Fin had said were finally working. I ordered a pizza and watched a squirrel writhe around in the kudzu from my porch while I ate.

Needing something to do, I wandered back out to the Mustang, making a list of maintenance needs. I replayed Fin's apology on a loop in my mind, the doubtful side of me looking for some misspoken word or sarcastic tone to latch on to in order to turn the apology around and have some reason to avoid Fin forever. I was glad I couldn't find one.

"Afternoon," Al called, knocking on the side of the garage. I hadn't expected him, but I should have since he told me he would be back on Wednesday. I sighed and straightened. I wrapped the rag I was holding around one hand and tried to offer a friendly wave.

Al started drooling and practically skipped toward me. "Oh, man! Look at this car! This is beautiful! *Wow!* Can I sit in it?"

I laughed and nodded. Al jumped into the driver's seat and made himself comfortable, tossing the folders he'd been carrying into the back. When he was where he wanted to be, he sighed like a very tired man getting into bed. Al grinned stupidly up at me.

"You have the best shit, man. This is amazing. I...hey, you all right? Kinda look like hell." Al's face went from genuinely satisfied to genuinely concerned, and he caught me off guard.

Al leaned across the seat and squinted at me. "This hafta do with Frank?"

I grunted and crossed my arms. Al put up his hands in defense. "I know, man, we aren't friends, but we aren't enemies anymore, either. I saw him there when I was up at Grace's for lunch. I was gonna go talk with him, but he was chin deep in his third sundae and a whole lot deeper in misery, so I didn't. I thought it was something with Rose, but if that were the case, Grace would never let him wallow like that. We have seen him down about Rose, somedays worse than a few gallons of ice cream could fix. But if it's *you*..." Al waited.

I didn't budge.

Al laughed and opened the passenger door. "Come sit in this beautiful car."

I did, but I made sure to look angry. I was worried. Whether I was present or not, I still seemed capable of causing Fin harm.

Al slowly flipped his ball cap backward and lounged in the seat. "Can't believe it is as bad as Frank lets on. Bet it was his doin', too."

"What, are you on my side now?" I didn't like Al blaming Fin, even if Fin was to blame. I was ready to take the blame for all of Fin's bad or low moods, but I couldn't take the blame for this one.

"I'm not *not* on your side. But fucking figure it out, man. You both look like hell." Al sighed and ran his hands over the steering wheel. "Back in high school, I know I wasn't the only one who gave you the idea to keep things a certain way with Frank."

"Coach?"

"Naw, Dad was just plain homophobic. I'd like to think I was looking out for Frank, and I could tell as soon as I started talking that *you* already had all those thoughts in *your* head. Which made my job easier, 'cause then I could just tell you *you* were right. Just like now, I can see that whatever happened between you two, you're thinking he did whatever because you're the bad guy, but *you're* wrong. And all three of us know Fin was wrong, too."

"Everyone can't be wrong." I felt both relieved and annoyed that Al could read me so well.

"Everyone sure as hell can be wrong. That's the beauty of being human."

"Like when?"

"Everyone was wrong about the world being flat. About DDT. That bananas are food—"

"Bananas *are* food."

"Bananas are trash." Al's voice grew very quiet and even. "People get all kinds of ideas, and so many of them are wrong."

Al's cool tone made me feel like I had a friend. It made me uncomfortable. The sun bore down into the unshaded car and Al continued to run his hands over the leather interior, making a soft swishing noise. I let what Al said sink in.

"I'm not paying you for therapy," I said after a few silent minutes.

"Advice is free so long as I get to sit in this car."

"You know your accent gets thicker when you're not minding your own business."

"You should hear me drunk. All right, let me get out of here before I offer to buy this, too. Speaking of which, you think about rent on this place?"

"Yeah. I have to hang around a bit longer, but…" I really didn't have a plan after I finished the business of Mom's estate, not to mention the pending problem of her remains. But Al didn't need to know any of that. Or maybe he should. At the back of my mind, I got the impression I should say something to someone about something. But I didn't.

"Right, well, you know how to reach me. I suppose you'll be at the City Founder's Festival?"

I gave him an *are you joking* look.

Al grunted as he pulled himself out of the car. "I know, but I think Lin is singing, and there's always beer."

We concluded our business with a handshake. I had heard every word Al had said. *It was Frank's doing. We were both wrong.* I cleaned up the mess around the Mustang and put the car securely back into the barn. I ate more pizza, put my phone on the charger, and took a shower.

Standing in my living room that night, I felt small and boring. I ached to see Fin, so I let myself send the text before I got too worked up over it. *Hey you wanna talk?* Then I surprised myself by sending *I can come over.* I was already out the door when I received Fin's reply of *yes* and *come.* I didn't really know what I was going to say. I would probably have to apologize for taking so long to accept Fin's apology, but I didn't want the night to just turn into me and Fin trading apologies, which was sort of how I expected it to go.

I also knew we had a lot more to talk about than just the hospital. Something had been on Fin's mind the other day when I told him about Al and me fighting. But he hadn't said what it was. We had never talked about that night in college either. But how do you start a conversation like that?

Ten minutes from my house and ten minutes from Fin's, it started to rain. I just sighed and kept walking. Either way, I was gonna get wet. It was a warm Southern rain, big fat drops that seemed to land on you even if you weren't standing directly under them. I picked up my pace only slightly. Lightning crackled around me and thunder pealed. I felt suddenly whole, free. The humbling, threatening urgency of the storm seemed to settle whatever was raging inside me. The peace gave me courage, so I didn't bother knocking, I just pushed into Fin's room through the back door.

"O!" Fin shouted, tossing aside the book he had been holding. He jumped off the bed. "Is it raining?"

"No, it's the new fashion," I said in a tone I hoped was more playful than anything else, holding out my dripping arms. I was soaked through.

"Just take off whatever is wet, and I'll get you a towel," Fin said, his voice and expression pure concern. He left the room in a few strides. I had only gotten a brief glimpse of him before he left. His face was pink and his hair damp and feathery, like he just gotten out of the shower. His clothes were casual for once, basketball shorts and a tank top. Seeing him again after only a few days apart shouldn't make my soul relax as much as it did.

I made quick work of the soaked T-shirt, hoodie, my undershirt, and my shorts. I also pulled off my wet, smeared glasses and tossed them on the bedside table. My hair was dripping down my back, so I untied the ponytail and shook it out. I was considering taking off my underwear, which was wet at the waist, when I heard a gasp. Fin was just standing in the doorway, staring at me. I felt a flush of embarrassment and looked down at the puddle I'd made.

"Sorry, I—"

There was an audible gulping sound, so I looked back at him. Fin was just standing there, pressing the towel to his face. Despite my fuzzy vision, I could see the deep red in his cheeks and the brightness and want in his eyes. I wondered at the expression for a moment. It took the darkening of Fin's eyes as I ran both hands through my wet hair to make me realize that Fin's longing gaze was completely for me. I felt myself smile.

I guess I was attractive, but I was more situationally handsome: dressed in a suit for Mom's promotion dinner, in leather on my bike, or in a band T-shirt with a drink in my hand at a dive bar. If people were looking for a particular type of guy, I could usually pull it off. I really doubted my ability to be the daily sort of attractive that kept the attention of a regular partner. But rain-drenched-nearly-naked Orion seem to be doing it for Fin. I wanted to be embarrassed that I wasn't like Fin, clean lines and fit, but the expression on Fin's face was enough make me say fuck it.

"Give me the towel, Fin," I said with a laugh.

"I don't think I will." Fin let the towel fall from his face, still clenching it in his hand. Bright white teeth bit at his pink bottom lip. He was shameless.

"Fin!"

Fin didn't move, didn't look away. He didn't even seem to be breathing.

"Fine, I'll come and get it." I crossed the room and put out a hand to get the towel. Instead, Fin filled my arms. He pressed his body against me, his mouth on mine. I heard myself make some sort of surprised noise and managed to steady us. It was the most relieved and terrifying kiss I had ever experienced. He'd said he wanted this, but the kiss seemed to prove it. It was also scary how every part of me seemed to draw him closer. My chest tightened, and my blood coursed with the sharp gravity that seemed to live in Fin's kiss.

Fin raked his hands hard through my hair, and holy hot Jesus, I liked that. My body vibrated in response. I was a hair guy, which is why I kept it long. Nothing turned my dial harder than a strong hand in my hair. A low whimper escaped me and Fin tightened his big hands harder in my hair. I slowly backed up until I was forced to sit on the bed. I pulled Fin down to straddle my lap.

"Oh my God, yes," Fin said into my shoulder, kissing my neck, writhing with pleasure. We hadn't been close like this since…and then I remembered why I'd come over.

"*Wait!*"

"What?" Fin said.

"I didn't come here for this. Well, not that—shit, I came to apologize."

"For what?"

"For taking so long to accept your apology."

"I accept."

"Just like that?"

"Of course. I figured if you wanted to come over, you must have forgiven me."

"Yeah?" I kissed at Fin's neck, tracking my hands up his shirt. I ran my fingertips along his ribs. I liked the way it made him tense and shiver, like he felt it all over his body.

"Yeah," Fin breathed, "just like that."

I did it again, his skin soft and his muscles hard, wanting to take in every sensation at once. There was so much doubt in me about things with Fin, but every time my skin made contact with his, I felt reassured. I chased that feeling all over Fin's body. Fin moaned, unashamed, and claimed my mouth again, rocking on top of me. *God bless basketball shorts.* They were doing little to hide how turned on he already was.

Fin's noises and breathing made me feel like no one else could fill this need for him except me. I was also insanely into Fin's constant motion, wriggling and vibrating. It was like holding on to pure energy. I needed his reaction, his responsiveness. Fin's attraction to me made me feel important. I wasn't important to very many people, but Fin made me feel it. And I wanted it so badly.

He was childish and funny and serious and capable. I liked that he had obscenely tidy hair, and that he blushed and that he cried during movies. I liked the grandpa way he drove, and the 90s style overshirts he wore and…shit. I didn't want to think anymore. I just wanted to feel.

I pulled Fin's hips down, his ass rubbing my lap, his dick grazing over my dick and stomach. Hell, I was so turned on, I almost couldn't breathe. Fin rocked his hips, thrusting and grinding. I wouldn't last long with that happening. I felt suddenly like I was in charge, like he was following my lead, and that sent a flash of anxiety through me. I didn't want to disappoint him.

"Tell me what you want," I breathed.

"Ah, fuck me," he said, half a statement, half a question.

P—penetration? Oh boy. I figured if we kept on the way we were going, we'd have reached that point eventually. But I might have to answer for leaving him in that hotel room once and for all. We'd only ever fucked once, that night. I guess it was different. He'd fucked me that night. This was him asking to be fucked. *Different enough?*

I looked into his face. He was blushing, but his eyes were intense, determined, and searching my face. It felt oddly like a challenge. He seemed to say, *I'm not going to say it if you aren't.* We both knew I wasn't. He combed through my hair with one hand and steadied himself on my lap with the other.

"You want me to?" I said.

Fin seemed surprised, too, but shrugged. "I didn't know how badly I wanted it until I said it. I mean, I won't lie. I had been thinking about it enough to prepare for it."

"Okay."

Fin got to his feet, and I scooted farther up on the bed. He seemed like he had something in mind, doing things with a determined expression. He first pulled the string that turned off the overhead light, leaving the room golden hued in the soft light of a lamp. Then he rummaged through his side table and knelt on the bed, mirroring my own pose. He seemed disquieted and nervous. He glanced around the room, looking away from me, then back, staring into his hands. I noticed the condom and lube he was clutching.

"Um, I guess we should have the talk about being tested. I mean we should have had it that first time, but it wasn't like...shit—"

I almost laughed, relieved. "Is that what you're so nervous about?"

Fin growled and flopped onto his stomach, raking his pink-tinted hands through his fiery hair. "I'm nervous for a lot of reasons."

"We don't have to do anything."

"I want this, but..."

I understood. I felt it, too. We had something instant and deep between us, born from our days together as teenagers, but there was also a lifetime of distance between us, a hundred unsaid things. I generally liked distance and kept it with most people, but not Fin. I wanted to help him relax and feel okay. I had an idea of how to do it.

"Okay, don't move."

Of course Fin moved, turning to watch me. I leaned over the bed and pulled my damp phone from my hoodie. I peeled it out of its case, dried it on the blanket, and thumbed on an internet radio app. The first suggested station was a singer Fin liked, so it seemed like a safe bet. As the music started, I tossed the phone somewhere near the pillows. I crawled over to Fin.

"What are you doing?"

"Just lie down."

Fin complied. I took the condom and lube from him and set them nearby, so he would know that wasn't where I was going with this. Then I placed myself behind him, straddling one of his legs. I delicately put my hands where his shirt met his shorts, then slipped them under his shirt and up his tight, muscular back.

"Want me to take this off?" he said, shyly.

I just grunted an answer. He pulled it off, revealing a long stretch of white, freckled skin. I felt warmth and interest flood me, something mesmerizing about the look of my brown hands running over his skin. I massaged, saying nothing. As the music and my hands worked, Fin's body started to relax.

"I would have never guessed you like this kind of music," Fin sighed after a while.

"Who says I do?" I said, going for coy.

"You're singing to it."

"Am I?"

"Yeah."

"Well, am I any good?"

He laughed and rolled his eyes. "I remember someone saying the only true music is the blues and that all other music wasn't worth listening to."

"Sounds like an ass."

He just grunted and settled back onto the bed. I started to massage a little deeper, Fin's breathing deepening in response. I wanted to answer his question about being tested, but it seemed weird to just blurt it out.

"Knock knock," I found myself saying.

"Who's there?" He sounded surprised I was telling a joke.

"Confused comedian."

"Confused comedian who?"

"And the pepper said, 'Shake her? I barely know her.'"

Fin laughed. And groaned. "That is the worst."

"Mom was full of 'em." I laughed.

"I remember."

"Um, so I'm not saying this to try and move things along, but you should know, I was tested about a year ago. Clean. Haven't done anything since."

"That long?"

"They tested me going into detox. Figured it wouldn't be fair to subject someone to me if I was that kind of mess."

A flush crossed over Fin's face and shoulders. "Six months ago. Negative."

"You're funny," I said.

"Why?"

"What kind of doctor gets nervous talking about STDs?"

"Sex doesn't come up much when studying cancer."

I grunted.

"I asked a guy once, and he told me it was a mood killer," Fin said after a moment.

"That's because he probably had something."

"You think? Thank God we never did anything. I don't know, I mean, it *is* kind of a buzzkill."

"Fuck that."

Fin turned and looked at me. I was serious. Not only was being safe a good idea, but Fin valued it on, like, an extreme level. All of the guy's lotion was SPF 30 or higher—his ChapStick was sunproofed, for crying out loud. I cocked an eyebrow at him.

"Okay," Fin said with a laugh. He nuzzled deeper into the bed and sighed as I smoothed my hands over him. I smiled and thought about what to say next. I liked this, whatever it was. Small talk maybe?

"What else is making you nervous?" I asked in a moment of confidence.

Fin nearly flipped us both as he turned to sit up. "You are, Orion."

I stared. Fin's words didn't compute. *I* made Fin nervous?

Fin turned red, his face going the color of his beard. "I mean, all else aside, we've known each other a long time, but not like this."

I absorbed Fin's words. The *all else aside* was an invitation to not talk about that night, so, okay, what then? *Like this?* I considered it for a few seconds. I couldn't figure out what Fin saw in me. But he saw something, and he said he wanted a thing with me. And I could feel how different it was, from any other time. There wasn't a name for that in-between place, that *I don't know where this is going but if it doesn't go somewhere I am going to be disappointed* place. I was speechless.

"You look like I'm about to hit you with my car," Fin said, placing a soft hand over mine. "I'm going to take that to mean you're nervous, too."

"I am always nervous around you," I said.

"I know."

I rolled my eyes, embarrassed. "Get over yourself, Franklin."

Fin laughed and lay back on his stomach. I was relieved to not have Fin's deep gaze on me. It gave me a moment to let my guard down. Feelings washed over me, a lot of feelings. The one feeling that stuck was that I was happy. More than that was beyond anything I had allowed myself to consider. But Fin was offering more.

My pulse quickened as I went back to massaging Fin. I chubbed up again as my brain considered the possibility of full on fucking Fin. That didn't mean I wanted to rush. I cleared my throat and scrambled for more to say, more questions to ask.

"How long have you been in town?" I wondered why we hadn't talked about these things. How can two people come so far just on the experiences happening in real time, ignoring the past?

"Year," Fin said, sounding nearly asleep.

"How do you live?" I said, not knowing the best way to phrase it. My brain was working hard to find the words as my blood pooled south.

"You mean money? Well, Rosey had a lot saved from when Dad and Granddad died—and Grandma, actually. And I had some saved from odd jobs. I do some long-distance work for the university from here. We do okay. How do *you* live?"

"Um, Mom worked for banks, so I can live on the investments for a while. Lin sends me a check every now and again for songs, too."

"Geez, are you serious?" Fin said.

"What?"

"You just sound like a bad romance novel character. Dark mysterious biker, rock star with investments and no job?"

I laughed. "Well, I am, didn't I tell you? Don't tell the Romantic Characters Guild I'm giving it to you for free."

"You're just a nerd."

"What about soccer?"

Fin flipped over, turning to look at me. "What are you doing?"

"Um…"

"Small talk? Back rubs? Music I am sure *you* regularly listen to. Yup—bad romance novel character."

"How do you know so much about romance novels?"

Fin gave me a squint, turned only a light pink, then rolled over. "Fuck off, Orion."

Fin pulled a pillow under his chest. I hesitated. Only one word could describe where I suddenly was with Fin, and realizing it was like a punch to the guts. *Safe.* Somehow we'd found safe. Safe was scary.

"You okay?"

"Yeah, sorry."

He winked at me. "You know, the foreplay can be over if you want."

I laughed, feeling sixteen years old instead of twenty-nine. "Will your mom hear us?"

"Naw, the washer and dryer and the bathroom in the master are between us. She sleeps with music on, plus drugs. So, let's go."

"Let's go?" I leaned over him, pressing my crotch against the back of his thigh, covering him with my body. "I think you can ask a little nicer than that."

"I think that was perfectly nice."

His breath was short. His body moved under mine, making the contact between us warm and tempting. His playfulness made the whole room brighter, and I didn't want it to stop. I wasn't holding him down, but I wasn't light either. He groaned as I pressed into him a little, and he lifted his hips into me. I kissed his shoulders and neck, sliding a hand down his side. I laughed as he cussed, his hands gripping the pillow under him.

"I think I would be willing to hear a little begging," I said.

"I bet you would."

"I mean, you could always return the favor. I think a back rub would be nice."

"I'd rather rub something else."

Damn his long-ass arms. He reached an arm behind him and was palming my dick before I even realized he'd moved. The sudden sharpness of having his hand on me made me gasp. Proud of himself, he stroked me slowly, with his fingertips. I had to catch his wrist and pin it down before I decided to let him keep going.

"Tell me," I whispered.

"Um..."

"Anything. Since you're so demanding, I want to make sure you get what you want."

"Hu—um," he breathed. I was slowly rubbing his back and sides with my hands, feeling the soft skin of his upper thigh, his lower back, the shape of his ass.

"Fin," I urged gently.

"Damn, touch me, please." He added *please* as if that would make me do more.

"I am."

"You are the worst. Uh, I like the way you kiss my neck." I repeated the kisses, marking my way down his back along his spine. Fin moaned, his whole body vibrating.

I adjusted so I was more completely against him, my cock resting against the crack of his ass, my chest pressed into his warm back.

"Fuck, why are you so cold?" he said when my hair grazed his shoulders. He squirmed, more in surprise than to get away.

"I was out in the rain and someone wouldn't give me a towel." I traced his ear and the side of his face with my mouth. Fin arched back, his ass and thighs pressing into me.

"Right, sorry."

"What else do you want?" I said.

"Please." He pulled his hand, and mine with it, under his body. "Touch me."

I gave him more room, and he lifted his hips for me. I took some steady breaths and followed the lines of his abs down to the hem of his shorts. Fin groaned. My pulse rose in response to the heat and need coming from his body. I slowly slipped a hand under the waistband of his shorts. He wasn't wearing underwear. Fin pressed up, giving my hand more room. I took the space, wrapping my hand around Fin's length.

"Fuck, Orion."

Aware of the way he liked to be stroked, tight and slow, I gripped loose and low on the base. Fin writhed. But I held still, held on, letting him chase the friction. I wanted this. I was scared it would end. I was going to make it last as long as I could, which meant finding some way to slow him down.

Fin arched back, rubbing against me, rubbing my dick along the crack of his ass. Hell, that felt amazing. I suddenly became aware of how hard I was, Fin's ass pressing against me. I hadn't given myself much attention, but I was fucking throbbing. I panted against his shoulders, pressing down on him. It felt like the world stopped when Fin rocked forward into my fist and drew back, the head of his dick grazing over my fingers, streaking them with pre-cum. Then he rocked forward again.

"Fuck, Orion, please?" Fin begged, rocking harder into my hand. "You are such a tease. Just fuck me already."

I groaned, enjoying the sound of him begging. Fin whined when I released him. I pulled his shorts down to his thighs. Yup, I really liked fooling around with some clothes on. It made things seem inexplicably seedy and sexy, being wanted or wanting so badly you didn't even bother getting fully undressed. I also liked that the shorts restricted Fin's movements a bit, reining him in.

I had to reach across Fin to get the lube and he caught my arm on the way, peppering it with kisses, lingering on the knuckles of my fingers. I just retreated, applied some lube to one hand and smoothed Fin's long back with the other.

Fin rocked into my fingers as soon as they made contact with his entrance. I relished the power Fin was giving me. I couldn't promise a painless continuation of safe, happy moments like these. I wasn't the type. Fin rocking against my fingers, taking more inside himself, reminded me that at least I knew how to do this.

I refocused on giving Fin pleasure, the idea of getting him off being enough to bolster my confidence. One finger quickly became two, and Fin was a panting mess. I wasn't much better, tense with need. I was so turned on, I was almost ready to beg myself for more. In a deep breath, I rasped out, "Okay?"

"Fuck, finally, please, shit."

I slipped my fingers free and moved for the condom. Just as I was about to put it on, he rocked back, knocking it out of my hands.

"Sorry, excited."

In that clumsy moment, I felt something that scared me more than anything else I'd experienced with Fin. Beneath the lust and the want and the guilt and the safety, under it all there was a flood of affection, the real kind, the kind that people called a specific four-letter word that changed everything. I hadn't ever had fun in bed with someone. There had been sexiness and frustration and enjoyment but not fun, not like that.

"God, fuck, aren't you ready?"

I picked up the condom, rolled it on, and applied lube. I was so far beyond the sex. I wanted it, but I wanted everything else more. However, more was for later. Sex was happening at the moment, and my feelings were happening, so I focused. I adjusted myself against Fin, pressing just barely, into place.

"Fin—"

Fin rocked into me hard, taking my full length in a single sharp burst. My vision filled with white-hot pleasure, and the forest fire that was Fin's body surrounding me burned away everything. We both gasped, clasping on to each other. Fin let out a rush of swearing, and I blinked away the spots in my vision.

"Fuck, did I hurt you?" Fin said.

"No, geez—are you kidding?"

"Sorry."

"Fuck. Are you okay?"

"Hell, yes. Jesus, this feels so fucking good."

Fin propped himself up on his elbows, head low between his arms. I appreciated the sight. It was all so urgent and needy, so immature and fun. I smiled. The love had always been there. It just took disarming myself enough to let me *feel* it.

"Okay?" I exhaled.

I didn't really know what I was asking, I just pressed my chest over Fin's body, trying to find some level in my whirling reality. Fin rotated his hips against me, dragging his body over my balls and thighs. That was making it hard for me to regroup. I took a desperate breath.

"Yeah," Fin said.

I pulled myself together. I rubbed a hand over Fin's back and made a small movement, an infinitely small thrust comparatively, and was surprised as Fin gave me control back. He just breathed and moaned. I moved again, drawing out and pressing in, drawing back and rocking forward, gauging Fin's reactions. Fin locked a hand over mine, steadying himself.

"Tell me," I whispered.

"Slow, long," Fin answered, almost voiceless.

I fucked slowly, rocking in deep strokes. Fin's body tightened around me, his hand still on mine, moans soft and low. In a few thrusts, I was so close to orgasming I could almost see it. Fin's body seemed to pulse with his want, and it was accelerating me over the edge. Every place he and I made contact sent shocks through me. The sight of the freckled skin, red hair, defined muscles, all of it was so perfect and nearly overwhelming.

"Fin," I said, feeling the need to explain how close I was.

"Close."

"Tell me how to get you there."

"Your hand, faster."

I didn't hesitate to fulfill the request. I lost control to Fin as soon as I wrapped my hand around his dick. I heard myself cuss as he set a pace, rocking back into me, hips colliding with ass, and then forward into my fist.

I was sure I came first, losing reality and cadence as Fin worked himself against me. The motion made my orgasm slow, long, and nearly painful with relief. I was giddy by the time Fin stopped, my hand warming with his release. And we were still for a while, until Fin shifted and my mind settled back into my body.

"Damn," Fin said, releasing my hand from his grip and relaxing.

"Yup." I flopped down on his bed and closed my eyes.

"Here," Fin said, tossing the discarded towel at me.

"I don't need this now. I'm pretty much dry."

He laughed and found a trash can for the waste. Fin was easy to love.

CHAPTER 16: FIN

I woke to the muffled shouting of my name.

"Fin?" Rose called again, knocking on the door twice.

I groaned, rolling over. "What, Ma?"

I looked over my shoulder at Orion, who had one arm wrapped tight around my waist. His eyes were still closed, but I was sure he was awake. Fucker managed to somehow steal all the pillows.

"Fay and the kids will be here in a few minutes."

"What?" My brain was not working, sleep was winning.

"It's noon, get up. Fay will be here in twenty."

"Yup, okay." I yawned and listened to her footsteps as she moved away from the door.

Waking up naturally was hard for me. When my alarm went off, I had no problem, but left to myself I was more likely to just fall back asleep. I considered setting an alarm for five minutes, but I didn't know where my phone was. I yawned and stretched, turning to smile at Orion. His eyes, brightly gilded and intense, were open and on me. I snatched a pillow from him and flopped face down into it.

"Morning," I said, trying to drag my blanket over my head.

"Hey," he said, his voice small.

"You okay?"

"You didn't go for a run?"

I looked at him. I didn't really know what question he was asking me. It sounded too simple to be that simple. I answered it anyway. "Naw, been going a bit hard the last few days. You're the excuse I needed to stay in bed."

I had expected a reaction from Orion and there wasn't one. "O, you okay?"

"Yeah, sorry. Why were you running so hard? Marathon?" Orion rolled onto his back, hooking his hands behind his head.

"I will have you know I don't run *every day.* I guess I was just angry and sad. It helps me think," I said, closing my eyes.

I never would have thought that would be what he wanted to talk about the morning after the night we had. I noted the looseness in the muscles in my back and shoulders. I made a mental note to let Orion rub me down more often. I also noticed the soreness in other places. My skin warmed as I thought about it.

"I can see you thinking about dirty things," Orion said.

I opened my eyes and glared at him, but he didn't notice. He was looking at his hands. They were thickly calloused and looked overworked and raw. I hadn't noticed the evening before.

"I understand," Orion said in a wistful way, his words almost lost to the quiet. I wasn't sure what that meant, but when he looked at me again, he seemed more present. And he smiled at me.

"So, what are you going to do today?" I said, closing my eyes again.

"Well," Orion started with a grunt. I could feel him shifting around on the bed, "I'm going to go home and charge my phone."

I noted the lack of music and opened my eyes to see Orion testing a dead phone. We had different phones, otherwise I would have offered him a charger. I considered picking one up the next time I was at the store. The idea of the gesture died as I watched Orion fish his glasses off the floor.

I had hoped the answer to my question would have involved me. The fact that it hadn't, and Orion's distance, made me nervous. Other mornings with Orion had been playful or cuddly. Orion would never admit it, but he was an extreme big spoon. Seeing as my family was coming over, I couldn't really blame Orion wanting to get out of here.

"Fin?"

I started at my name. I wasn't sure if I'd dozed off again or what, but Orion was closer, staring at me. Orion put out a hand and ran it down my arm. I couldn't stop the hope the gesture caused.

"Sorry, I was thinking. I am not really about seeing Fay today."

"Still owe her an apology?"

"Yeah."

"You can come with me. We could sneak out the back."

I grinned, liking the idea. A slight knot had formed in my guts. The idea of Orion leaving me was always in my periphery. And I had known going into it I probably wasn't enough to make him stay—

"Fin?"

"Stop watching me think."

"Think quieter, then."

"Yeah, okay. Let's go."

While Orion intended that we just sneak away, I sent Rose a text explaining where I would be. She told me I couldn't hide from Fay forever. *Me too.* I followed Orion out the back door into the sunlight. We walked across the field between our houses at a slow trudge, the land still muddy and wet from the rain. The Starr house was just coming into view through the trees when I thought to ask Orion, again, what was on his mind.

Before I could say anything, Orion coolly slipped one hand into the pocket of his shorts and the other into my hand. We had never held hands before, not really. I hadn't ever given it much thought. I almost laughed at the idea, and I tightened my grip around Orion's warm, tough fingers. The knot in my gut tightened, too. It was a weird, ominous seed of doubt that had lodged in my soul, and the light of my hope couldn't kill it.

Then there was humming. I looked over and Orion was absently humming as we strolled. I wanted to punch myself. *Why can't you just enjoy this.* Everything that happened the night before, the hand holding, the soft smile, the humming. All of it was mine, and I couldn't enjoy it. Not fully. I knew that Orion *left* places, and whether he meant to or not, he left people.

It was probably the sex. We had met up in Rhode Island and stayed in a hotel one night. We had sex, and I woke up completely alone. It was a year before I heard from him. I hadn't woken up alone this time, but the fear was there.

"You are never this quiet," Orion said, holding the door to his house open for me.

"Sorry," I said, trying to focus on Orion. I wondered what might be the most focused thing I could do at that moment, and I did it. I kissed Orion. It felt like such an ordinary and extraordinary thing to do. Like breathing. Orion hummed his approval.

In the kitchen, Orion plugged his phone in near the stove and went upstairs for a fresh set of clothes. I put on the coffee, even though it was late and already too hot. Then I went to the fridge. The groceries I'd filled the house with were gone, replaced by a box of pizza with a single slice in it and a handful of sauces that came with the pizza.

"Don't judge me," Orion said, coming back into the room.

"I'm not. We can go to the store if you want."

"I don't need taking care of."

I felt my judging squint before I could stop it. "That's not what I am saying."

Orion sighed and shook his head. "Right. I know."

I sensed a *but*, but it remained unsaid. My phone buzzed in my pocket. I didn't like the tension between us. It was probably my fault. Orion had been in a good mood most of the morning. I had to wonder if he could tell what I was thinking. I didn't like the doubt I had.

Frustrated, I looked at the message on my phone. It was from Lin, wanting to meet for lunch in the city. She seemed like a good bridge. Lin would know what was in his head. I ran the risk of exposing myself since Lin's blunt observations were universal, but maybe I needed an ally in the attempt to solidify this, whatever this was.

"Fin, I didn't mean to snap at you."

I set the phone on the counter. I sighed, endeared by Orion's confession. I felt my expression soften. "Would it be so bad to let someone take care of you?"

The question went unanswered. Orion's phone burst to life, turning itself on after charging a little. It buzzed against the counter with urgency. Orion and I watched as texts and other messages filled the screen.

"Damn," I said when it was done.

"What the hell?" Orion crossed to it, and I went to look over his shoulder. The first two texts were from me. The next few were from Lin.

"What video?" I asked Orion, reading one of the messages over his shoulder.

He started to reply but lost the sentence, concentrating on the rest of the messages.

There were two from Al, the same set I'd received from Lin, two from his brother, Corvus, and one from his lawyer, Shively. That one had Orion's attention. It said simply *no change.*

"No change?" I said.

Orion set down the phone without answering any of the messages.

"You're popular," I said, trying for a lighter tone.

"How the hell did that happen?" Orion said, looking completely put off by the idea that people wanted to talk to him.

I leaned against the island to give him space. "Is everything okay?"

"Isn't it? Is everything okay with you?"

"That's not an answer."

Orion sighed and raked his hair out of his face. It was loose and wild, untamable from the rain, sex, and sleep.

"No. Not *everything* is okay, but I don't want to talk about it."

"Fair enough." I was pleased to have gotten at least that much.

Orion looked for a moment like he was deciding something, then he came over to me. He put his hands on my chest and rested his face against me. I put my arms around him before I could question it. It was so vulnerable and so unlike Orion.

"I won't push," I said into the tangle of black hair, "but if you need help, all you have to do is ask."

"Help me buy food. What do humans eat?"

"How did you make it this far?"

"I dated a pizza guy for a while."

"You are the worst."

"What did Lin want?" Orion said after a moment.

"Um, she wants us to go to Atlanta and have lunch with her."

Orion pulled back and looked up at me. "Is that something you want to do?"

I tried for a noncommittal shrug. "I think it would be nice. We don't have the car, though. Would you want to take the bike that far?"

The smile that crossed Orion's face was so beautiful I wanted to take a picture.

"You buy a car or something?"

"When do we need to be there?"

"Since it's afternoon now, I guess dinnertime."

Orion didn't hesitate. He crossed back to the phone, thumbed a message to Lin, tugged the charger from the wall to bring along, and pulled open a drawer in the island. Surprisingly, it was full of sunglasses.

"Geez, why do you have a thousand pairs of sunglasses?"

"Just grab a pair and let's go."

I grabbed my own phone and a set of aviators, and followed a very excited Orion out to the garage. I could only whistle as Orion pulled the tarp off the white muscle car. A memory of Marge speeding around town in it came to me.

"It still looks great."

"Want to drive it?"

"Me?"

"Yeah, just promise you'll speed a little." Orion gave me that big smile again, a wink, and tossed me the keys. I let them fall into my hands and watched Orion hop in the passenger side. It was all too much. The knot of doubt became a lump of certainty. The minute Orion left town, I would be decimated.

I sighed, the revelation giving way to in-the-moment joy. I hopped into the car, started the engine, and tore out of the drive. I talked Orion into his seat belt, and he fiddled with the radio. We didn't say much after that, the wind and radio drowning out all other sounds. I watched Orion from the corner of my eye. He was draped over the edge of the car, his head resting on his arm, his face serene.

I wondered if he thought of this car as his mother's or his. I had a few of my father's possessions, nothing as cool as the car, though. As the road slipped beneath, I wondered what my father would have thought of Orion. I'd considered it before. To me, my father and Orion had never existed together on the same planet. There was the world with my father in it, and there was the world with Orion in it. Dad used to roll his eyes every time I mentioned a crush. The memory of that made me laugh out loud. Orion looked at me suspiciously. I just shrugged and reached my hand out to him. Orion took it.

Orion's phone rang four times in the time it took to drive to the city. He didn't answer any of the calls, merely side-eyed the phone. Each time it rang, he tightened his grip on my hand. I was more interested in Orion's reactions to the calls than in the calls themselves.

By the time the third call dropped, I could feel the anxiety vibrate from Orion's hand to mine. I didn't ask about it, though. I just drove a little faster.

❖

"Well, well, well," Lin said as we pulled up to the restaurant. She was sitting alone on the sidewalk patio and waved as I parked.

"Hi, Lin," I said, kissing her cheek. Orion didn't say anything, he just kissed her, too.

"Damn, I can't believe you two."

"What?" we said together. Orion sat, tossing his glasses on the glass tabletop. I popped open the umbrella in the center of the table, shading myself and most of Lin. Orion squinted into the sun as he tried to pull his even more unruly hair into a band.

"I had this whole plan to get you two in the same place, see if I couldn't get either of you to quit being such sad sacks about each other. But you beat me to it," she said, putting her feet up on the empty fourth chair.

"I wasn't being a sad sack," I said.

"I have photo evidence of both of you."

"What?"

She laughed and pulled out her phone. She first showed us a photo of me, taken while I was alone at Grace's.

"Shit—how did you get that?"

"Gracey."

"Delete it."

"Wouldn't matter. Orion already has a copy."

He shrugged. "She sent it to me. She also yelled at me."

"I did," Lin said proudly, a very big margarita making its way to the table for her. She continued before anyone could say more. "*And* his reaction to that photo was this."

She thumbed past the photo, and a video started to play.

"Shit," Orion said, unable to hide the bashful smile spreading on his face. We listened to Orion's song. I noted the strain in his hands and voice. Band-Aids were all over some of his fingers. He looked like he'd played nonstop for hours, all day even. I felt the blush spread, no longer embarrassed but charmed.

"OMG, if you two keep this up, I'm going to need another fucking marg."

"What do they have here," Orion said, picking up a menu.

We chatted freely until my fiesta burger, Lin's nachos, and Orion's burrito came. Orion and Lin discussed band matters, then Lin and Orion chatted about Al being bisexual and secretly in love with me. I didn't have anything to say about either of those things. I just drank in their happiness.

The cheer died a brutal but swift death as Orion's phone buzzed against the table. Lin and I both watched as Mr. Shively's name bannered and disappeared. It was the second time he had called. Then the phone beeped to show he had left a voicemail.

"So, radio silence then?" Lin said, her tone dark. My skin prickled as Orion and Lin exchanged a heated look.

"I don't have to answer my phone," Orion said, not breaking the stare.

"I know that. I should count myself lucky, right? The mysterious Orion Starr answers at least *half* my phone calls."

"What the fuck do you want, Lin?"

"Nothing. I was just pointing it out."

Orion side-eyed her. Lin stared at him critically. Then I understood. Lin's questions were calculated. She was gauging something. And Orion's remarks were just as calculated. It was like a secret code, words with double meanings.

"Any word on your mother's ashes?" Lin said pointedly. Orion's answer was an eye roll. Lin had cracked him. Embarrassment and guilt crashed through me. I had never once thought to ask about Marge's remains. I hated myself as I observed the pain that crossed Orion's face.

Then Orion looked at me. Without looking away, he spoke to Lin. "I don't want to talk about it."

Lin turned her steel trap of a gaze on me, her eyes dark as she spoke to Orion. "Huh, I wonder why."

"It's not his fault." Orion's voice was quiet but stern. He turned toward the car.

I felt suddenly like I had no idea what was going on. I was a bystander, observing people who knew each other better than I would ever know either. But this was what I'd wanted, wasn't it? For Lin to lay Orion out for me. So why, then, did I feel suddenly at odds with them both?

"I know it's not, but look at you," Lin said. "It must be something. One phone call and you can barely sit there. You can never just *be* somewhere."

Lin could see it, too. The idea that Orion was ready to bolt was now a solid confirmation in my mind, coming out of Lin's mouth.

"It wasn't just one phone call."

"You're missing the point."

"Right, okay. Well, call me when your band takes up permanent residence somewhere," Orion said, crossing his arms.

"We aren't here for me."

"No one asked you to be here for me."

Lin sighed. She took up a chip from the greasy paper basket and chomped it noisily. Orion stared into his lap. I tried not to look anywhere. At some point in the long silence, I ended up looking at Orion and was startled to find he was looking at me. It was a hard, critical gaze I didn't understand.

"Is this why you wanted to come?" he said, his voice flimsy but his stare hard.

"I don't understand."

"You wanted Lin to help you figure it out."

I knew my blush gave me away. "Not only that."

"What else, then?"

"I just wanted to spend time with you." I looked down at my plate, not missing Lin's amused expression.

"You *had* my time, Fin. Why this? Are the details of my shitty life so important you have to call in backup?"

"Orion—"

"Oh, better say your goodbyes now, Finny," Lin said, her voice dark.

Orion seemed to know what she meant by it, and he backed down. He stood and snatched his sunglasses and phone from the table. "Fine. Fuck, I can't fight you both."

"This isn't a fight," I said.

"We are on your fucking side," Lin said.

Orion put his hands up and went into the restaurant.

"Where are you going?" Lin said.

"To pay, we're leaving."

Alone with me, all of Lin's defenses collapsed and she sighed.

"You okay?"

She wiped a hand under her sunglasses. Tears. I was surprised and was instantly ready to cry with her, but I didn't. It all seemed so out of place, the argument, the scent of Tex-Mex and tequila, the bright evening sun, tears. All of it belonged somewhere else, some *when* else.

"I'm fine, Fin. Sorry. I didn't mean to throw you under the bus. I just don't know how to get him to understand."

"Leave before you're left, right?" I said.

Lin heaved a deep, clearing breath and downed the rest of her margarita. "Yup. But he has a point, too."

"Yeah?"

"My bus will roll out of here. Hell, we should have left four nights ago. And someday you'll go back to Rhode Island. We aren't really prime examples of sticking around for him, are we?"

My heart broke then and there. I hadn't thought about it that way. I sighed and sat back in my chair. "Fuck."

Lin looked like she was about to answer when Orion came back to the table.

"You ready?" he asked me, his voice distant. I couldn't say anything. I just took in a deep breath and stood.

Orion considered Lin for a moment. She looked up at him, the parts of her face visible around her glasses stoic. Orion put a hand on top of Lin's and sighed.

"I hear you, okay? It's not that easy," Orion whispered to her.

"Of course it's not."

Orion went to the car, not waiting for me. I crossed to Lin. She stood and let me hold her in my arms.

"Finny?"

"Lin?"

"Be honest with him," she said. Her voice had something else in it. Something stronger. But I didn't know what it was. I released her and got into the passenger seat of the Mustang.

❖

The drive home was silent except for the wind blowing around us. Orion kept to himself, practically crammed against the driver's side door. He chewed his fingers, thinking. I slunk down into the passenger's seat. I didn't notice when I fell asleep, just woke up to the glaring fluorescence of the gas station lights.

"You want anything from inside?" Orion said, his first words since leaving the restaurant.

"Water." I rubbed my face with the inside of my button-down. I tried to wake up completely while he was gone. When he was back, he set his water along the side of the seat and handed the other to me. Orion slipped the key into the ignition, but he didn't do anything else. I sipped and waited.

"Do you agree with Lin?" he said.

"About which part?"

Orion ran a hand through his hair. "Do you think I should stay?"

Every cell in my body wanted to say yes, but I couldn't. Orion staying in Georgia meant nothing if I didn't stay, too. And I wouldn't. I had a degree to finish. But Lin's words rang in my head, so I considered what an honest answer would be.

"It doesn't matter what I think. If you found something to stay for, you'd know it."

We shared a long stare. His expression was nearly blank. I tried for a smile but knew it missed the mark. Orion started the car, and we headed toward town in the twilight.

We made it back to Rose's just after nine. I knew there was no inviting Orion in and that I wasn't going back to his house with him. I didn't know what it meant in the long term, but I knew the night had been decided.

I wondered what I should say, but I couldn't think of anything. Then I did something desperate. I leaned across the car, getting into Orion's space, and I kissed him. I forced every emotion I had about him into that kiss. It was hard and clumsy and hopeful.

Orion kissed me back. I could have died with relief. The kiss he returned was as desperate and messy and filled with countless emotions as the one I offered. Then I pulled away, left the car, and went inside the house. From inside, I could hear the Mustang speed down the street.

CHAPTER 17: ORION

I had hoped my house would just reclaim me. That hope was shattered the next morning with a nine a.m. phone call from Colonel Sanders. I didn't answer it. It was followed by the beep of a voicemail. Then the chirp of a text message. Then the hum of another call. By eleven, my skin was crawling.

I didn't want to think about my mother. I didn't want to think about Lin. I didn't want to think about staying in Georgia. And the problem with not thinking about those things was I had to think about them anyway because I couldn't stop thinking about Fin and Rose and Mom. And none of those people would be on the other line if I answered the phone.

Lin called it radio silence, but what she never seemed to get is that the silence was the only way I could keep things from getting more fucked up. As the day coursed on, there was a stream of beeping and vibrations from my phone, and on the tablet, and from the laptop. It felt like high school after I was arrested. That year had been constant calls with lawyers and school districts and case managers. Now it was fucking Shively and funeral homes. Every call or message added to the anxiety and the fear and the disappointment. Each message was someone trying to reach someone I didn't know if I could be: friend, client, adult, bereaved son.

Shively would just tell me Mom's ashes were delayed again. And the appraisers would just ask what I planned to do with her things. And Al would ask about Fin or renting the house. And Lin would try to apologize. There were even two phone calls from two schools I had applied to—both rejections, I was sure.

Pacing the house got me through the first day. I disconnected all the devices from their chargers, but they would take days to die, and turning them off seemed like a whole special level of dysfunctional. And then it was dark. Then I woke up. The next day was quieter but still marked by people trying to reach me.

I was afraid of what the news about Mom would be. Even if it wasn't another delay, what would I do with her when she was finally ready? I had thought about spreading her around the house, then I had thought about sending her to Corvus. Then I thought about nothing. Memories of her started to rush in two or three at a time, and I couldn't find the space to sort it out.

The most unsettling part of it all was that Fin didn't call or text. *Fin.* I craved the steadying impact of Fin's hand in mine. All through the drive to the city, Fin had held my hand, and the phone ringing was dulled in comparison to my overwhelming affection for that hand. But none of the messages or calls or emails were from Fin.

I really lost it Monday afternoon. I couldn't handle the hot summer and the house and the constant barrage of the technology and memories. So, I took off on the bike, driving in as long a straight line as I could manage. I wondered how far I could get. It wouldn't be hard to leave GA. There was another state in every direction. I just had to pick one.

But for once, the drive wasn't helping. It was making things worse. I almost ached with the urge to leave and was equally pained by the urge to stay. As I sped over the highways, making a large square around my hometown, I considered every option available to me. The only thing I could really do was wait. And the idea of waiting just made me drive faster.

I was rounding a corner just inside the town limits when my only outlet for my sorrow and anger died as the front tire on the bike hissed and fell flat. I growled and pulled to the side of the road. I was stranded with a large nail in the tire.

I stood looked around to get my bearings. Then I went to the nearest street sign and screamed, shaking the sign by the pole. I spun in a slow circle, looking for people or cars on the street. It was noon and I was alone. I sighed and went back to the bike to inspect the damage.

I hadn't been crouching there for more than a few minutes when the lights and sharp warble of a police cruiser nearly scared the shit out of me. Anxiety sparked in my chest, but I knew I was doing nothing wrong, so I just had to stay calm. *Right?* Still, I stood and lifted my hands enough to show that I was harmless.

"What are you doing, son?" the officer said, stepping out of his cruiser. He was a young guy, but I didn't recognize him. I hated that he had called me *son*. I was no one's son, not anymore. Besides, I probably had three or four years on the guy.

"My bike has a flat, and I'm just trying to figure it out."

"Your bike?"

"Yes."

"Can I see a license and registration?" He pulled a pad of notes and a pencil from his belt.

"Am I doing something wrong?" I said, putting my hands down.

"Standard procedure. License and registration."

I pulled my wallet from my vest pocket and handed over the license. I was fishing for the registration in the saddlebags when the officer grunted. I looked over my shoulder at him.

"Orion Starr?"

"Yeah."

"You got a middle name?"

"Hunter," I said, panic rising since I couldn't find the registration for the bike. I tried to think where I might have put it, but he kept interrupting my thoughts.

"You're from New York?"

"Yup."

"What are you doing in Painted Waters?"

"Mom died."

"When is your birthday?"

"It's on the…" I stopped. The man was giving both me and my license a critical eye. I had been bounced from enough bars at eighteen to know he thought it was a fake.

"Registration?"

I sighed and knew I was in some real shit.

❖

It took about twenty minutes for the officer to load me into the cruiser, read me my rights, and pull into the station. I didn't say anything until I got to booking.

"I want to call someone and let them know I am here," I told the cop behind the counter.

The man ignored me for the most part. He had me put my loose things into a basket including my glasses and hair tie. They let me keep my boots since they didn't have laces. Then I was fingerprinted. I wanted to scream as my first set of prints came up on the screen from my arrest in Atlanta nearly a decade and a half ago.

"See, my license is real."

"Sir—"

"Just let me make my call please?"

"Sir—"

Another cop came up behind me and put a hand on my shoulder, taking me to a holding cell. They didn't take the handcuffs off, either. They just left me in the cream-colored stone room and shut the red metal door behind me. I sighed and pressed my eyes shut. It was fucking impossible. It was impossible to just live. I banged my head against the stone. It was about an hour before anyone came to talk to me.

"You wanted to make a call?" the new officer asked.

"Please."

The officer led me back to the booking desk and placed a phone on the high counter in front of me. I put my still cuffed hand on the receiver and froze. I didn't know any numbers by heart. I racked my brain trying to figure out anyone's number. A cold sweat started to pool at my lower back, and I wondered how far I could get with a desk phone as my only weapon.

Then it was in my mind. Ten numbers. I wanted to bash my face against the counter. I had joked at the time that the number looked like it belonged to a taxi service, the number four repeating except for the three at the end. Al had laughed, saying he got calls from drunks needing a ride home all the time. *Al.* I had no one in the world I could call besides Alexander Fucking Jefferson. The cop near me grunted with irritation, so I jammed in the number.

"Good afternoon, you got Alexander."

"Al, it's Orion."

"Really?"

"Yes, really. Just, fuck…I was arrested, and you are the only phone number I could think of."

"Oh, shit. What for?"

"Never mind. I need you to get hold of my mom's lawyer. He'll help you get someone to get me out of here. You have his number?"

"I have his card back at the office."

"Good. I mean, can you help me?" I felt suddenly stupid. I was suddenly asking a former bully to bail me out.

"Yeah man, don't worry about it. I got you."

"Tha—" I was about to thank Al when another voice cut in and my heart stopped. The other person asked Al if everything was okay. I would know that voice even if I'd gone completely deaf.

"Al, is Fin with you?"

"Yeah. You want to talk to him?"

"Fuck no! You can't tell him I'm here. Don't tell him you're helping me."

"Why not?"

"Al, I don't have time to explain, but come on."

"You're being really dumb."

"Al, now is not the time for you to play therapist, okay? Just get me out of here."

"Fine."

I sighed as the line went dead. My heartbeat was sharp in my chest. How could I face Fin? This was just one more reckless, embarrassing thing to add to the list. One more reason I would never be good enough for him. One more thing that made me hate myself.

It took five hours before anyone came to get me. The officer pulled open the door and held out a hand like a butler. "You have been cleared for release."

"Have I?"

"Yup, your buddies got hold of your lawyer. They're waiting for you in the lobby."

"Bud*dies*?"

I wanted to tell the officer to put me back in the cell and forget about me. I sighed instead and followed him to the booking counter, where my stuff was waiting. I slowly loaded up and went through the metal detectors to where Al and Fin were waiting.

"You okay?" Al asked.

I nodded and looked at Fin. Fin looked angry, his arms crossed over his chest. He gave me a quick once-over, meeting my eyes for a moment. Then he turned his gaze back at the desk where the cops lingered.

Al was cheerful enough for the three of us. "Come on. They said your bike was on the street, so I brought the truck. Figure we can tow it back to your house."

"Thanks. Al. You talk to Shively?"

"Yeah, he says you need to call him as soon as you can."

I just grunted. We left the station in silence and I hunkered down in the front seat of Al's truck. Fin got in the back, and Al took his place behind the wheel.

"I can't fucking believe those people," Fin said. Al looked at him in the mirror as he started the motor. I didn't say anything.

"Yeah, well. It happens," Al said.

"It shouldn't."

"I agree, but you marching around there like you got some kinda power doesn't make things better," Al said. I looked at Al. "Fin lost his shit in there. They threatened to arrest him for acting like he was owed something. I thought he was going to punch a cop."

I looked in the mirror at Fin's angry face. He didn't seem like he wanted to talk to me, so I didn't say anything. Thankfully, Al filled the silence, chattering the whole drive back to my bike. I felt small and ridiculous in the large truck.

After fifteen minutes of nothing but Al talking, Fin put his hand on my shoulder, bringing me suddenly out of my mind back into my body.

"What?"

"Where were you going?"

"Nowhere," I said, knowing that wouldn't satisfy him.

"Were you leaving?" he said, slouching back into the back seat. His words were pointed and hollow all at once, like a needle full of poison.

I rolled my eyes. I didn't want to talk, especially about this. What could I tell him? Saying I wanted to leave would hurt him. But I couldn't promise I'd stay. I knew what he wanted to know. Was I leaving him? Well, fuck that. If he wanted to know where I was, he could have called at any point over the last three days.

"Not this again," I said.

"It's a simple question, Orion," Fin said, his voice dark with anger.

"Fin, I was just fucking arrested, give me a break."

"Wrongfully—" Fin shouted.

"Why did you bring him?" I heard myself asking Al.

"He was already in the truck."

"Didn't want me to find out?"

"No, I didn't."

"Why? One more thing to *not* tell me? Another secret you and Al could keep for another eight years?"

"Excuse me for not wanted to be judged," I said.

Fin sat forward at this, doing his best to look at me. "I have never judged you."

"Not you, Fin. People."

"You didn't want to tell me so other people wouldn't judge you."

"Yes." *So they won't judge you for knowing me. I don't need to be the reason people hate you.* But I didn't say that.

"That makes no fucking sense." Fin sat back again. I knew that was the end of it for the moment.

I seethed in the passenger's seat, fueled by rage at the cops, myself, Al, Fin, and countless other people. I ignored the rising tide of guilt, choosing anger. It felt like I was going to burst into ten thousand pieces. I felt like I needed a drink.

We found the bike where I had been forced to abandon it, and the three of us made quick work of getting it into the truck. While Al and Fin strapped the bike down, I hovered inside the passenger doorway. I didn't know whether to get in it or help, so I did neither.

"You got it from here?" Fin said as he jumped from the bed of the pickup.

"Yeah," Al said. Fin thumped the back of the truck definitively with the flat of his palms and started walking back the way we'd come.

"Wait, where ya going?" Al said.

"Home."

"I can take you."

"Naw, it's fine. I need the walk."

"Fin." I heard the name escape my mouth before I could think. Fin stopped, hesitating. He drew up his posture like he was about to fight and turned.

"You can't just leave," I said, my mouth outpacing my brain by a few heartbeats.

"Hypocritical coming from you."

"What? Just tell me what you're mad about."

"What I am mad about? You were going to leave. You were just going to skip town and never look back because that is what you do. And what the fuck was I going to do? When you left the first time, I at least *knew* you were going. The second time I didn't, and it nearly killed me. Things are so much bigger now between us, Orion, we are— were—fuck, I guess if you were just ready to go, we aren't anything, are we?"

"You're the one who stopped calling."

This sentence seemed to hurt and surprise Fin. He sighed and looked away. I wasn't sure he was going to answer, but he did. "I stopped calling because I couldn't ask you to stay."

"But you can get mad at me for leaving?"

"No, I can get mad at you for leaving *without* telling me you were going."

I didn't have an answer. I was angry, hands clenched into fists, and the anger would never let me explain my feelings. After everything I had been through, now Fin wanted to fight with me about that night.

Well, that sucked for him because I had nothing left. I couldn't explain that I wasn't leaving. I was staying because of him, which made me a shitty person because I should have been staying for my mom. I couldn't explain that even if I *was* there, we shouldn't happen because I was the type of guy to who got arrested and bullied and fired and kicked out, and Fin deserved better than that.

I said, "Everyone leaves, Fin."

"Sure, Orion. But I think the Starrs do it especially well. I think that's all the Starrs are good for."

Those words were like damp wool on my fiery rage. I knew Fin's words were a challenge for me to be different. But I had nothing left to meet that challenge with. As my own rage burned out, I could actually see Fin's transform. His angry face softened and shallowed until the only thing left there was hurt.

When he spoke again, his voice was very small and very broken. "If this is all that it can be between us, well, at least I'm not surprised this time."

Fin seemed to sense my inability to speak. His shoulders slumped, and he shrugged. Then I watched as he disappeared down the road. Al whistled low and long as he too watched Fin leave.

"You okay?"

I wasn't ready to meet his eyes. I just got into the truck. Al finished what he was doing in the back and hopped into the driver's seat. I stared out the window.

"You know, I'm here if you wanna talk…"

I didn't even let him know I had heard him. I was struck with a sudden realization. Even in person, I was silent, always knowing I should say something. *Radio silence.* Sure, it kept me from having to say everything, but it also left no room for other people to say anything either. Being the person who did all the talking was probably just as tiring as being the person who said nothing.

Fin was the person who said things. And now Fin was saying nothing. Did he just get tired of reaching out? It was possible for silence to kill people's will to reach out. I had just seen Al do it. He had offered his company, but his sentence died before he even finished it. I turned so suddenly that Al jumped.

"Hey," Al said, pulling the truck into my yard. Al wasn't who I should be saying things to. Other people deserved to hear a lot more from me. But Al was *there,* reaching, and all I had to do was reach back.

"I wasn't trying to leave."

"I figured."

"How?"

"Your bike was on the way back *into* town, not going away from it."

I sighed, the logic too complete to argue with.

"Orion, why didn't you tell that to Fin?"

"I don't know."

Al nodded and patted me on the shoulder. Then I was helping Al get the bike out of the truck. Then I was lying on the floor of my bathroom. Then I was nothing. But I promised myself I wouldn't stay nothing for long.

Chapter 18: Fin

I made it home after Rose was already in bed. I took a long shower and went to sleep, determined to return my life to normal. My run the next morning was a nightmare. As I ran, I did the math. It had been only three weeks. Three weeks and Orion was as deeply embedded as he had ever been, maybe more so. I didn't want to accept it. I'd had relationships four times as long, and those guys were lucky if I could remember their names. *Not Orion.* Every minute with Orion seemed like a lifetime. And I was tired.

And I was pushing my run. It was a cool morning, and my raw muscles took a while to warm. Then I pushed the pace, my lungs burning, my heartbeat like a hailstorm against my chest. And in all of that sensation, I couldn't shake the gentle brush of Orion's lips during that first kiss, or the heat of us together in the kitchen, or the warmth and safety we'd had only days ago.

I was rounding a corner when my vision blotched with white spots and my throat tightened. I had to stop running, and I puked near a tree in a park. Thankfully it was early enough that no one was around. I hadn't pushed myself to puking since freshman year. I stood upright, and my legs and back felt like they were made of steel. I started walking back toward my house. Without really knowing how, I made it home. I ate something and punished myself more by taking as cold a bath as I could manage. Rose was waiting for me when I came out of my room.

She crossed her arms. "What is the matter, Frank?"

"Rosey," I said, pulling at the hem of my shirt. I didn't know how to say the next part without bursting into tears, so I took a deep breath. "I think things are over with Orion."

She didn't say anything. She just opened her arms and accepted me against her. And I did cry.

CHAPTER 19: ORION

Days passed, unchecked. I lay in bed watching movies on the old TV in my room. Every device in the house had finally died, so there was no longer a constant parade of callers. I didn't notice what day it was until Friday morning, when I awoke to the sound of glass breaking downstairs. I was out of bed accessorized with a bat in no time. My heart was beating in my throat and I was annoyed. I mean, why break a window if you wanted to rob me? It wasn't like my doors were locked.

But it was only a picture that had crashed to the floor. I laughed, feeling stupid, and crouched amongst the glass. That photo had hung by the door since the day we had moved in. It was a photo of a red bicycle leaning against a pastoral stone building. Mom had that photo since she was a kid. The day we'd moved in, she'd hung it on the wall by the front door. And it proceeded to crash to the floor at least once a year.

Hunter. Mom's voice came to me. I had been teasing her about hanging the picture for the fourth time. *This picture deserves to be picked up just as much as any of the rest of us. We all fall, Hunter.*

I sighed and went for a broom. Mom had always said things like that. She believed that no matter how hard a person fucked up, they could always do the work to pick up the pieces. As I pushed glass into a dustpan, I considered her words. I poured the glass into an empty pizza box and stuffed it into the trash. Mom's words repeated. Again. And again. I had fucked up, I guess. But getting arrested and my mother dying weren't really my fault, so maybe I just *felt* fucked up. And that was something to consider.

How do you feel less fucked up? It's like riding a bike, I thought stupidly as I picked up the bike photo and propped it on the table by the door. *You just gotta pick yourself up.* I hate me. *One piece at a time*, my brain added.

"All right, that's not helping," I said to myself.

When I wanted Crow to think I wasn't fucked up, I showered. So, I showered. When I wanted Mom to believe that I was fine, I called her. The first thing I did after my shower was put every device in the house back on a charger. It took a few minutes to get my phone back online. And it took a few more minutes to work up the nerve to call Shively. Al said Shively had handled everything about getting me released, even going as far as having my bike registration and birth certificate faxed to the police department, so they didn't have a choice but to hear him out. I felt embarrassed as the phone rang.

Shively answered after a few seconds. "Ah, so calleth the free."

"Yeah. I, uh...wanted to say thanks for helping me, I know you are not a criminal lawyer or whatever."

"Ah, I am not. But nor are you a criminal, so there we have it."

I grunted, but his words made me feel slightly better. They echoed Fin's outrage at the injustice, and my own insistence that I hadn't done anything wrong. I said, "Still, I know you didn't have to—"

"Your mother was a good woman. *Mr. Shively*, she said to me, *help my sons if you can.*"

"Well, you do—did."

"Right. Have you had the chance to hear my other messages?"

I sighed and sat on the edge of the coffee table. I ran a hand through my wet hair. "No, sir."

"That's fine. I can detail the information now if you're ready."

I wasn't sure I was, but I said yes anyway.

"Your mother is ready for you," he said.

"I...what?"

"Her remains have been prepared. I know this can be a bit much, so I took the liberty of having them carried from here in the city to the funeral home in your hometown. I thought the reduced distance might ease some of the stress."

I sighed, relieved. "Today?"

"Yes, today, although your mother once said, 'There's no reason to be in a hurry over the dead; it's not like they're going anywhere.' She was a funny one."

I just laughed. I hadn't intended to deal with Mom. Then I looked across at the bicycle photo. Maybe it was time.

"Text me the address?"

"I already have."

I found some coffee, cleaned out my voicemail, and was at the funeral home in time for my two o'clock appointment. I waited in the parlor for the director. He was a short man with a fake tan and trimmed ear hair.

"Mr. Starr," the director said.

"Mr. Fleet."

"This way." Mr. Fleet turned and went toward the back of the main coffin showroom. "Mrs. Margery Starr." Mr. Fleet gestured.

I stopped dead in my tracks. He was indicating an ornate urn on a stand. The jar stood nearly two feet tall and had carved gold snakes for handles. A scene of a unicorn stabbing a goose standing in a field was painted on the front.

"That?" I gasped after a second.

Mr. Fleet gave a terse nod and went over to the urn. He pulled a card from his pocket, slammed his feet together, and looked down his nose at the card.

"Ha. Ha. Just kidding," Mr. Fleet read blandly. He then reached behind the urn and pulled forward a sleek silver canister that could have easily been a coffee thermos.

I felt my mouth hang open. *A joke.* It was a joke Mom had orchestrated, and it was so much better Mr. Fleet had to be the one to tell it. My heart did that thing it did when there was something happening that was worth its attention.

I took the canister from Mr. Fleet with a sigh. "Didn't see that coming."

"Indeed," Mr. Fleet said before turning to leave the hall. I followed, looking down at the futuristic object in my hands.

"She also instructed that you have this," Fleet said, holding an envelope out to me. I took it quickly, afraid of what it might be.

Midge. With the canister in my hands, I felt a calm wash over me. I had a sudden sense of the proximity of my mother, not in the canister, but all around me. I hadn't felt her at the funeral. But she was there, with her tacky jokes and sleek canister. And strangely, the debt collectors for all the things I owed my mother were silent.

"Instructions for caring for your loved one. Have a good day, Mr. Starr," Mr. Fleet said, handing me a sheet of paper. He did not wait for me to answer before he went back into his office.

It was raining by the time I made it back to the car, the rain drumming on the ragtop. I looked at the urn in the passenger seat. My mother. *Midge*. I looked at the envelope and at the handwriting on the front. It was nearly unintelligible, but I knew what it said. *Hunter*. I reminded myself that I could do this as I slipped my fingers under the envelope tab.

I wasn't surprised to find a handwritten note scrawled across a few sheets of legal paper. I flipped them open and smoothed over the words with my hand. I read.

> *Hunter,*
>
> *I figured you wouldn't read this until long after my funeral so I'll start by saying don't be mad if no one comes. I didn't want them to. I wouldn't want you to, either, but I knew you wouldn't listen. I also knew you'd have a hard time reading this letter, so I just left it with someone until you were ready.*
>
> *Don't worry, Hunter. I'm not in any hurry. Put me in a box or toss me out on the highway, it doesn't matter. Whatever you do, I know it will be because you love me, and I know it will free you.*
>
> *I wanted to apologize. I look back at these last few months, and I wish I hadn't been so selfish. I suppose what they tell people about terminal shit is that you have the right to live your last few moments the way you need to or want to. I wanted to live them in a way I thought was normal. I wanted to live them in a way that I thought would cause the least amount of damage.*
>
> *Did it work? I'll never know. Or maybe I already do. I am sorry I might have deprived you of something you needed. Closure maybe?*

I have always told you "no guilt." I also know advice is easy enough to give and that I carried a lot of guilt for a long time. But you don't have to. Especially not toward me. I am dead, son. No one is coming to collect.

I hope the time you spent waiting on me didn't make you too crazy. I know you hate GA. I left you the house because you're always looking for a home. But as I write this, I realize you weren't ever like Crow and me. We just wanted somewhere to BE. You aren't like your father either. He just wanted somewhere to GO. But you were always mine, and you're probably lost now. You were always looking for SOMEONE. I was always someone you could be sure about. But you are going to need a new someone. So let yourself find them.

Find someone who will check on you and let them care about you.

I almost couldn't read anymore. I missed her with every part of my soul. Her words brought Lin and Corvus to mind. I owed them so many apologies. I wiped my eyes with the backs of my hands and looked back at the page.

Find someone who can share in your victories and help you heal when you are defeated.

I thought of Rose and Al and Grace. People who were somehow happy to see me. People who were interested in what I was doing.

Find someone who you can love, and let that love anchor you. You may never find SOMEWHERE to be, but you can find SOMEONE to stick to. You deserve people who love you, Hunter. You deserve to love yourself. You deserve things. You are so hard on yourself, thinking you had to be perfect or good to be worth the love I have for you, or worth your brother's love, or whoever. You don't have to be anything but you. You can have people all over the world who love you.

And of course, the only person who came to mind was Fin. I didn't know if Fin loved me, but I had fallen hard for him. Love had worked its way into me.

> *Don't worry, you aren't as lost as you think. When you dump my ashes, I will melt into the earth and spread like water, then I will be everywhere. And you will always be home.*

I lost it. I cough-cried into the sleeve of my shirt, the letter bunched in my fist. I almost couldn't breathe with the rush of emotion. It took me whole minutes to regroup enough to be able to see the few remaining words on the page.

> *I guess I should also tell you that your father called me. He wanted to talk with you boys and was sorry to learn I was dying. I told him to fuck off and that if you or Crow wanted to see him, you would look for yourself. I took down his address anyway. He missed out on the best part of watching you and your brother become good men. And if you never reach out to him, I won't lose any sleep over it. I got the good stuff.*

I looked at the address. My father's name was written there, Dave Starr. The address was for some town in Arizona. I knew my parents met there, but I was surprised. After all these years I had never once thought about where my father might have ended up. I returned to the letter.

> *Don't lose your brother.*
> *Don't hold on to me too hard. I am always with you.*
> *Since you never check anyway, I will tell you, I dropped 10,000 in your bank account. Don't tell Crow. I knew you would give him all the cash, but I didn't want you to want either. Since I have never written a posthumous letter I'll say goodbye the only way I know how.*
> *Knock knock*

Tears flowed with fresh abundance as I laughed, but these tears were different. Up to those two words, all the other tears had been grief and loss. Mom's joke brought the kind of tears people cry when something beautiful happens. I felt suddenly light, radiating. I imagined that that was how my mother felt, what she meant by *free*. I read on.

> *Who's there?*
> *Interrupting cow*

Halfway over the top of the words *interrupting cow who?* was a giant red sharpie *MOO!* I laughed. There were only three sentences left. The last three sentences my mother would ever say to me. Going forward everything would be a memory, but for one moment more I had something new from her. And that something new turned out to be the most ancient thing a mother could say to a son.

> *I love you. I love you. I love you.*

Those three sentences dripped into me and soaked into my bones. And that was it. I sat in the car, rain flowing all around me, and I cried. I cried because I really, truly missed her. I wasn't exactly sad that she had died, I wasn't exactly lonely because she was gone. I was homesick.

When the tears finally stopped, I carefully folded the papers and put them in the glove box. Then I looked at her ashes.

"Home, I guess," I said to her and started the car.

Arriving home brought a new sensation as I carried Mom into the house. I glanced at the instructions and considered where to put her, at least until I could figure out where to spread her ashes. I considered the mantel, but she had always said a fireplace in Georgia was dumb. I wondered what her favorite part of the house had been. The answer was simple.

I carried her up to her room and was surprised to find my guitar on the bed. I didn't remember leaving it there. Putting Mom's ashes down on the nightstand, I crossed to pick up the guitar. Then I saw a photo on her dresser that I hadn't noticed before. It was me and Fin at the lake, the same photo on the desk in Fin's room.

Fin. I didn't know how to think about Fin. I looked down at the guitar and strummed. Then Fin's voice drifted into my head. *I think that's all the Starrs are good for.* Mom's letter said I deserved people who loved me. I barely liked myself. Then again, her letter also said I deserved to love myself. I sighed. I loved Fin, and I had a feeling Fin loved me. Mom loved me. My brother loved me. Lin and Rose and Grace and maybe even Al. I didn't know about deserve, but maybe I had it anyway.

I took the photo and the guitar downstairs. The photo sat by the guitar on the couch while I was in the garage getting the rainwater off the Mustang. Then I came inside and started to play. I couldn't fully focus on the words Fin had given me, but I knew there was a song there. Instead I played through some others. When I looked up again, it was dark and my stomach growled. As I ordered Chinese food, I vowed to go to the store in the morning.

And I did go to the grocery store. Filling my fridge and cabinets gave me a nostalgic feeling. I thought about watching Fin fill the kitchen. I guess if I wanted to make Fin think I was okay, I would have to buy groceries. I wondered how people did this. How did other people move on? I guess counseling? I didn't know. After breakfast, I picked up my guitar again. I was working to pull together a song from the last few words I had shared with Fin. Some hours later I managed a first verse and chorus:

> *Stars streak across the sky. I scream, but they pass me*
> *I wish I may I wish I might, but what's the point no one's listening*
> *I wish to take back the words I didn't mean*
> *I wish for the chance be what we could have been*
> *but nothing's changed and the night turns to dawn*
> *a thousand wishes and you stay gone*
> *Wishing for you, wishing for time*
> *Trying to force the stars to align*
> *Wishing for right, wishing for free*
> *Wondering what you must think of me*
> *Wishing for peace, wishing to heal*
> *Asking the universe to make a deal*
> *Wishing for sleep, wishing for trust*

Hoping you remember what was great about us
Wishing back what we had before
But wishing is all the stars are good for

"*Oh my God!*" a woman screamed, breaking my concentration. I screamed and jumped from my stool, hauling the guitar over my shoulder like a bat. I had it poised to strike when I recognized Lin. Even through my fright, I was happy to see her. She looked like the star of a music video as she grinned at me, her hair falling over one shoulder, her sheer overshirt slipping off the other.

"For fuck's sake, *Lin.*" I slipped back onto the stool. She laughed and put a coffee down on the counter. I assumed it was for me since she had another in her hand.

"You wouldn't have hit me. You like that guitar."

"I have better ones. What are you doing here?"

"I heard through the local gossip channels that you were arrested. And you're an asshole because you called Alexander fucking Jefferson instead of me."

"I couldn't remember your number." I took a sip of the coffee.

"And you could remember his?" I recited Al's number. Her eyes went wide. "Yup. That is easy to remember. So, tell me everything."

Lin found a stool of her own and propped her elbows on the counter. I considered opening with an apology. *Ending radio silence.* But the look on her face and the coffee gift told me we were good. I loved Lin. I steadily told her the whole story.

At the end, I expected judgment or criticism, even from her. But Lin just slammed her palms on the counter, angry but not at me. "Fuck! Orion, those fucking cops! I can't even. And Fin…he wow, I can't even with him, either. Is that what the new song is about?"

"Yeah, that was sort of the last thing he said. More or less."

"What a dick."

"I thought you liked Fin," I said, strumming to cover my nervousness.

"I love Finny, but you are my soul mate. I will defend you to the grave. Are you gonna play the song for him?"

"It's not finished."

"Well, let's finish this shit. It's so beautiful, O."

Something occurred to me, like an echo resonating deep inside. "Why don't you ever call me Hunter?"

"Thought it was your mom's thing."

"Crow does it. You call Crow *Crow*."

Lin nodded resolutely. Then she said it like she had said it a hundred thousand times. "It's so beautiful, Hunter."

CHAPTER 20: FIN

The weekend passed in a blur of work. The days were measured by the completion of manageable tasks. I graded four different assignments for the two professors I worked under. I wrote a report. I analyzed data. I wrote emails. I answered voicemails. I searched for reference papers for my own research. I read chapters of medical books. And most importantly, I didn't think about Orion.

At least, not until after dark. Thoughts of Orion were unstoppable when I was lying in bed. I would try to fall asleep, but all I could think about was his arms around me. Then I would wake with the fantasy that Orion would be lying with me. Or that Orion had come in the night, slept, and was gone before I woke. None of it happened. And I felt stupid for wanting it. So I kept my head down and tried to force my life forward.

Rose didn't ask questions about what happened. She had just heard me out when I needed to vent. Then she hugged me and left it alone. I didn't even realize it was Monday until Al asked me to lunch. I waited for him to show up at the house. Then got in the van. Before I thought too hard about it, I was sitting at a table in a diner holding a menu.

"Frank," Al nearly shouted.

"What...sorry." I knew he had been talking, but I had not been listening.

"Come on, man, what is going on?" Al punctuated his question by drumming his fingers on the table.

"You already know."

We were a town over, at a diner Al's sister worked at, but she didn't appear to be on shift. It was Al's favorite place. The interior was robin's-egg blue and chrome, with red leather booths surrounding a horseshoe bar. The cooks worked in the middle of the bar so you could watch them flip pancakes and brown sausage. It was a twenty-four-hour place on the edge of town, and it only served breakfast. Al and I were sitting in a booth along the windows. I caught the eyes of a passing man who glared at me, so I looked at my menu.

"All right, fine, but what're you so upset about? You broke it off with him, man."

"He was *leaving*." I slapped down the menu. The waitress jumped as she tried to put down coffee. I felt myself blush as I helped her mop up the spill. I said to her, "Sorry."

"That's all right, hon. Al, it's good to see you. How's Kel and the girls?"

"Thanks, Gladys, good to see you, too. The fam is great. The older ones start soccer soon."

"Sounds nice. What can I do ya for?"

"Can I get egg meal number two," Al said, handing the woman the menu. I heard Al order but didn't order myself, I didn't even look up from the coffee cup. Al grunted with annoyance. "Get him an egg meal number two and an Oreo milkshake."

"Sure thing, love."

I could feel Al stare at me with ten thousand questions just waiting to be asked. We were silent for a moment. I didn't look around. I didn't think. I didn't feel. Because all those things led back to Orion.

"He wasn't leavin', you know." Al's voice was soft and slightly muffled by the coffee mug at his lips.

I looked up, unsure what I had just heard. "What?"

"He told me."

"When? What? Al!"

"Don't shout, man. He told me in the truck. He said he wasn't leavin'."

"What the hell was he doing then?"

"Drivin'."

I could have died. Unsure of what to do, I raised the mug off the table. *Orion wasn't leaving?* Why would Orion stay? Why wouldn't he leave? I couldn't even manage enough focus to sip the hot beverage, so I lowered the mug back to the worn dark blue tablecloth. Before I committed to a real reaction, I asked Al, "You believe him?"

"Yeah. He was on his way back into town when he got a flat. I mean, think about where his bike was."

I folded up in the booth and moaned into my hands. I had been so worked up from the trip to the city. And Orion hadn't contacted me after. I hadn't contacted Orion either. I was sure Orion was ready to go. I was sure Lin had said her good-byes. And I had been so surprised by Orion's anger at me. And that made me even angrier. *What right did Orion have to be mad at someone for not contacting him? He never contacted anyone. So why did it matter what I did?*

I sighed and tried to regroup. I was so easily distracted by my own anger that I didn't hear Al's words. Not really. So, I repeated them in my head. *He was on his way back into town...he was on his way back into town.* Why? Did Orion want to stay? How much of it was me? How much of it was Marge? I sighed, slumping on the table.

"He really wasn't leaving?"

"Naw."

"God, I'm an ass."

"Yup."

"Fuck, why didn't he tell me himself?"

"You were yellin' at him," Al said with a laugh.

"I am glad you think this is funny."

Al just shrugged.

"Why did he tell you?"

"I wasn't yellin' at him—"

"Fuck you, Al."

"Naw, I'm serious. You and Orion are exactly the same. Both of ya want words of affirmation from people but neither of ya know how to say shit."

"I say things."

"No, you yell things. They say if you're yellin' you ain't listenin'."

"Who says that?"

"It's in one of Kel's books."

"She reads relationship books?"

"Yup, she reads and I listen. You yell," Al said, not letting me off the hook. I couldn't disagree anyway.

We were silent for a few minutes. Gladys brought the food and Al dug in. I just poked at my eggs and sucked the milkshake through a straw. I replayed that day in my mind, thinking about Orion and the bike and the words I said. I said so many terrible things.

"Al."

"Frank."

"Am I nuts?" I said, dropping my fork loudly. The other patrons turned to look at me.

"For?"

"For caring about him as much as I do?"

"I married Kelley after two months. I knew I loved her the day I met her."

"Yeah, but that's you."

"Damn right it's me. I don't waste time like you," Al said, drawing my plate closer so he could eat my potatoes.

"What do you mean?"

"It's been a decade."

"No, it's been less than—"

"Naw. If you get back with someone, it all counts, all the time then and all the time in between. You both seem pretty hell-bent on bein' stuck in the past anyway. You cared about him then and never stopped. So…" Al said with a resolute shrug, stabbing the potatoes into long rows on his fork.

"It seems crazy."

"So what?"

I sighed and pulled my plate back. We ate in silence. Then I considered Al. Al was a good-looking man, all blond hair and light brown eyes. He could have been a model, not like a traditional one, but the dad bod kind. Al had been my best friend since middle school. Al had loved me in one way or another since we were kids. I loved Al, too. So why was it Orion and not Al? Or anyone else in the world.

"Quit lookin' at me like that."

"Sorry. Why him? Why him and not anyone else?"

"Who cares?"

I was suddenly exasperated. "What do you mean *who cares*?"

"You want him, he wants you—what does the why matter for? Better yet, can you think of a reason why *not* him?"

Al seemed to be getting frustrated with me now. I had seen less and less of his temper over the years, especially since he had kids, but the way he was chewing the inside of his cheek, I knew his buttons were being pushed.

"And ta be honest, Frank, it's that attitude right there that made it so Orion didn't want you at the jail. He thinks he's not good enough for ya, and if you go around asking *why*, he sure as hell won't ever believe he is."

"He doesn't think he is good enough for me, and being arrested, he didn't want to seem even less good for me?"

"Ah, welcome to reality, Dr. Ness. Can I get you more coffee?"

"Ugh, I really wish he would get off that horse."

"Well, he had a lot of people telling him to get on it, so cut the guy some slack."

"Did he?"

"Hell yeah. Why'd you think he was so easy to bully? He was told that when his dad left, when he got kicked out of his old school, when I was up his ass—the whole damned world tells him he's not good enough just for being brown. I get how he feels a little. Someone has to tell us we're doin' something worthwhile, that we *are* fucking worthwhile. His mom's gone, Frank, and the guy has, like, one friend. Fucking cut him some slack. Damn, I'm worked up now." Al pulled his hat off and slapped it on the table. "Listen, he needs people in his corner, so quit fighting him."

"I tried that, and he stopped talking to me for six years."

"Come again?" Al blinked at me.

CHAPTER 21: FIN

I considered the best way to tell Al the story. I sighed and poked my eggs. "You remember when I had that busted hand in undergrad, and I told you I got it in a fight and you laughed and said I was probably just jerking off too hard?"

Al snorted, looking around at the other patrons. We were practically alone. Everyone around us had pretty much left, and only singles were coming in and sitting at the bar. Al looked at me. "What, you were really in a fistfight?"

I nodded. He stared. I sighed. "A week before that fight I went to one of Lin's shows in the city."

❖

It had been a hot summer in Rhode Island. I felt like I was sweating my nuts off, and that was saying a lot since I was from Georgia. I had to stand in line for nearly thirty minutes waiting to show the bouncer my ticket and ID so I could go inside. I was so relieved to finally get into the bar.

I saw Lin right way, putting CDs in stacks on a table. The area around her was covered with band merchandise, and she was surrounded by people. It took some elbowing, but I made it across the crowd. I tapped her shoulder and she practically climbed me with excitement.

"Finny!"

"Hey, Lin! Good crowd."

She grinned as I set her on the ground. "Naw, I mean yeah—they're for the headliner, though. We're just the opening act."

"Well, good. The crowd will be sober enough to remember you."

She brightened. Then she glanced over her shoulder at a guy behind the table. He had been talking to a potential customer when I'd walked up, so I hadn't really looked at him. But once I did, I knew who it was in an instant. Lin caught my hand and started to pull me toward him.

"Orion," she called once we could be heard over the din. He turned, saw me, and looked like he was about to piss himself. Then he smiled. That stupid smile.

"I think you remember Franklin," she said, patting my hand.

"I remember."

"Good, sell him a shirt," she said, walking away.

"Did she plan that?" Al said. He was so enthralled by my story that he let his coffee get cold. I waved Gladys over to refill our cups.

"I wouldn't put it past her."

"What did he say?"

"He said, 'what size?'"

"What size? Lord almighty! Is that how the dudes were doing it in those days?"

"That's what I said. He meant shirt."

"Oh, sure."

"Anyway, he gave me a shirt and I ended up behind the table helping him sell merch all night. When the headliner was doing their encore, we were making out in the bathroom."

Al rolled his eyes and sipped his coffee.

"Fin," Orion breathed into my neck. He had me backed up against the wall of the stall. I almost couldn't hear him over the sound of my own breathing and the pulse of the music. I couldn't think with his hands on my hips, his body pressed against me.

"I have to go," he said, sounding genuinely sad about it.

I laughed. "No way."

Then I kissed him, wrapping my arms around his body to keep him against me. I pushed him up against the other side of the stall, pressing him into the graffitied metal. He grunted with a sound I took for satisfaction. He kissed like he was drinking me in. Then he seemed to remember what he was doing and pulled back.

"Fin, I don't want to. I have to."

I stared at him.

He swallowed and ran a hand over his short, messy hair. "Listen, I can't believe this, but I've got to get the next train back to New York. I have to be at work in seven hours."

He had to pull his phone out of his pocket to check the time.

"Oh, okay," I said, backing up to lean against the other side of the stall.

He looked at me, gold eyes alive with mischief. "You know, there's a train back here next weekend."

"What?" I didn't have enough blood in my brain to think straight.

He laughed. "Give me your phone number."

"You want to see me again?" I said, pulling my phone out of my pocket and handing it to him.

He shrugged. His comment was casual, but his eyes were too alive for me to believe it. "I wouldn't say no."

"So," Al said when I paused to drink more of the melted milkshake.

"So, we talked on the phone for the whole week."

"Baww."

"Stop it or I won't tell you the rest."

He held his hands up.

"So, then he came back the next weekend. He booked a hotel and was going to stay Saturday into Sunday."

"Was going to?"

"Well, things were great. We had dinner, I showed him campus—"

"You showed him campus?"

"He wanted to see it."

"Nerds."

"Whatever. Anyway, we decided to go out for a drink."

Al's eyes went wide. "You didn't."

"I did. I took him to Mark's."

"Geez, I can't imagine a worse place for a guy like him," Al said. I agreed.

❖

Mark's was the last place Orion would be comfortable. It was a posh med school bar in the center of the city. It had overpriced drinks and dickhead patrons who thought they were smart shit because they were in med school. It was a huge mistake. But at the time, I thought it would be fine. My ID was still pretty new and Mark's didn't harass me about my age. Orion looked out of place amongst the white and pink polos and pale skin.

"This…is a place," Orion said, following me into the bar, the chains and buckles on his clothes making a distinct clatter.

"Yeah, all the med school students come here. Is it okay?"

"It's fine," he said, but I couldn't place his expression.

We ordered at the bar, and I tugged him into a booth near the front of the room, hoping it would make him more comfortable. It didn't take long. He sat facing the door, with the rest of the bar behind him. I watched it become more crowded with faces from my classes and labs. But Orion seemed only interested in talking to me. And I felt like I was the only person in the world.

Then the shit hit the fan. I got up to go to the bathroom, and he went to the bar to get another round. On my way back, I overheard a guy say, "But that's that kid from Byron's class. Ness something."

Of course, I stopped to listen.

"So what?" a second guy said.

"Well, look at who he's with."

"So? Let him slum if he wants to," a third added. That raised my blood pressure a little, the first tendrils of rage starting in my guts. But I didn't say anything. The three guys were the overly clean, neat types who had memberships at expensive gyms and wore boat shoes everywhere. I had seen them in my class, sitting in the back, harassing women and the occasional gay kid who sat too close.

"Yeah, more like Slumdog Millionaire," the second guy said.

"Listen, if that twink wants to spend his life getting stopped by TSA agents, then let him."

I almost couldn't see, I was so enraged. I stepped up to the group. "Wow, homophobia and racism all in one sentence."

The three turned to me, no shame or remorse in their faces. In fact, they looked pretty happy to see me.

"I don't know what you're talking about," the first guy said smugly.

"Playing dumb doesn't have as much of an impact if you're *actually* dumb."

The guy made a move toward me, but one of his buddies caught him.

"Fuck off, fag," the second guy said.

"Whoever smelt it dealt it," I said, stupidly. Who knew that would get under their skin? The second guy was off his stool and in my face in an instant.

"I'm not a fag."

"And my friend isn't a slumdog."

"I thought *you* had bad taste, but maybe it's your friend who's slumming."

"Well, he *was* with your mom last night."

I'm not sure who punched me, the bones below my eye burning and the room taking a steep tilt to one side. Then there was a blur and Orion was shoving his fist through one of the guys' teeth. The third one came after me, but I got to him first, my hand connecting with his huge nose. Then my hand was on fire. The room exploded into a commotion as people swarmed to break up the fight. Orion and I were carted outside and told to go home.

"I can't believe those guys," I said, flicking blood off my dripping hand. We started walking away from the bar toward nothing, just away.

Orion pulled his bandana off his vest where it was tied and wrapped it around my hand. "At least our drinks were free."

❖

"I honestly thought it was fine after that," I told Al. He was staring at me.

"But?"

"We made it back to Orion's hotel in what I would have called a good mood, aside from being beat up a little. But then the school called."

"The school?"

"Well, my coach. He told me the bar owner had called the school, and they had called him. It was like one in the morning."

❖

I was sitting on the bathroom counter of Orion's hotel room, and he was leaning over my hand inspecting the wound. I hadn't wanted to go to the hospital, and he was trying to see if he needed to change my mind. I was inspecting the gash he had above his eye. The phone rang, and without thinking about it, I put it on speaker.

"Hello."

"Ness? It's Coach Michaels."

"Hi, Coach."

"You know why I am calling?"

"I can guess."

"What the hell were you thinking? You know who called me? A dean. And do you know what he said? He said if anything like this happened again, you'd be out."

"Out? Like what, suspended?" Orion was doing a decent job of pretending like he wasn't listening.

"Damn near. They said it violated the terms of your admittance, and that by all rights, you should lose your scholarship. I reminded them that your grades were good, and from the way the guys on the team who were in the bar tell it, the assholes you and your friend punched were making comments."

"They were being racist homophobes. And it wasn't just about Orion, it was about me, too. Am I still in, then?"

"Yeah, Ness. But this is your one and only warning. Your scholarship is the only reason you're here, so keep that in your head. I will see you tomorrow. We aren't done talking." The coach disconnected the call before I even got the chance to say goodbye.

"That was close."

Orion looked at me with a hard expression, but he didn't say anything. He finished wrapping gauze around my hand and secured it with surgical tape. Then he left the bathroom and went to the window.

"O?" I said, following him. "You okay?"

"I don't think this will work out."

My stupid heart snapped in half. "Care to tell me why?"

"I don't want you to get kicked out of school."

"What does that have to do with us?"

He sighed and faced me. "You got in that fight because of what those guys were saying about me."

"And what they were saying about *me*," I said, hoping it would change the course of his thoughts. "But it's not like it will happen again—"

"It might."

"Might is nothing."

"Think about my life, Fin. How many fights have you been in? How many times were you arrested for it? It happens to me—"

"Once."

"Once is enough to change everything." He slumped and landed on the bed. "The arrest, once. The fights, too often. People say shit about me, Fin. And if your first reaction is to punch them all, then we will have serious issues."

"It's not my first reaction. Orion, I'm not afraid of that."

"That's because you don't know how bad it can get."

I was floundering. I didn't know what to do. He was so earnest. I stared into his sad eyes, and I could already see that he was leaving me. I wanted him back. Back in the hotel with me. Back in my life. Back. I reached out for him.

"Orion," I said, kneeling in front of him. I slipped a hand under his chin and raised it so he would look at me. He let out a breath like he had been holding it. "Look, let's talk about it tomorrow. I've enjoyed our night together. We can talk about it when it's not so close."

He nodded.

❖

"Oh shit," Al said.

"Yup."

"What happened?"

"We had sex."

Al choked on his coffee. He stared at me through watering eyes. I stared back.

"Then he left. I had fallen asleep. I woke up, and he was gone. And that was all the contact until this summer aside from an email or two and a phone call."

"Wow."

"I know, but thinking about it now, I guess I hear it. I understand how he could have been so worried he thought the best thing was to leave. He was expelled for fighting because he loved his mother. Then you and Coach warn him not to mess with me—"

Al groaned and scrubbed his hand over his hair.

"I know, I know. But then he gets in a fight at a bar because of his feelings for me. Then he got arrested the other day. I get it. But how do I get past it?"

"I don't know, but I'd try if it was me."

I rolled my eyes. I felt my face burn with shame and my guts ache from finally talking to someone about that night. I hadn't even given Rose all the details. But I was seeing everything Orion had been trying to tell me for the first time. I was so caught up in what I wanted from Orion that I didn't see *why* he was doing it.

"Have you really not heard from him?" I said. Al shook his head. But it was a prophetic moment, because Al's phone chirped. I watched him idly, thinking it was most likely Kelley with a cute photo of something one of the girls was doing. Al's face brightened with surprise, then dipped into concern. Then he looked at me.

"Something wrong?" I put a hand up trying to catch a waitress. One came and I ordered pancakes. Al watched and waited to answer.

"I just got a *thanks I owe you a beer* text from Orion."

I felt myself pale. I tried to keep emotion from my face. I didn't know if it was a good thing or a bad thing or both. Happy for Al. Sad for myself. Proud of Orion. Surprised, unsurprised. Annoyed. Indifferent.

"Neat."

"Neat?"

I went to open my mouth when my own phone vibrated. I nearly dropped it on the floor trying to get it out of my pocket. I did manage to land an elbow in my eggs. I could feel Al's eyes on me, but I didn't look at him. I just wiped my arm and thumbed open the notification. I knew my expression had fallen because Al gave me a sympathetic look.

"What happened?" Al said.

I had to swallow before I could answer. "It's a new video on Lin's YouTube. It's Orion."

"Oh. You gonna watch it? I could watch it with you."

"No, I…" I put the phone on the table and stabbed my pancakes. "Can we talk about anything else?"

Al gave me a soft smile and started recounting some of the cute and funny things his girls had been up to. I loved Al's kids, so I was happy to sit and listen. And while I listened, I considered ways to be better. I considered ways to approach Orion, ways to do things differently so it wouldn't have to end the way it always had.

I waited until Al was done with his stories and was working on getting the check so we could go. "Al."

"Yeah?"

"Thank you. You're a great friend."

"All right, all right." I didn't miss the embarrassment on his face.

I grinned and then froze, my phone vibrating again. I looked down, Orion's name shining up from the screen. I looked at the phone. I looked at Al. I looked at my empty plate.

"You gonna answer?"

The phone felt like it weighed a thousand pounds as I pulled it up to read. *Hey. Can you help me with something? Come over tonight? 8?*

"Damn, what's that mean?" Al said.

"I don't know."

"What'll you say?"

I stared at the words. I had stopped expecting the text, maybe never expected it. But there it was. I knew what I wanted to say, which was some combination of I'm sorry and I love you. But that seemed wrong. *Sure. Should I bring anything?*

No just yourself. Orion's response was surprisingly fast. Orion had never been a texter, but he was texting me.

And I blushed and typed *Okay. Hey, I saw the new video, well not watched it yet but saw it was up.*

Oh.

Yeah. I am proud of you. You've done a lot with your music, and

I didn't really give you credit for it. I tease you a lot, but I also wanted you to know I am proud of you, too.

Thanks. I got things to do, but I will see you later.

Stay out of jail! I doubt they will let you have a guitar in there. Can you play a harmonica?;)

Fuck off, Franklin.

I could almost feel the shine of Orion's smile in the message. I had taken a risk by adding the joke but I wanted to reduce the impact of the out-of-character conversation. He called me Franklin, so he found it annoying but amusing. I was just about to type more when a text came back from Orion.

Thanks for saying the thing. See you tonight.

I beamed into my phone as I read over the conversation again. I didn't know what it all meant, but it was something. And I was going to hold on to that as hard as I could.

"Damn, we need to leave. I can't take this," Al said. He tossed some cash on the table for the check. I tossed some in, too.

"What?"

"You were hard to watch when you were sad, but this gooey-looking dope is worse. What'd you say?"

I passed over my phone as I drew myself out of the booth. Al did the same, still reading the messages. It wasn't until we were out on the street that Al spoke. "Damn, you guys are cute."

CHAPTER 22: ORION

I spent Monday morning calling the people on the list I had compiled from voicemails and emails. I wrote it on one of Mom's half-used legal pads, which made me feel like I could complete the list, my tense handwriting following pages of Mom's confident scratching. Calling the appraisers was no problem. Calling the investment agents was no big deal. Calling my New York landlord about my apartment was sort of annoying. I had a constant low-grade anxiety, but I was feeling pretty proud as the list of calls shrank.

I had received two voicemails from colleges in Georgia and Boston, both for music therapy graduate programs. Anxiety over the calls forced me to leave the room. I wandered my house for twenty minutes before I found the resolve to dial up Georgia. I got a voicemail, so I left a message I'd practiced and hung up. Another round of pacing and a few sips of coffee later, I called Boston. I mostly listened as they told me they wanted to send me paperwork and wanted me to come visit.

I just tried to write down what she was saying without thinking about it. If I thought about it while she was talking, I would have hung up. I looked over the page of notes after the call ended. *A place in the program. Music therapy.* I smiled and almost cheered. I wanted someone to tell, and the first person who came to mind was Mom. So I just said it out loud and hoped she heard. Then I thought of Fin. Fin was on the bottom of my list, but he was on it. Then there was Lin. I sent Lin a message with details about the offers and expected to leave it there. Lin had other ideas, and she turned my phone into a vibrating firecracker as she sent message after message.

I called my bank next to tell them I was, in fact, in Georgia so they would reactivate the cards they had stopped. After that there were three things left. I sighed and looked at the clock, thumbing the paper. It was barely noon. I was so tired of saying things and doing things, and because I had been a coward about doing it earlier, the three remaining things were the hardest: text a thank you to Al, call Fin, and get a new tire for my bike. Well, the last wasn't that bad.

"It's not that big a deal, right?" I sighed, looking at Fin's name.

I opted to text Al first. I knew I should have called, but—well, baby steps. That left Fin or a new tire. No contest. I hopped in the Mustang to go get a tire. But instead of making a left, I made a right. And instead of pulling up to an auto shop, I parked the Mustang alongside the Ness house. In order to buy time to figure out what the hell I was doing there, I cranked the top up over the car and cranked the windows up. Then I stepped out and shuffled to the door. I stopped at the door poised to knock.

"Good day, Mr. Starr," Rose said.

I was so engrossed in working out what to say to Fin that I didn't see her kneeling in the garden by the door. I went stiff. After realizing it was her, I let out a sigh that was really a stifled scream.

Rose laughed, offering me her bandaged hand. "Stop looking at me like that and help me up."

"What are you doing?" I said, helping her up.

She sighed and wiped her uninjured hand on her shorts, smearing them with dirt and leaves. "I'm working my good hand to a nub pulling weeds."

"Why?"

"Well, kiddo, sometimes you have to do something crazy to get to feelin' normal."

I stared. That made perfect sense, my fingertips still red and throbbing from the hours I spent perfecting the new song.

"I see what you're thinking, you get it. Here, come on in. Fin's not here, he just left. He'll probably be an hour, maybe a bit more. But I have something for you while you wait."

I glanced at the car, considering a retreat. Rose gestured for me to follow, so I didn't have an option. Rose offered me a seat at the little kitchen table. I tipped the salt shaker over and started pushing the grains into a shape.

"What's making you feel crazy?" I said to Rose as she turned on the tap and washed her hands.

Rose let out a dreamy sigh. "I was missing Fin."

"You said he'd be back."

Rose laughed and shut off the water. "Not my son. My husband."

I squinted at her.

"Fin never told you his father was called Fin, too? And his grandfather!"

"How'd you keep 'em apart?"

"Our Fin, we just called Frank or Junior when more than one of 'em was around, my Fin was Fin or Freddy, and his father was Elder Fin or EF."

"Freddy?"

Rose started doing something at the counter that I couldn't see from my place at table. "Yup. From the oldest to youngest, you have Francis Irving, Fredrik Ivan, and Franklin Ian Nesses."

"And you still miss him?"

"On occasion. Freddy would come home from deployment and would help me in the garden. He'd say, 'A woman named for a plant pulling up plants is like bad Shakespeare.' He was the worst."

"Have you ever thought of remarrying?" My salt pile was taking on the shape of a star. I wanted to talk about anything else in the world but me, even if that meant talking about Fin's dead father. Rose crossed the room with two plates, each with a piece of Fay's bakery cake on it. The cakes were brown and spotted, with green and orange frosting. My best guess was carrot cake. Rose slid one to me and tossed a fork my way.

"Sure. No one excited me like Freddy could, though. Maybe someday. Lord help me, I loved him. Now, how are you? Have you decided where to take your mom's ashes?"

"No, not yet. I have them now and..." My thoughts trailed off. I appreciated Rose's directness. She gave me time. Eventually I was able to finish. "I was pretty worked up about her ashes. There had been so many issues and delays, I thought the longer she was in limbo, the worse. Like I wasn't a good son or something."

I faltered and Rose waited. I thought of Mom sitting on her dresser with a view of the beautiful yard. "She was never in any hurry, though," I said. "Now that I have them, all that pressure is gone. Still nowhere to take her, but I feel less crazy about it."

We were silent for a moment. Well, I was silent, and Rose respected that. I combed over memories of my mother. I hoped I missed her enough. My deeper memories started to surface like the blue fortune from the depths of a Magic 8 Ball. I couldn't stop myself from saying more.

"Mom had a great singing voice. She could outsing anyone." I laughed as I mashed the cake and scooped the mash onto my fork for a quick bite. "But she couldn't remember the words of a song to save her life."

"What?"

I sat back in my seat, the memories getting close to being too sad, held back by being too funny. "You know the Michael Jackson song 'Billie Jean'?"

"Of course."

"Midge could sing along when it was playing, but on her own, she would sing shit like: 'Billie Jean is not my mother. She's just a girl who claims that I am undone—'"

Neither of us could do much but laugh at that point. After a moment I wiped the tears from my eyes. "Man, she would tell these awful jokes all the time. I remember so much. I regret being away most of her last years. She told me I had fought enough for her, and that she was fighting for me now. She was always fighting for me, though. I can't imagine I ever did shit for her, not really. Sorry, I don't know why I can't stop talking."

"She was truly amazing. You tell a good story, Orion. Probably helps that you got a good singing voice, too. You should become a narrator."

I rolled my eyes. "Sure."

"You can talk to me about your mom any time. I loved her. Everyone loved her. She made me laugh. Once she said to me, 'Rose, we're from the South. We'll fight our wars and make up the ending later.' I laughed at the time, but after all this, I can understand what she meant now."

"From the South? That's funny. She was born in New Hampshire."

"Well, her kids are from the South, so I guess we can let her stay."

"I was born in Connecticut and Crow in Arizona."

Rose slammed her fork down and gasped. "Fin said you were from Atlanta!"

"I went to school there before moving here."

"After all this time, my son and a Yankee," Rose said in a deeper-than-usual Southern accent, rolling her eyes. She made an inappropriate gesture with her hand and peeled some frosting from the side of her cake.

I laughed but sank a bit in my chair. "Knowing Fin, he would have told you why we had to move. Midge was so determined to make sure that I was okay, she gave up everything she had in Atlanta to come here. She would say if this city won't stop punishing you for a crime you already made up for, we will just move to a place where they don't know about it. Everyone found out not long after we moved here. I didn't tell Midge how hard it was to make friends 'cause I didn't want her to move us again. If it hadn't been for Fin and Lin…well, I'm surprised you knew and still let him around me."

Rose slid her mostly intact piece of cake to me. "Here eat this. I'm going to get one with more frosting, and I'll tell you a story."

I finished my own piece and pulled Rose's closer. I wouldn't say no to more cake. I waited for Rose before taking a bite. I watched as she scraped the frosting off the edges of the box and cardboard base and piled it in a colorful mess on the top of her new piece. She put her cake down at her place and held up a finger before disappearing around the corner. She came back with a bottle of pink wine and two coffee mugs.

She sat back down, poured the wine, took a bite of cake, and wiped the fallen hair out of her face with the back of her hand. Then she started.

"So, when I graduated high school, I was two years into being a mom and one year into being a wife. I was so proud. They called Freddy's name first and then me. *ROSEY JO NESS.* I marched across that stage and snatched that diploma, worried someone would try to take it from me. When the ceremony was over, I was standing with the Ness family when I heard a girl talking to one of her friends about my situation. 'I hear her parents abandoned her.' 'Well, at least she graduated. I'm surprised. She had a kid at fifteen, how bright could she be?' By then I was lit like a firecracker. I handed Frank to Freddy, marched over to those girls, and clobbered one in the face, my diploma still clenched in my hand."

My eyes were wide as I listened, one hand wrapped around my coffee cup of wine, the other holding a fork in the air between my plate and my mouth.

Rose blushed in a way that reminded me of Fin. "Well, sure as the night is black, they arrested me."

"They arrested you?" I had never met anyone else in my life who had been arrested—well, not anyone I considered *good*. It's not as common as most think.

"I *was*. They carted down to the jail for assault. I was so angry, sitting there, that I didn't even think to cry."

"I did," I said into my coffee cup.

"Well, I probably should've. Anyway, I was there for nearly five hours before Kevin, the sheriff, said I had been released. I strutted from that cell expecting to see Freddy. I nearly died on the spot when I saw Elder Fin standing there. *Alone.* Elder Fin was tall but was three or four times as wide and was pure muscle. He spent fifty years on the railroads, and he was the biggest man I had ever known.

"I was never more ashamed than I had been in those few steps it took to follow EF out to the truck. It was dark, and I had missed my graduation party. He asked me if I was hungry. I just nodded. He said they had leftovers, and we went to the store for more buns. I told him I'd go inside, but he ordered me to sit. I waited, staring into the clock on the dash wondering how long EF would pretend before he kicked me out of his house. Finally, he got back and he put the groceries on the seat between us. I didn't look up until he cleared his throat. When I turned, I about died again. He had two vanilla soft serve ice cream cones, and he was offering me one."

By now Rose's eyes were wet with memory, and I had forgotten all about the cake and wine. Rose swirled her frosting into a brown mess on top of her cake. "I didn't understand, so I set to stammering. He told me to hush, so I shut up quick and took the cone. He started the truck and I tried to eat it even though my stomach was in knots from the shock. Then he said, 'Now, there are many times in this life where you are gonna want to knock someone out. I think you learned a pretty good lesson about why that's a bad idea. There's no good reason to lay hands on someone, but if you're gonna do it, standing up for yourself and your family is the best of the wrong reasons.'"

Rose put a big scoop of frosting in her mouth and sighed. I was amazed. I could picture it all, the small, blond woman with baby Fin. Elder Fin was a little harder for me to imagine, but I had seen at least one picture of him. I knew Rose wasn't finished, so I sipped the wine and waited.

Rose let out a long, teary sigh and pressed on. "So…one day, many years later, I was sitting right here in this spot and Fin came bursting through the door. 'Rosey, we need to go to the store!' he hollered at me, and then he slammed a box on the counter."

"Your Fin impersonation is spot on."

Rose laughed. "It should be. I've had to listen to him for a billion years. Anyway, I said to him, 'You know where the store is. Where'd you get that cake? Why is your hair a mess?' He came over to where you're sitting, and he looked very serious and very grown up and said to me, 'I made a new friend, and I invited him over for spaghetti. We stole that cake today, but I promise he's a good guy.'"

"I hated when he talked to me like that. He sounded just like Freddy. He still sounds like that, but I learned that was just his way. Anyway, I heard what he said and I couldn't believe it.

"You stole one of my cakes?"

"Yup."

"Why?"

"Orion and Principal Yeager have the same birthday."

"So why did you steal the cake? Who is Orion?"

"My new friend. He took it 'cause he didn't get a cake. He was just acting out. But he saw me sitting there and asked me to help him, so I took it and we drove off."

"He drives alone? How old is this guy? Who is this guy? What kind of car?'"

"'Rosey! Calm down and let me tell you. He's eighteen today! And it wasn't a car, it was a motorcycle. And we went to that railroad bridge over the river and ate the cake then he brought me home—we missed last period—and I told him to come here for a proper birthday tomorrow and he agreed. At least I think he agreed. He does this weird eyebrow thing instead of talking."

"I was furious for one reason out of that whole story. I was so mad. I reached over and snatched him by the ear, and I said, 'Franklin Ian Ness, if you ever ditch a class again, I'll make sure you know what hell looks like. Do you understand? He just laughed and said, 'Right, sure, but spaghetti.'

"He was so happy he started talking again a thousand miles a minute about the rest of his day and how he wanted to get you a real cake, and he wanted to use Freddy's meatball recipe, and eventually I stopped him because I just had to ask him how he knew you were a good guy. He said, 'He knocked some kid's teeth out at his old school for talking shit about his mom. Sounds like the best of the wrong reasons, you know.' And I did know. I still know."

If I were the blushing type, I would have. I had never heard that part of the story. I remembered approaching sixteen-year-old Fin with the cake, then sitting with him on the bridge, and then watching Fin carry the rest of the cake into the house before I went home. But I had never thought about Rose's reaction to it all. I was also trying to figure out what she was telling me. The best of the wrong reasons. I was okay by her? I was a good guy? I had a bunch of questions.

I looked at Rose, who was watching me. "You think...man, this is weird, but—"

"Yes, Orion. I think you're good enough for Fin. You are a great guy. Now, if you asked if he was good enough for you, well..."

I laughed, knowing she was joking. I opened my mouth to say something but stopped short. *The cake.* I still hadn't been able to land on what I would say to Fin, but I hadn't known what to say to get Fin's attention when we were teenagers either. The cake had given me a place to start. The cake had given us a chance. The cake was the place to start again. I stood up so fast I startled Rose.

"I need to go."

"What?"

"Also, I need directions to Fay's shop. I forget where it is."

We shared a look, and she understood. She winked at me and jotted down directions to the bakery. "He also likes beer, and he won't admit it, but he likes flowers, too."

I beamed. I took Rose in my arms and kissed her cheek. I laughed, setting her on the ground again. "Don't tell him I was here."

I started toward the door, then turned. "Um, thank you."

I drove off in the direction of Fay's shop. As I pulled up to the little bakery, alone on its block, I sent a text to Fin.

Hey. Can you help me with something? Come over tonight? 8?

I didn't want to say too much. Asking for help and asking for someone to come to me were already weird enough; details would give me away. My heart rattled in my chest as I locked the phone, trying not to anticipate a response. It came all too soon. Before I could catch myself, I was in a text conversation with Fin. And it felt so good. Fin was there massaging my back and saying nice things and—I had to stop myself.

"You really are a fucking romantic," I said to myself. I sent a message I hoped would end the conversation, even though I didn't want it to end, and I went into the shop.

Fay saw me coming. She gave me a huge smile. With a knowing, almost giddy look, she pulled a box from behind the counter.

"On the house. It's his favorite."

I looked at the plain, white frosted cake. Then I looked at Fay.

"Rose texted you?"

"Yup."

"Thank you."

I took the cake and went back to the car. I considered the time. I had five hours. I stopped and got beer and flowers. I may or may not have googled how to set up a mood or whatever and made adjustments to the lighting and music in my kitchen and bedroom. Then I showered, preparing for any possible outcome for the night.

I was high on the idea that things might be okay between me and Fin, that I might have something tangible in life. It made me hopeful about other things. Could I really do a graduate program? Could I make it work even when Fin when back to Rhode Island or if I went to New York? Would Crow want to come back to Painted Waters for the holidays? It was so distracting that I lost track of time. I was slipping into a fresh pair of jeans when I heard my name being called from downstairs. I jumped and looked at a clock. One minute past eight.

"Shit." I grabbed a T-shirt and made for the stairs.

CHAPTER 23: FIN

I took my keys and went out the door in my room, not really wanting to talk to Rose about where I was going. I paced myself, trying to walk like a normal person. I figured whatever I was going to do, whatever Orion needed help with was probably about Marge. I didn't dare think it was about us, if there even was an us. And that was okay, I wanted to be there *for* Orion.

I came to the back porch and vaguely thought about going around front to ring the bell, but that seemed too formal. *Was it supposed to be formal?* I honestly didn't know. I could see a warm light through the white curtains in the kitchen windows. The back door was never locked. *But should I ring the bell?* I decided to do what I had always done and let myself in.

"Orion," I called. My heart stopped, and I had to blink hard before I could process what I was seeing. The eat-in area of the kitchen was being warmly lit by candles. There was a cake from Fay's at the edge of the table, and in the center a small vase of yellow flowers. The table was set for two, each plate paired with a bottle of my favorite beer.

Orion trotted into the room, stopping in the doorway opposite me. He shyly adjusted his glasses and slipped his hands into the pockets of his pants, shrugging and grinning. Orion was the most fantastic part of it. He looked happy to see me, his eyes brightly catching the firelight. He had trimmed his beard and braided back his hair, still damp from a shower. Hell, even the clothes he had on looked clean. Orion motioned for me to come into the room. Just like that, as if I had not rudely told him off a few days ago.

I wanted to reach out and hold the flowers in my arms. I wanted to hold Orion in my arms. As I crossed the room to the table, I considered crying. Orion stared at me, waiting for me to do something. *Fin, do something!* My next words surprised us both.

"Did you steal this one, too?" I said, pointing to the cake.

Orion laughed loud and long. "Fay gave it to me."

We both sat down.

"What is all of this for?"

"It's…I," Orion said, running a hand over his hair, "I didn't know how to get you to come back."

"So, you bought a cake?"

"It got your attention the first time."

"You always had my attention. You don't have to bribe me."

"I know, but I didn't want it to be *just* me when you got here. I feel bad for letting you walk away again and for falling off the face of the earth, *again*. I wanted to tell you that I…" Orion's words sort of spilled out of his mouth and seemed to run out pretty quickly. He sighed and looked down at his hands.

I laughed. "Really? I say fucked-up shit to you, and your reaction is to buy *me* a cake?"

"What things?"

I felt my face warm. "I shouldn't have accused you of leaving."

"I *wasn't* leaving."

"I know, I just…Well, I'm glad you are still here." Orion looked as if he were going to interrupt, but I held up my hands. "We don't have to talk about that right now. I know we will, probably. For now I came to help you. But I guess I really came for this?"

I'd been tricked.

"I don't think what you said was fucked up. I mean, it *was*, but I get it. I would suspect me of leaving, too. I just don't know how to be wanted."

"Meh, I'm an ass. It's fucked up to bail a guy out of jail and then yell at him for not doing what you want even though I never really told you what I wanted. I care about you and I want to support you. I don't show it well. I can't even imagine why you still talk to me."

Orion blinked at me.

"What?" I thumped the edge of the table with my fingers. Orion's slow reaction was making me nervous.

"I guess it was refreshing."

"Come again?"

"Being arrested was stupid. It always has been. And people make a big deal out of it, but it didn't seem to matter to you. Like when we were younger. You accept that sometimes I might get arrested, and you want me around anyway."

"That sounds like a very different way of thinking from the guy who left me in a hotel once." I tried to make my voice as neutral as possible. Orion flinched anyway.

"Fin, I'm sorry. I just panicked. I couldn't—"

"Orion, I think I get it. If I'm wrong, let me know, but when you had to leave Atlanta, you were pretty convinced it ruined your life and your mom's life. And in high school, you thought it would ruin mine because of stupid Al. And maybe you thought college would be different?"

"That's it, but it wasn't."

"And you got arrested again now."

"I did."

"So?"

"Your mom told me she got arrested for the same thing in high school."

"My mom?" I said, my voice betraying my surprise. "She told you about that? When the fuck did you talk to her?"

"This morning. I went looking for you, but she wanted to tell me that story."

"Well, what did she say?"

"She said I was a good guy, even though shit like that happened. You know, I think you have her temper."

"Don't start with me," I said. "I shouldn't have reacted that way to those guys in that bar. I knew better, but I couldn't stand them putting you down. I shouldn't have said what I said the other day. I was just afraid you would get scared off and not...I don't know."

"Not try?" He looked at me, then at the beer on the table. He ran a hand over the condensation on the glass. "I was too scared to try then."

"Too scared?"

"Of everything you had to lose. I wouldn't have been able to handle if it had been because of me."

"And now?"

"Now I'm here, and I'm trying."

"I liked the new song. It sounded familiar," I said, lamely trying to change the subject. I could feel the heat on my face. I couldn't even begin to imagine the shade of red it might be.

"I hope it's okay that I used your words."

Orion's face was so expressive, even beyond what I already knew. His eyes looked clear and he looked certain. There was no malice or snark in his words. His face was so beautiful, and I almost didn't hear him. *The song, Fin.* I had listened to the song. I listened to it in the car with Al, lost my shit over it because the song was so beautiful and forgiving.

"I'm honored, even if I'm horrified. I meant it when I said I was proud."

"Thanks," Orion said, a look of embarrassment crossing his face.

"It's a good song."

"It'll do."

"You're so ridiculous. You are a good guy *and* a good songwriter and singer and don't roll your eyes. I have proof."

"What proof?"

I smiled at him. "The band sells more shirts that say *I'm not one for speeches, so here's a song* then they do Leather and Lace shirts."

"Sounds fake."

"I will call Lin."

"Jeez, don't. Fine, I give up. How do you do that?" Orion leaned back in his chair. I hadn't noticed until Orion slunk away that we'd edged closer to each other. We had almost been touching when he moved.

"Do what?"

"Just *say* stuff. If that's what you, I don't know how to…" Orion faltered.

"Orion, if I worried about what you could or couldn't *say*, I would have done it in high school. I get it. The only thing I want is to know what you want. Simple. What do you want?"

Orion sighed and leaned in, slipping his hand over mine on the table. "I want you to just be here."

I felt my skin flush at the touch, and I couldn't have stopped myself from smiling even if I wanted to. "What do you say we eat this?"

Orion went to find a bottle opener, and I pulled the cake toward me, ignoring the plate. I cracked back the lid and piled a huge mound of airy sponge onto my fork. I was shoving it in my mouth as Orion came back to the table. I shamelessly moaned. "I love this kind. How did you know?"

"Rose told Fay I was coming, and she had it ready when I got there," Orion said, opening the beer.

"Rose? Fay? Good Lord," I said, my voice taking on a distinct Southern sound. I reddened at my accent and took up another bite.

Orion detailed everything that had happened while he was with Rose. Then, to my surprise, Orion kept talking, almost as if he couldn't keep the words in. He told me about his conversation with Corvus and the coming holidays. He talked about Al and Lin, and his mother's ashes. All the while he talked, I stared at him, unblinking and fully immersed.

"Shit, O," I said when Orion finally finished his stories.

"What have you been doing?" he said.

"No, wait." I proceeded to ask as many follow-up questions as I could manage. It felt good. And Orion seemed responsive. We had been talking for hours, and I noticed only because half the cake was gone.

"So, this new song—" He finally stopped. "Naw, now you."

I gave him a slight glare, then shrugged and started to tell Orion about the things I had worked on while we had been apart. I quickly lost track of my own stories, though. I was distracted by the glint of candlelight off the fork as it slipped between his lips. I tried not to stare at the way he thumbed the neck of his beer. I liked the gold shine of the light on his hair. I liked the absent way Orion played with the hem of my shirt, his hands dangerously and innocently close to my crotch. Mostly, though, it was the deep gold of Orion's eyes. I heard our words, but it was murky outside the drunk feeling of lust. Orion's growing arousal didn't go unnoticed, and it didn't help me focus at all on the conversation.

"Okay, when will you finish your degree, though?" Orion said.

I side-eyed Orion and grinned. "Why do you care so much about school?"

"I care about your school."

I wasn't buying it. "Naw, this is different."

Orion looked as if he would say something, but I suddenly yawned. I apologized.

He glanced at the clock on the oven. "It *is* after midnight."

"I—"

"Stay," Orion said. I blinked at him. "I would like it if you stayed the night."

I smiled and felt a wave of relief. I nodded. We lazily cleaned the kitchen and doused the candles. I followed Orion up the stairs into his room. Again, I was surprised. The room was lit with strands of small yellow LED bulbs. I looked around at the soft glowing beads and turned to Orion, who was reaching for his phone. He thumbed on some blues before looking up at me.

"I am impressed," I hummed, warming.

"I may have googled some things," he said, running a hand nervously over his neck.

"The Romance Novel Characters Guild would be proud," I said, turning to look at it all over again. Orion gave me a nervous laugh. Neither of us had ever tried a more traditional style of romance on the other. It had honestly never occurred to me, and now that it was happening to me, I was at a loss. The expression on Orion's face wasn't helping.

Orion stared at me, not moving from the edge of the room. I watched as he looked me over. Starting from my bare feet and scanning up to my hair, Orion looked appreciative and interested. I couldn't handle keeping eye contact, my heart beating too hard. I knew we needed to decide what we were. But Orion had asked me to stay, so the only thing I had worked out so far was staying.

"I want you to take off your shirt," Orion said, his voice hoarse at first but building confidence as he reached the end of his sentence.

My heart leapt into my throat, and my mouth went dry. I stared, but he didn't shy away. I felt my fingers moving before my mind had a chance to doubt the request or the man making it. Slowly, without taking my eyes off Orion, I pulled off my button-down shirt. Underneath was a black tank top, which I pulled over my head. I tried to go slow, savoring the wanting way Orion looked at me. It felt weird, but the longer Orion stared, the longer I could stand to let him stare.

Orion gave me a smirk. "Take off your pants."

I laughed and bit at the side of my lip. I paused a minute, deciding. Orion's smirk returned to something a little more desperate. I recognized his vulnerability. For once in our relationship, we had talked, and now

I could see the need to return to the safety of physical communication. Our ability to explain ourselves with our bodies was always better than our ability to talk to each other.

Slowly, I hooked my thumbs into the waist of my jeans, just above the pockets. I waited for Orion to break eye contact and watch what my hands were doing. Orion watched, enthralled and practically drooling, as I traced my hands along the waist of my jeans, meeting at the fly. I popped the button and slid the denim down, stepping out of the pants and tossing them aside.

I didn't look up at Orion right way. I closed my eyes and breathed, feeling exposed and semi hard. I did look up eventually, especially when I didn't hear anything. Orion had backed against the wall, bunching his shirt in his fist over his heart. It was a look of desperation and gratitude and, if I had to put a word to it, love.

I crossed the room in less than a second and slammed my mouth against his. Orion pushed back, wrapping his arms around me. The contact of our lips and bodies sent waves of tingling heat through me. For a moment it was confusion, both of us desperate to find some hold on each other. Orion raked his hands over my whole body, not lingering in one place but trying to cover all of me at once. I panted against him, pressing into him looking for more contact. He was fully dressed, and I wanted that to change, but I needed him to slow down.

I pushed Orion back against the wall. Steadying myself with both hands on the plaster, I pulled back just enough to breathe. We looked at each other, half laughing. He seemed to understand that I wanted to take my time, to look at him like he had with me. He rested his hands on my hips and waited. Gently, I reached up and removed his glasses. I was going to work my way down Orion, savoring everything. Orion's only response was a deep breath.

I pulled his shirt over his head and smoothed over the soft skin of his belly with my hands. The lights made Orion look like he was cast in gold, lined with a glowing, expensive, ethereal haze. I pressed my bare chest against his and kissed the tops of his shoulders, one broad and tan and blank, the other broad and tan, and tattooed with a night sky with three constellations visible in the black: Corvus, Orion, and Ursa Major.

Slipping my hands down his strong arms, I kissed his neck, under his chin, around to his jaw, then his earlobe. Orion stretched his hands over my back, slowly tracing a path over my skin. I liked the feeling of being memorized.

I remembered him standing in my room, his damp hair a halo of waves around his face. I liked the way he looked, hastily undone. With one hand, I unwove the braid in his hair. I watched his eyes close and his mouth fall open with pleasure. I felt his dick surge against mine with each stroke of my fingers on his scalp.

"Damn, I could watch you enjoy this all night," I said, working my other hand into his hair.

"I'd let you."

"Tempting, but I have a few other things I'd like to touch."

I let my lips fall on his, softly, only as the start of a journey. I kissed his lips, his chin, his chest, and his belly button, working my way onto my knees. He groaned, his hands at his sides like he didn't know where to put them. Kneeling before him made my pulse race. I learned early that I loved being face-to-face, so to speak, with dick. Orion's was grade A, heavy and hard and thick and fucking gorgeous as far as dicks go. I unbuttoned Orion's pants and slipped them down his legs.

"This okay?" I said, slipping my fingers into the hem of his briefs. It took a lot of willpower to keep from rubbing my face against his bulge.

"Fuck, be my guest." Then he went back to leaning against the wall with his eyes closed. It was a vulnerable expression, like he was waiting for the roller coaster car to crest the hill.

I rubbed myself against him, kissing and caressing his inner thighs and lower torso. I took my time to free him and tried not to tip him over as he stepped out of the briefs. With the same slowness I had tasted the rest of him, I let his cock slip into my mouth.

"Fucking fuck," Orion groaned. I agreed. I wasn't down there to get him off, but I did want to get him close. I sucked gently and traced the underside of it with my tongue. He shuddered and moaned. As I worked the underside of his cock and the head, I massaged his thighs, tracing where his legs met his torso and caressing his balls with my thumbs.

"Fin," Orion groaned.

I pulled back. "You taste amazing."

I wrapped my hand around his base and licked the length of his shaft. "I fucking love having you in my mouth."

"God damn it," he breathed.

I sucked him back in, taking him in only until my lips met my hand before I sucked, leisurely letting him in and drawing him back out. His body trembled, and he rocked only slightly, his control and steadiness impressive. I wanted to see him let go. I wanted him to fuck into my mouth until he came.

"Holy fuck, I, damn it," Orion babbled.

I moved my hand, stroking while my mouth drank him in. I drew my fingers over his balls, holding and rubbing. I wondered if I could get off just giving him head. The rub of my boxers was a far cry from enough friction, but the sounds of Orion taking his pleasure in my mouth was doing some work on my own self-control.

"Fin," Orion groaned, his hands suddenly on my shoulder. "Shit, you have to stop."

I released him and looked up at him. He looked down at me. His face was a languid mask of pleasure. He smiled. "I…I don't want to come like that. I mean, I do, but I…Damn."

He offered a hand to help me stand then practically tackled me onto the bed. Orion vengefully tugged at my boxers, pulling them down and off in a hurry. He lay his body over mine and rocked our bare dicks together. He was so warm in the cold room and perfectly heavy, pinning me against his bed. Orion seemed eager to press all my sex buttons. He ran his hands over my nipples and down my ribs. He used his weight to rub his cock against mine. He bit at my lips and sucked my neck. I felt like I would shred apart.

But I could play the game, too. I bit Orion's neck and grabbed handfuls of his black hair. And whenever Orion pushed our groins together, I rolled my hips, turning the crushing pressure into a long stroke between our bodies. Orion hissed and moaned and cussed, and I knew it was all because he wanted me. I could have lived in those moments forever, unrushed and thirsty.

Then Orion pushed away and got a hand around my cock. He stroked and watched. I nearly orgasmed then, the grip of Orion's hand tight. My dick remembered the feel of his hand stroking me while his dick filled me. I knew Orion was savoring this by the way he was touching me, wanting to get me close but not get me off, wanting to bring me as much pleasure as he could.

"I fucking love the way your hand feels," I said. I kissed the inside of his arms and used my legs to pull him over me. "I want more."

Orion did the opposite. He stopped moving, which left me panting and off balance. I looked up at him.

"You okay?"

"I would…" He paused and laughed. Then he shrugged, "I was thinking maybe you'd want to fuck me this time."

"Oh, fuck yes," I cheered. Then I thought about it. "Are you sure?"

Orion cocked an eyebrow and gave me a perfect, shy smile. "As a heart attack."

I laughed. "The man tells one joke, and suddenly he's a comedian."

Orion shrugged, and we shifted so he could look for something in the desk drawers. I watched him. I had been worried about being with him like this, which is why I'd offered to bottom the last time. He'd bottomed that night in the hotel, and I was pretty sure I was in love with him then. Us together now felt infinitely different and bigger than that had been. It was primal and scary, but it was also safe and familiar. This would be an intimacy extreme.

When he found what he was looking for, Orion rearranged himself under me. My thoughts burst and blinked away like fireworks. He looked up with gold eyes, and I concentrated on the gentle affection there. Orion kissed me as he rolled the condom onto my length. I tried not to fidget at the contact, instead running my hands through his hair. He held up the bottle of lube and offered some to me. I obediently and eagerly held out my hand. Orion added some to his own palm.

I let Orion move first as he added his lube to the lube already coating the condom. I had to remind myself to move slowly when Orion gave me space. I was fucking excited. I reached between us, then between Orion's legs. It took fumbling from both of us for me to comfortably access him. Orion hissed at the first contact.

"Sorry."

"It doesn't hurt. How is your hand this cold?"

"It's not my hand."

Orion laughed too, breathing at the intrusion of my finger. *Lord almighty!* He was so warm and the tension of his arms around me, his legs around me, his body around me was perfect. I pressed in, watching his face.

"You are amazing," I said, slowly drawing back and sliding in.

"Hell," Orion started. I think he meant to say more, but he didn't. He just moaned as I repeated the movement.

I worked slowly, massaging until Orion's breaths turned from slight winces to inhalations of pleasure. I made sure every action was one he liked. I added fingers and more lube, and he let me enjoy him. Everything seemed to be happening with intention. It was quieter, and we both concentrated more, as if we knew something needed to be said, and it took getting this right to say it.

Then Orion broke as I focused on that spot inside everyone, that one place that turned everything from wonderful to mind-blowing. Orion gasped and writhed, and I held still until he seemed ready for more. Then I moved again, aiming and watching his composed face flush and change with want.

"Fin, damn it."

I adjusted and placed my cock where my fingers had been. I took a long breath and letting it out, pressed deeper. Orion's eyes opened for a moment to look at me, then closed, tight. He looked momentarily pained, and I did my best to pause.

"You okay?" I said, the warm tightness of Orion's body making me eager and needy, but I forced myself to be patient.

"God yes," Orion said. He put his hands on my back and arm, pulling me toward him, into him. I pressed and felt Orion give and accept. I breathed into it, burying my lube-free hand in his hair. It felt like it took forever, even though it wasn't as slow as it should have been, then all at once, I was fully inside him.

I paused, enjoying the feeling of Orion all around me, his body strong and warm. He opened his eyes, and I kissed him. We smiled, nearly laughing at each other. With a satisfied hum, Orion more completely wrapped his legs around me. I responded by rolling my hips, coming out, and sliding back in. Orion growled, throwing his head back. *Yes please to this.* I did it again, reveling in the pleasure I caused.

"Yeah, I like it slow like this."

Good, I thought sarcastically, *the one pace that will make me crazy.* I kissed him and found a pace with the music playing.

I wanted to give Orion what he wanted and more. Nothing was any more certain about our relationship or our future than that morning except now I understood we were in a relationship. I didn't know where in the world we would be together, but he had asked me to stay that night and there was no doubt in what that meant. Orion had asked me for this, some version of vulnerable and safe. I wanted Orion to know he deserved it, that he deserved things he never thought he was good enough for.

"Orion, God, I love being inside you."

I worked hard to keep a slower rhythm, holding back my own urgent need to drive in faster, harder. The look on his face was enough to make it worth all my self-control. Orion hummed and groaned and purred. It all went straight to my guts, straight to my dick. I could feel my orgasm swelling, but I managed to hold it back. I wanted Orion to come first.

"Fuck, Fin, this feels so good. Fuck, I want more of you."

"How?" I said, barely finding the word.

"Hand."

I fisted his cock with my lube hand. Orion bucked and gasped at the touch. Orion's moans became more audible, his voice melodious and rasping. His eyes were shut tight to the intensity and bliss.

As if to even the score, Orion suddenly took back some of the control. He put his hands on my hips to restrict my movement, and instead of me thrusting down into him, Orion bucked up to fuck me, riding my dick and fucking into my hand. I had to admire that. The pace changed and the sensations shifted, and suddenly I was everywhere and nowhere all at once. I hadn't known a sensation as big or overwhelming as us fucking, and the reality of it became more honest and unrestrained by the minute. Orion pulled me down to kiss him, sloppy with friction and moans.

"Fuck, Orion, I am so—"

Time seemed to slow after that. Orion's pace became more desperate, and his body tensed around me. I tightened my grip on all the parts of him I could hold on to. I felt heat moving through me, pulling my orgasm to the surface. As an orgasm erupted from Orion, my own release stormed through me, sending jolts of electricity spreading all over my body.

After a few breaths and a few moments, my head started to clear.

I had managed to keep myself propped up instead of collapsing onto Orion. I looked down at his bliss-softened face. His eyes were bright and on me. I leaned in for a kiss, sending an aftershock through us.

We didn't say anything. We just breathed and tingled. Eventually, I went first to clean up, then Orion. Orion flipped the music to something that suited my sleep habits and got back into bed with me. The gold lights remained on. And I got the luxury of feeling Orion fall asleep in my arms.

CHAPTER 24: ORION

I woke to the searing incandescence of the sun through the window. I had spent the night with my arms wrapped around a warm, wonderful man. But I woke alone. Groaning, I rolled into the place Fin had occupied. I felt suddenly old. My limbs ached from sleeping on them weird, my head ached from the sugar hangover, and I felt completely exhausted. I missed Fin. I wondered if I had dreamt it. The longer I was alone, the more I noticed the stirring, the guilt and doubt.

In the passion of the night, I had found relief from my guilt. Fin's steadying kiss, his kind words, his hard body. It had been just me and Fin. The affection, the love even, had come back, warm and flowing, filling me. And yet. Despite Fin's words and the sure way he kissed, I was worried. Was it all really as okay as I thought it was?

I was about to get up when Fin's voice floated into the room from the direction of the stairs. I smoothed my hands over the pillow Fin had used and pulled it under my body to hold. He wasn't gone. I hadn't expected him to be and he wasn't. That was something.

"No. Okay, well, I thought we already did that…*okay…Rose!* That…no…Ugh yes…is that Fay? Tell her she is not funny. I am hanging up now. Love you."

Fin ended the conversation as he came into the room, his perfect red hair and beard looking uncharacteristically untidy. My body reacted to the sight of him walking back to me in just his underwear. But I didn't act on it, I just watched. Fin held two glasses of water. He handed the waters to me, tossed his phone on the desk, and slid back under the blankets. I knew I had a stupid grin on my face.

"Mom says we have to come to dinner tonight," Fin said with a sigh, nearly chugging his whole glass of water. I sipped and raised an eyebrow. "Yeah, Fay and Obie got some deal on ribs or whatever, and they are going to barbecue at the house. We have a smoker? I don't know."

I tried not to squint as I set aside my glass. Fin caught my expression anyway. I wanted to see Fin's family, but I also wanted to stay as long as I could with Fin alone in my room. We were safe. But I also didn't want him to get the wrong impression.

Fin merely shrugged and propped an elbow under his body. "I know, I don't want to share you either, but Mom is *Mom*. Can I have my pillow back?"

I responded by burying my face in it. Fin laughingly snagged my abandoned one and snuggled back down in the bed. He closed his eyes and reached a hand out to me, lacing our fingers together.

Fin didn't seem to notice what he was doing, but it struck a mournful chord for me. Fin had said "Mom," the word standing alone. He hadn't said my mom, rightfully claiming Rose, but said simply Mom, as if she were somehow both of ours. That was a dangerous way to think. I wanted a mother. I wanted *my* mother. Knowing she was, in part, in the other room wasn't the same, and it didn't seem fair to want to latch on to someone else's mother. I also wanted Rose, a friend, I guess. I knew she wasn't mine. But something in Fin's words pulled me toward the idea.

"Dinner is at six, which leaves us eight hours. I wouldn't hate spending it all right here," Fin said sleepily, drawing the back of my hand to his lips.

That gesture explained it. I was *Fin's*. I knew it even if I thought it was too soon to say anything. And by being Fin's, I was Rose's by proxy. Which meant I was going to dinner.

"You okay?" Fin said, opening his eyes a little to look at me.

"Yeah. I just miss Midge."

"Do you want to talk about her?"

I snuggled into the bed until one side of me was flush against one side of him, our hands still linked. Fin waited a heartbeat, and when I didn't offer up a memory of my own, Fin found one.

"I remember first meeting her."

I didn't move. I didn't dare breathe and risk the memory being disturbed. Fin continued, unaware of how fragile the moment was.

"We were on the bike, going to the bridge. This white car pulled up next to us and the woman inside screamed, 'Share the road, damn kid.' I was horrified. Then you took off your helmet and screamed back, 'Watch where you're going, witch.' I thought we were gonna die, she for sure could kick both our asses. Then you guys laughed. She was like, 'Witch is a new one.' And you shrugged and said, 'I feel like Halloween.' Then you introduced me. Your mom told me, 'Fin, if my son says ten words a day, three are about you.' I just stammered like an idiot—"

"You didn't stammer. You said thirty percent? I should work for at least passing."

Fin groaned. "I hate me."

"She liked that."

"I liked her."

I turned to Fin and kissed him, thanking him in the way only a kiss could.

We slept for another hour, then went for a drive in the Mustang, getting coffee and breakfast burritos. I let Fin drive again. Fin actually did speed this time, sending the car streaking down back roads and country lanes. I couldn't just sit, though. The future was threatening to force itself in between, prying me away from him. I could talk about it, though. I had to learn to talk about things. I could talk about it.

"Fin," I shouted over the roar of the car and the wind.

"Yup?"

"Are we dating, like officially?"

Fin's face broke into a smile. "Okay."

I was half satisfied. I didn't know what it meant to date officially. "Fin, I don't know how to…I can't make any promises."

Fin considered me for a moment. I couldn't see his eyes. He turned back to the road after a moment. My heart drummed in my chest as he pulled the car to the shoulder and killed the engine. We were at least an hour from town, lost in the winding mix of forest, farms, and abandoned county roads.

He turned to me, pulled off his glasses, and sighed. "I am not looking for promises, Orion."

"How do people do this without promises?"

"I don't know, but so far promises don't seem to be our thing. I mean, you have never made any, and I can't seem to stop expecting contradictory things. I expected you to leave *and* to stay. I expected you to call or text *and* to be silent. So, maybe promises aren't for us."

I sighed. The college offers were on the tip of my tongue. I wanted to tell Fin about them. I wanted to announce that if Fin stayed and wanted me to stay, I could go to the school in Georgia and stay with him. And if Fin left, I could go to the school in Boston. But I knew Fin had a point. I wasn't even sure I wanted to go to either school. But I was starting to appreciate having something to look forward to. I liked the sticky note of plans I had with my brother. I liked the idea of at least a fall semester. And I wanted something to hold on to with Fin.

"So, what then?" I asked. "How are we supposed to do this?"

Fin was working hard to suppress his grin. I figured I must be saying things he liked. He said, "Well, we seem to be able to do this in real time. So, what if we just scale back."

I wasn't following. "Scale back?"

"Yeah, instead of promising something big, we just do the best we can today. Like, I know my family can be a bit much, so I promise that we can leave if you are feeling overwhelmed. You just have to let me know and we can leave."

"I like your family."

"So do I, but Fay has, like, forty kids and I just want you to be comfortable."

I considered the suggestion. I wondered what I could do for Fin, what could I do today that would make our relationship a little better. It was a lot of pressure, but not nearly as much as trying to do enough to ensure forever.

"I will do my best to tell you." The words escaped me before I could overthink them. We had agreed to one more day. And that was enough for me.

❖

We walked to the Ness house that evening, Fin practically dragging me behind him, his large steps outpacing mine. I didn't mind. I smiled, liking the pull of Fin's fingers on my hand. Fin seemed sort of revved from the drive. He had been talking about work pretty much since we'd got back into town. I tried to follow, but the deluge of names and science was a bit much. So I just soaked in Fin's voice. As we entered the house, I felt saturated by his energy.

"*Mom?*" Fin called from his room.

"Here," Rose said, muffled and quiet, sounding like she was in multiple places at once. Fin seemed to know where she was, though. So again, I just let myself be pulled along. We crossed the room, the hall, and the living room, but Fin stopped just before he reached the front door. He turned nervously to me.

"I…" He pulled my hand between both of his. His skin flashed red in frustration and embarrassment.

"You okay?"

"It's just Rose, Fay, and Obie and the kids, but if you don't want to show them…I mean public affection can—"

"Fin, your mom and aunt helped me plan last night, I don't think we can get any more public than that."

"Fair enough."

We shared a quick kiss and entered the front lawn together, hand in hand.

"There you are, Fin. Come help me with this," Rose called.

She and Fay and were trying to set up a folding table. Four children, ranging from ten to three years old, ran around the front yard trying to pour water from bottles on each other. The only one who really ended up wet, though, was the toddler, and she didn't seem to mind.

"Orion, it's good to see you, man," Obie, Fay's husband said. He was standing at a grill coating the cooking meat in sauce. Obie was a surprising man. He was a big hulking guy, a personal trainer by trade. His skin was beautifully dark, but warm. His eyes were bright and smiling. It seemed perfect; a person needed to be a giant to keep up with Fay.

I took Obie's large hand. "Hey."

"Know anything about barbecue?" Obie said, flipping a set of tongs to me as if it were a sword.

I eyed the utensil. "I know how to eat it."

Obie laughed large and loud.

As things got set up on the lawn, the adults piled into the house, gathering the last of the things we would need. Rose stacked dinner plates and silverware into my arms while Fay and Fin fought over which insect repellent to use. Obie hoisted folding chairs, four or five under each arm. Everything was nearly sent crashing to the floor by the extremely sudden crash of the front door banging open.

"*Roooossseeee!*" Lucas screeched, rushing into the house.

"In here!"

Lucas raced into the kitchen and set his daughter on the ground. She wandered over to the table and stared at me as I set down the plates. Lucas crossed to Rose and scooped her into his huge arms. In his hand. he was holding a yellow folder. Everyone else in the room stood stone still and alarmed.

"What is going on?" Fin said. Lucas sucked back tears and put Rose properly back on the floor.

"I have news," he said with a grin. He handed the folder to her and took a step back. Rose looked at Fin, waiting as he came to her side. She looked around the room at Fay, Obie, and me before turning to the folder. Feeling awkward, I looked at the child at my side. She didn't seem to want anything, and unlike her father, she didn't seem upset. She stared up at me. I offered her a chair and she climbed up, standing on small wobbly legs. She took my hand for balance. The room would have been silent if it weren't for the sound of Lucas trying to hold back sobs.

Hands shaking, Rose peeled the folder open and read from the note at the top. "Please request a reservation in the outpatient program. Mrs. Ness has shown consistent and substantial improvement..."

She didn't finish reading. She dropped the folder and put her arms around her Fin. He had been in tears since she had started reading. I understood enough to know Rose's cancer was in remission. *That was it.* The hope was clear and sharp and bright around us.

Fay screeched and took Obie in her arms, sending the chairs crashing to the floor. Fay's children ran in from the other room to stare. I watched, uncertain, my heart thudding with joy and seizing up from the pain. I felt the sorrow because my mother's cure never came. But I didn't focus on it. I focused on Fin's affection and my own joy for Rose. As if I had reached out to him, Fin looked up and our eyes locked, and I felt welcome in the moment. The torrent of tears and screaming around the room ballooned my heart.

Lucas let out a howl and took both Nesses into his arms. "I am so happy. This is it!"

Rose suddenly started shaking and pushed both men away from her, "No wait. I have been declared in remission before, but it was wrong. What if this is wrong?"

Lucas shifted from happy mess to semi-professional mess as he coolly explained, "That was with a less promising treatment solution. The results of this treatment are much more reliable and conclusive."

Rose tossed her head back and screamed, loud and tangibly happy. The little girl at the table started screaming, too. Fay ran to Rose, and they landed in a crying pile on the floor. Lucas bear-hugged Fin, who had found a chair to collapse into, trying to absorb the reality. I started toward him and was pulled into in a hug by Lucas. I tried to pat the giant man's shoulder as his arms crushed my rib cage.

"Orion, go in there and get the coffee mugs. Lucas, get Kyoko over here! We are going to celebrate!" Rose whooped as she pulled herself off the floor. Fay stayed down, too overcome to move.

I laughed and found the cups Rose and I had drunk from the day before. I found an assortment of other mugs for the rest of the people, including some Disney ones for the kids. Rose had the wine uncorked by the time I came back in the room. She handed me the bottle.

I put a portion of wine into each adult mug. Lucas clapped me on the shoulder, nearly knocking me down, Fin took his mug, and with a soft, ridiculous smile, Rose hugged me and proceeded to hold my arm, poised to make her toast. Obie held Fay and their kids in his arms. There was a hush as the room waited for Rose to say something. She just looked around.

"Oh, I never thought of what to say," she said with a partial laugh.

She looked at Fin, who was beyond words, big rivers of tears streaking his red face. Even Lucas was too elated to speak. Eventually, as they realized none of the others were capable of finding a proper toast, they all turned their gaze to me.

I laughed and held up my mug and said the only thing I could manage to land on. "Fuck cancer."

The adults cheered, shouting after me, holding up their mugs. Fay's kids carefully selected the word "frick," watching their mother for confirmation. Lucas's little girl held up her water and chirped, "Fuck cancer!"

The rest of the night became the most phenomenal makeshift party I had ever witnessed. Lucas's wife brought flowers. The whole family ate out on the lawn, crying and laughing and celebrating. The food was delicious, despite my nearly setting all of Obie's work on fire. The children found some music and games to play, and the adults talked about what Rose should do next. And Fin kept my hand tight in his.

I couldn't remember when I had celebrated something with a crowd. It was always been just me, my brother, and Mom. Holidays, birthdays, graduation, all just the three or the two or the one of us. I didn't know what it would have been like to celebrate my mother's life. Rose had so many around her, so much love. I was a part of it now, but how much of it was actually mine?

"You okay?" Fin said to me, the evening light casting him in hues of pink and indigo.

"Yeah, I was just thinking."

"About?" We were standing alone at the edge of the crowd, looking in at the joy and fun as if it were a living museum piece. I could feel Fin's love and peace. And I was suddenly worried that my own turmoil would ruin it.

"Your family is so crowded," I said after a moment. "How do you have this much love? How do you not get lost?"

Fin grinned and squeezed my hand. "Only you would think ten people was a crowd."

I sighed.

"They're your family. too."

"Are they?" I tried.

"You don't think so? Why don't you go over there and tell Rose you aren't family."

I considered Fin's sarcastic tone. Rose would throat-chop me if I said anything like that to her. But I still wasn't sure. It wasn't just Rose. As long as I was with Fin, Rose was family. But Fay and Obie, and Lucas. How could I keep anyone? I had never had to keep people before.

Fin sighed and pulled me back toward the celebrators. "O, you are so funny."

"Why?"

"You can't even see how loved you are."

Just then, Lucas's little girl placed herself in between Fin and me, prying our hands apart. She placed her small hands in ours and demanded that we swing her. I considered the child. Then Fin. Maybe

I could have faith that Fin was right. Maybe that would be my promise for tomorrow. *Maybe.*

"That is a pretty good lyric, Fin," I said, helping Fin swing the giggling child into the air.

"O," Fin said after a minute, talking to me over the sound of the child giggling. "I'm, well, if this made you sad or if your mom—"

"It's okay, Fin," I said. "We don't have to talk about her."

He turned to me, his expression serious. "We can. Orion, she is a part of you. And I don't want to pretend like this is easy for you."

"It's not easy, but it helps not to pretend."

He gave me a resolute nod and looked for his mom in the crowd.

"You don't have to worry," I said as the child screamed into the air, and other kids started coming closer to get in on the fun. Fin looked at me. I knew exactly what my mom would feel if she were here. I said, "Mom would have been thrilled."

CHAPTER 25: FIN

I was just stepping into the driveway as my boyfriend rolled up next to me on his motorcycle. It was weird for me to think about Orion as my boyfriend. We hadn't really talked about labels, but in the last few days since we'd had called it official, the title seemed to be at the end of every sentence in my thoughts. I felt my face warm as I watched him pull off his helmet. Good thing I had just finished a run, I could blame it for my blush.

"Running late?" he said with a wink.

I rolled my eyes. "Who knew you were so cheesy."

Orion seemed in a good mood as he laughed and kissed me. We still weren't sure how to greet each other. Then again, we hadn't been apart much, but Orion had gone out with Lin the night before, and I had been busy going over paperwork with Rose. Mom was days away from starting the outpatient program, and the hospital had an extensive information process. Seeing Orion was a relief, like stepping into a cool lake. I followed Orion up to the house and into the living room.

"Mom?"

"Hey," Rose said, coming into the room.

I nearly walked into Orion as he stopped short. I looked at him, then at Rose. Rose was wearing one of her head scarfs. Up to this point she had only ever worn her wigs when he had been around. She rarely wore the scarfs. Rose's hand went to the scarf, noticing that it had been noticed, in a way that was both defiant and self-conscious. She was bald from the treatments and hadn't made up her mind about whether to be out and proud about it or to let it remain one of the many secrets illness created for people.

"What are you two up to?" she said, sounding determined to not think about her scarf.

"Run," I said, shoving Orion out of the way so I could take off my shoes.

"I was on the bike scouting places to spread Mom's ashes," Orion said almost tonelessly. His eyes were mischievous, though, and he shoved me back, nearly knocking me to the floor as I balanced on one foot.

Rose mulled it over, gracefully plopping onto the couch. "Well, when it came time to lay the elder Nesses and my Freddy to rest, we spread their ashes at the abandoned orchard."

"What?" Orion said, turning to look at Rose instead of watching me.

Rose shrugged. "I don't know, some guy thought he could make his money down here in alcohol. He planted a bunch of apple trees for cider down by the river, where it flattens out into big stones, but he went bankrupt before there was ever any fruit on the plants. Now all those trees just sit there, most of 'em covered in vines or swamp moss. They say that he helped found the town."

Rose stopped talking as an enormous grin spread across Orion's face.

"That wouldn't be Painted Waters Orchard, would it?"

Rose stared a second, then blinked. "Yeah, how our town got its name."

Orion laughed and shook his head. He moved suddenly to sit in the chair by the door, as if his thoughts were too heavy to carry. I looked at Rose, then at Orion, who had covered his mouth with his hand. Rose watched him, amused and uncertain if what she had said was good or bad. I stood balanced on one foot, hands working the knot out of my laces. Honestly, I didn't know either. I had never seen Orion look bemused or dumbfounded or whatever emotion was playing at his eyes.

Recovering as if it never happened, Orion stood up with a stretch and a yawn, rubbing his hands through his hair. He winked at me again. "Rose, have you ever been on a motorcycle?"

"*What?*" Rose and I said together. I nearly tipped over again as I pulled off my other shoe.

"Well, if Midge is gonna get to the orchard, it has to be us three who takes her." Orion's expression was smug as he pulled the bike keys off the chain in his pocket.

"But a car, or...no, I haven't," Rose was alarmed, but I could see the angsty look she got, the same that said she was about to do something that would make me nervous.

"There are plenty of cars. What do you mean the three of us?"

Orion just shrugged. He stared out the window, thinking it over. "I only have room enough for two—three, since we have to go pick Mom up. Fin, you're kind of gross. You can shower and meet us there."

"I get to go on the bike?" Rose cheered. "*The bike.*"

"Yup."

"*Car!*" I shouted as endless images of my mother and my boyfriend dead in a traffic accident filled my head.

"Shower," they said together. Rose and Orion each pointed down the hall with matching expressions of mock sternness. I knew I didn't stand a chance. I stood staring, barefoot and sweating, as my mother and boyfriend conspired against me.

"I don't like this plan." I knew I was fighting a losing battle, though.

"Fine. Don't shower, then," Orion said, his voice amused.

"It's not about the shower, it's about Mom on your bike."

"You ride it all the time," Orion and Rose said together.

I felt my face heat while the rest of me chilled with annoyance. Orion's face was pure confidence. Rose's beamed with the prospect of the adventure the bike offered. I couldn't blame either of them.

"Does it have to be the bike?"

"Mom would want it that way," Orion said, his voice nearly pleading. I knew if I protested enough, Orion would give in and take a car. I realized it was only myself I was fighting, worry and a need to protect trying to make me stop them. I knew I would let them go. I didn't want to ruin anything for Rose or Orion. I loved how much they loved each other, forming a bond beyond mutually loving me. I sighed. *Love* was another word trying to creep into every thought I had about Orion. *Damn.*

I crossed to Orion, placed my hands on his shoulders, then hooked him in a headlock. "Today's promise? Do whatever you have to to keep her safe."

"Man, you are so gross."

"Frank, this is dramatic."

"You're next," I threatened her. "Be safe."

"I promise," Rose said, laughing. "Just don't touch me."

"Me too. I promise," Orion said, working his fingers under my ribs in a sharp jab to get me to let go.

"I will meet you there," I said with a grin despite myself. Every impatient and protective part of me wanted to scream and protest and put a stop to it all. Orion didn't ask for a promise, but I offered a silent one anyway. *I promise not to parent either of you.*

Orion looked at Rose and gestured grandly to the door.

"Oh, right now?" Rose said, looking alarmed again.

Orion ran a hand over his hair and straightened his glasses. "I mean, Midge can wait. But why not?"

"Okay, will I have to change my clothes or hair?" She nearly giggled. She started fussing with the wrap on her head. Orion faltered and remained silent.

Rose gave him a reassuring smile. "Oh, Mr. Starr, I know what you're thinking. I don't know, I guess to me a woman with no hair who is sick is different from a woman with no hair who is healed. Now, do I have to change?"

"Pants, closed shoes, might need some sleeves, I think your wrap will fit under the helmet if you want."

Rose gave Orion a thumbs-up and trotted to the back of the house. Orion looked around the room for the answers to what seemed like every question imaginable. I put a hand on his shoulder. He looked at me, eyes full of requests, but face stoic.

"It takes about ten minutes to get down to the orchard. I can shower fast."

"Okay."

"It doesn't have to be today," I said to him in a feeble attempt at comfort.

He cocked an eyebrow. "I've been looking around for over a month and nothing. I've talked about it with everyone, and I walk in here today and Rose gives me the answer."

Orion looked like he didn't know how to continue.

I smiled. "Feels like a sign?"

Orion put his hands on my arms and kissed me, careful to avoid the rest of my sweaty body. I felt everything in that kiss.

"All right!" Rose chimed, coming into the room.

"I'll see you in a few." I let go of Orion and patted my mother on the head as I passed her to go to the bathroom. I heard the bike over the shower.

❖

I remembered standing in the orchard with Mom and Fay and my grandparents as we spread my dad's ashes. I never told anyone it made me happy to do it. I should have been sad, but I wasn't. I was sad my father was dead, but I didn't want him to spend forever locked away. I wanted the world to know my father had been there. And my grandfather, and grandmother, now Midge. I let the shower water wash away the warm, joyfully sad tears.

I caught up to the bike in the car as it zipped through an intersection. I turned and followed. Rose waved over her shoulder. A few turns later, and the county road we were on came to a T, and beyond the intersection was the orchard. It was a beautiful, haunting sight—rows and rows of trees, each heavy with aging fruit and Spanish moss. Wildflowers had filled the spaces in between. Orion stopped the bike on the shoulder of the road, and I pulled the car in behind him.

"I love this place," I barely heard Mom say as she took off her helmet and hopped off the bike.

Orion offered her a hand. She handed him the helmet and turned to watch me approach.

"That was so fun. I can see why you like it," Rose said to me.

I grunted.

"Don't be such a baby, Frank." She laughed. She turned to Orion "Do you want me to stay with you, or do you want me to give you some time?"

"Um…" Orion said, dismounting slowly. He didn't answer. Instead he looped the helmet over the handles. As he stared out at the trees, his black hair fell over his face, hiding any emotion I could glean from his eyes. He turned toward the saddlebags, slow to get the silver canister.

"I am going to grab a handful of those flowers," Rose said.

She brushed a hand down each of our arms. I nodded. Orion seemed more nervous at the abrupt and unsubtle way Rose left. He ran a hand over his hair. I was nervous, too. I looked into my love's eyes and wondered if I could do this without crying.

"You will probably say you aren't the type, but...Well, I got them a while ago but since I wasn't sure. I knew you would never think of this for yourself so, I got these." I pulled a small black cardboard box from my pocket, put it into Orion's hand, then folded my arms over my chest.

Inside the box were two small metal vials each on a length of leather cord. Orion stared into the box for a second, and I couldn't read his expression. He shook the box slightly. I remembered when Orion first noticed my metal charm. When I was sixteen, I kept some of my father's ashes in. The light glinted off one of the vials and brought the memory back full force. It had been summer, and we had decided to go swimming.

"What's with the necklace?" Orion said, watching me reassemble my outfit. We had spent most of the day at the lake, but I was starting to look more lobster than human, so Orion offered to buy me a milkshake. Neither of us were much for swimming, but we had fun pushing each other into the water.

I simultaneously tried to pull my shirt over my head and look at the charm. "What do you mean?"

"It's kinda cool. Edgy. Just a bit of metal, seems too cool for you."

Orion had meant it as a joke, but I didn't laugh. I just sighed. "Huh. I wish it was."

Orion didn't understand, so he waited. I finished dressing and sat next to him on the stone steps leading to the path back to the car.

"It's got my dad's ashes in it," I said.

It hadn't been that long ago, and I felt sort of childish for wearing it. It seemed strange to me that a young man should carry the ashes of a Solider and Beloved Father. It seemed less meaningful than the flag they placed in Mom's hands or the dog tags they handed to Fay. But I had been desperate for anything, some acknowledgment that my father had considered me in the event of his death.

"I was sitting in the car at the memorial," sixteen-year-old me explained, picking up the story from where it left off in my head, not doubling back to tell Orion the rest. "And another solider came over and asked to shake my hand. She said my father was a good man and a hero, and that they had been good friends. She asked me where I was going to keep it. I didn't answer her, but she said she wore her father's ashes around her neck every day and kept her brother's ashes on the rearview mirror of her car. I figure if a Marine could be comforted, then I probably could."

Orion listened, then finally said, "Are you comforted?"

I nodded.

❖

Orion gasped once he remembered. I got one for him and one for Corvus. He didn't say anything. He just stepped forward and put his arms through mine. I accepted the hug immediately and pulled Orion as close as I could. We stood in the flowers, in the sun, holding each other. When we parted, we both needed a minute to wipe tears off our faces. Orion was half crying, half laughing.

"Thank you."

"Least I could do."

Orion looked into the box, then at the canaster in his hands. Then he looked at me. There was a question there.

"Oh, I have no idea how to do it," I said.

We stared at each other for a heartbeat, then we shouted. "Rose!"

We watched as she gracefully filled the tiny vials with ash. She handed one to Orion. He took it and slipped it back in the box for Corvus. Rose smiled at me as if to tell me she was proud I had thought of the gift. She passed the second vial to Orion, and he slipped it around his neck.

He stood looking at the little charm, his face a swarm of private thoughts. Rose and I just stood by. I didn't know what to do for Orion. I didn't know what Orion would want. I knew that the vial was never going to be enough, but maybe it was better than nothing.

Rose waited. She wasn't much of a crier. Even when she stood in that field with her husband's ashes, the tears were scarce. I remembered watching her face, waiting for her to show the same ocean of emotion I had. But she didn't. She felt for Orion, though. I could see it in the gentle way she looked at him.

"This is sort of funny," Orion finally said.

Rose looked at me expecting me to answer. I didn't. I just squinted at my partner.

"Mom wrote me a letter, and I read it the day I picked her up. She said, 'And when you spread my ashes I will melt into the earth and spread like water, then I will be everywhere. And you will always be home.'"

"That's lovely," Rose said.

Orion looked at her with a slight grin. "I guess if I have this, her ashes here with me, I guess I'd better figure out how to be at home with myself."

Rose looked stunned. Orion was always looking for home, looking for love. I wondered what Orion needed to hear. I wondered what I could say.

"You better figure out how to buy groceries," was what came out of my mouth. Orion laughed, fully and loud.

"Fuck off, Franklin."

"You'll figure it out. You're worth it," I said in as casual a voice as I could manage. Orion looked at me, smiling bigger than I had ever seen.

"Ready," Orion said.

"Well, Marge, you are in good company. My family will be good to her," Rose said.

"The Nesses have always been good to the Starrs." Orion shrugged like he could have been talking about anyone.

Together we turned our backs to the slight wind and Orion sighed. His hands shook as he took the canister.

"Is there something you say at these things?" Orion said, his voice breaking.

I gulped. "Say whatever you want."

Orion got a distant look. "Mom and I have been looking for Painted Waters Orchard since we moved here. We called it 'tainted waters' just 'cause we both didn't want to be here, to commiserate or something. I think it's funny that this is here. A real place."

"Are you sure you want to do it here? If she hated it?" Rose said.

"Sure, she would have thought it was funny." Orion laughed and shrugged. And just like that, he tipped the canister. What was left of his mother was carried off in the wind. We watched her leave. We watched her fill the space and the air and the universe around us. And for a moment, Orion seemed lighter. When she was gone, Orion put the lid on the silver canister and stared at it.

"Don't worry, you can take it back to the funeral home," Rose said with a laugh, knowing what his look meant.

He grinned and pulled her into a hug. "Thank you."

"You're going to make Fin take it back, aren't you?"

"Hey!"

"Naw, I am going to leave it on the mantel of my house just to creep out Al when he moves in."

"Al?"

"Moves in?"

Orion laughed. "I'll explain later. Let's go."

"Home?" Rose said.

Orion winked at her. "Naw, I have an idea. Guess I should make it up to Fin for sticking him in the car."

Rose, Orion, and I stopped at Grace's for sundaes. Wilhemina Grace was pleased to see us. She hugged Rose and almost broke an ankle dancing around her restaurant celebrating the news of Rose's remission.

CHAPTER 26: ORION

The rest of August was extremely busy. The small town came alive as children returned to school. Fin talked more and more about the busses crowding his morning runs. It just reminded me every morning that Fin would eventually have to go north. Rose was persistent about Fin going back to work and school, and she pushed him to return to his program and his life. Quietly, I pushed him too.

With the help of the Nesses, I managed to empty out my mother's house. I put a lot more of it in storage than I thought I would or should. Some stuff was donated, some given to friends, and some was packed into the Ness barn so I could take it back to New York someday. Really it was my secret plan to sell it all eventually. I hadn't yet told Fin about the graduate programs. I had explained to the schools what was going on, and they would both hold my place until the spring, which gave me time to find a way to make it work with Fin. I reflected on all of that as I stood in my empty room. I stared up at the little plastic stars and felt like I was losing something.

"You okay?" Fin asked casually as he came into the room.

I shrugged and picked up the last box. I was having a hard time talking to Fin. We hadn't been together for long, not really, but almost every time I opened my mouth the words *I love you* threatened to spill out, making it impossible to say anything sometimes. Those words and the ideas about the schools made my future with Fin seemed very possible. And that was scary.

"You really do like those stars, don't you?" Fin said.

I rolled my eyes and started to move toward the door.

"You can't hide from me anymore. I know what kind of sap you are."

I had agreed to let Al and his family move in. I had Shively's help, but it almost wasn't worth the paperwork to get a rental agreement in place. I almost regretted it until I met Al's girls, and they all thanked me for their new home, each handing me a homemade card. I felt like a hero. I let the large family move in in September for a lot cheaper than I should have.

I accepted an invitation to stay the rest of the summer at the Ness house instead of in the small bed-and-breakfast at the edge of town. I felt awkward that first night holding a duffel bag of my own stuff. I didn't know where to put it.

"Here," Fin said, taking the bag and tossing it into a chair in the corner. "I have something that might make you feel more at home."

He flipped off the lights. I watched as a hundred little stars started to glow on the ceiling. I didn't say anything, I just took Fin's face in my hands and kissed him.

Fin sighed. "I could get used to this romantic crap."

"Are you gonna put up stars everywhere I go?" I said, feeling content. Fin just shrugged and left the room.

Mid-September hit, and the force of Fin's return to Rhode Island became silently urgent. We learned to share space in what Fin liked to call *functional company*. Fin spent a lot of hours at his computer or on his phone working out his return. I mostly sat around and tried to calculate the small plans of my own. Without telling anyone, I drafted the acceptance letter to Boston.

One night, sharing our functional space, I was trying to work up the nerve to tell Fin what I was planning. Fin was on the bed simultaneously typing on his laptop and writing in a notebook. I sat at an old desk, pretending to tune my guitar. Fin sighed for the millionth time and I couldn't stand it.

"What are you even doing?" I cried suddenly, looking up from my strings.

Fin was balancing a pencil between his upper lip and nose when I called out to him. He jumped slightly and quickly removed the pencil. I laughed.

"I was looking at flights, and they aren't bad if I don't take any luggage at all, but one bag and—*hey*!"

The word "flights" sent me into action. I nearly jumped on Fin and snatched the laptop from the bed. I ungracefully slapped it shut and held the computer between my hands as if it would pop open and bite me.

"Um, sorry," I said, trying to regain some composure. "I just had an idea."

"I can see that," Fin said with a laugh, taking the computer back.

I sat on the edge of the bed and stared at the bedspread as I spoke. "Well, I was thinking. What if I drove north with you in the Mustang. Then I could stay with you for a while."

Fin was completely surprised by the offer. "Really?"

"Sure." I took this opportunity to look at him. Fin was staring at me open mouthed and wide eyed.

"What about your bike?"

"I can have it shipped."

"It's so expensive to drive."

"That's nothing to worry about."

"How long would you stay?"

I stood and crossed the room, "I'm not sure. I was accepted into a music therapy program in Boston."

"What? Fuck, yeah! Really? That is amazing."

"Yeah."

"So, you'd be nearby! Tell me more!" Fin launched into a seemingly endless stream of questions and praise. I watched and waited. Then Fin stopped suddenly and looked at me. "Oh shit, O. Did you want to *move in* with me?"

"Look, if you don't want this to happen that's fine. I just figured… well, I…" I was foundering. I was embarrassed and annoyed. Fin's reaction wasn't what I had expected. I wasn't sure what I had expected, but it wasn't that.

"Wait," Fin called reaching for my hand. "I'm proud of you, and I was just surprised."

Fin caught my arm and pulled me back to the bed. We sat across from each other, inches apart, but not touching. Fin seemed to chew on his words, staring at my face. I looked everywhere except at him.

"I didn't want to assume you and I are something more than we are. I don't really know what it is. *Official*, sure, but I just go with what you're doing and hope…" Fin fumbled with his words for a second, then shrugged. "I guess I figured it made sense here in town, you being with me. I just didn't want to kid myself you'd want more, let alone follow me to Rhode Island. I was so worried about being heart—heartbroken when we finally parted that I never figured you would want to come *with* me. I do want you to, though. I don't really care how it works out, and I am sorry for being overwhelming. I just…"

Fin rubbed his hands down his shorts. He pulled at the hem of his shirt. He waited. I watched him and could have laughed. Fin really must care about me to have put up with mixed signals for so long.

"It's sort of funny," I said. "I guess I just figured you could tell I am in love with you."

Fin looked up at me and instantly turned bright red. Unable to hide his embarrassment and surprise, he curled into a ball and covered his face with a pillow. I knew my own grin must have been pretty stupid-happy. I felt like melting from the brightness of the sunny love I felt for Fin. And Fin's embarrassed giggling was all I needed to know that I was loved back.

After a second or two, Fin crawled over the side of the bed. "I'm going for a thing."

I laughed as Fin left the room. I didn't need to hear him say that he loved me. Fin was probably running to tell his mom. I lay on the bed and flipped Fin's laptop open. I bypassed the tabs for the flights, the university, and social media, opting for a game.

My phone buzzed. I looked at without unlocking it. It was a text from Al.

What is in the silver canister?

The phone buzzed again and new words flashed.

Is this an urn?

I laughed, but didn't bother replying. Al sent a number of other texts guessing at the contents of the silver canister and I ignored all of them. With a laughing yawn I said out loud, "You should have left me the unicorn one, Mom."

About the Author

Sander completed his master of science from Purdue University in 2017 and has been published in scientific journals and a speaker for Ignite Talks and is a published poet. Wanting to see more of himself in fiction, his works feature LGBT characters and characters of color. He lives in South Florida with his partner, his best friend, and their many pets. As a Colorado native, he spends too much time telling Floridians how great the mountains are.

Books Available From Bold Strokes Books

Best of the Wrong Reasons by Sander Santiago. For Fin Ness and Orion Starr, it takes a funeral to remind them that love is worth living for. (978-1-63555-867-8)

Coming to Life on South High by Lee Patton. Twenty-one-year-old gay virgin Gabe Rafferty's first adult decade unfolds as an unpredictable journey into sex, love, and livelihood. (978-1-63555-906-4)

Death's Prelude by David S. Pederson. In this prequel to the Detective Heath Barrington Mystery series, Heath discovers that first love changes you forever and drives you to become the person you're destined to be. (978-1-63555-786-2)

His Brother's Viscount by Stephanie Lake. Hector Somerville wants to rekindle his illicit love affair with Viscount Wentworth, but he must overcome one problem: Wentworth still loves Hector's brother. (978-1-63555-805-0)

The Dubious Gift of Dragon Blood by J. Marshall Freeman. One day Crispin is a lonely high school student—the next he is fighting a war in a land ruled by dragons, his otherworldly boyfriend at his side. (978-1-63555-725-1)

Quake City by St John Karp. Can Andre find his best friend Amy before the night devolves into a nightmare of broken hearts, malevolent drag queens, and spontaneous human combustion? Or has it always happened this way, every night, at Aunty Bob's Quake City Club? (978-1-63555-723-7)

Death Overdue by David S. Pederson. Did Heath turn to murder in an alcohol-induced haze to solve the problem of his blackmailer, or was it someone else who brought about a death overdue? (978-1-63555-711-4)

Every Summer Day by Lee Patton. Meant to celebrate every summer day, Luke's journal instead chronicles a love affair as fast-moving and possibly as fatal as his brother's brain tumor. (978-1-63555-706-0)

Everyday People by Louis Barr. When film star Diana Danning hires private eye Clint Steele to find her son, Clint turns to his former West Point barracks mate, and ex-buddy with benefits, Mars Hauser to lend his cyber espionage and digital black ops skills to the case.(978-1-63555-698-8)

Cirque des Freaks and Other Tales of Horror by Julian Lopez. Explore the pleasure of horror in this compilation that delivers like the horror classics…good ole tales of terror. (978-1-63555-689-6)

Royal Street Reveillon by Greg Herren. In this Scotty Bradley mystery, someone is killing the stars of a reality show, and it's up to Scotty Bradley and the boys to find out who. (978-1-63555-545-5)

Death Takes a Bow by David S. Pederson. Alan Keys takes part in a local stage production, but when the leading man is murdered, his partner Detective Heath Barrington is thrust into the limelight to find the killer. (978-1-63555-472-4)

Accidental Prophet by Bud Gundy. Days after his grandmother dies, Drew Morten learns his true identity and finds himself racing against time to save civilization from the apocalypse. (978-1-63555-452-6)

In Case You Forgot by Fredrick Smith and Chaz Lamar. Zaire and Kenny, two newly single, Black, queer, and socially aware men, start again—in love, career, and life—in the West Hollywood neighborhood of LA. (978-1-63555-493-9)

Counting for Thunder by Phillip Irwin Cooper. A struggling actor returns to the Deep South to manage a family crisis but finds love and ultimately his own voice as his mother is regaining hers for possibly the last time. (978-1-63555-450-2)

Survivor's Guilt and Other Stories by Greg Herren. Award-winning author Greg Herren's short stories are finally pulled together into a single collection, including the Macavity Award–nominated title story and the first-ever Chanse MacLeod short story. (978-1-63555-413-7)

Of Echoes Born by 'Nathan Burgoine. A collection of queer fantasy short stories set in Canada from Lambda Literary Award finalist 'Nathan Burgoine. (978-1-63555-096-2)

www.ingramcontent.com/pod-product-compliance
Lightning Source LLC
Chambersburg PA
CBHW030513020726
47494CB00004B/1075